What was he thinking?

He was lonely, that was all. But he had family now. Jonathan was enough.

A whistle sounded in the distance. He looked down at his brother and smiled. "You hear that whistle, Skipper? That's another steamer telling us to get out of her way, that she's coming into the dock."

"Boat!" Jonathan twisted around and pointed out on the lake.

"That's it. That's the steamer." He looked out over the water, focused his attention on the other vessel.

Clarice turned to face them, smiled and straightened Jonathan's stocking. He glanced down and met her gaze, and the oneness, the sharing of the moment he'd craved, happened.

"I think he could wiggle right out of his clothes."

There was a proprietary tone, a touch of motherly pride in her soft words. She smiled, and the warmth in her eyes, the gentleness in the curve of her lips, sailed right by his common sense and lodged firmly in his heart.

Award-winning author **Dorothy Clark** lives in rural New York. Dorothy enjoys traveling with her husband throughout the United States doing research and gaining inspiration for future books. Dorothy believes in God, love, family and happy endings, which explains why she feels so at home writing stories for Love Inspired Books. Dorothy enjoys hearing from her readers and may be contacted at dorothyjclark@hotmail.com.

Books by Dorothy Clark

Love Inspired Historical

Family of the Heart
The Law and Miss Mary
Prairie Courtship
Gold Rush Baby
Frontier Father
An Unlikely Love
His Precious Inheritance

Pinewood Weddings

Wooing the Schoolmarm
Courting Miss Callie
Falling for the Teacher
A Season of the Heart

Visit the Author Profile page at Harlequin.com for more titles.

DOROTHY CLARK

His Precious Inheritance

HARLEQUIN® LOVE INSPIRED® HISTORICAL

Recycling programs for this product may not exist in your area.

LOVE INSPIRED BOOKS

ISBN-13: 978-0-373-28327-9

His Precious Inheritance

Trust in the Lord with all thine heart;
and lean not unto thine own understanding.
—*Proverbs* 3:5

To my husband and sons—you all continually demonstrate the gentleness and safety to be found in a man's strength. Thank you for teaching me how to write real heroes.

And Sam. Once again, you've gone that "second mile" and hung in there with me through the deadline crunch. You're a true cowboy hero—always galloping to a lady's rescue. Thank you.

*Commit thy works unto the Lord,
and thy thoughts shall be established.*

Your Word is truth. Thank You, Jesus.

To God be the glory

Chapter One

August 1878
Chautauqua Lake, New York

"What is amusing you, Clarice?"

Clarice Gordon met her mother's gaze in the mirror and her smile turned into a grin. "I was remembering the flabbergasted look on the milliner's face when I refused to have any adornment put on my hat." She settled the brown felt forward of the thick knot of hair at the back of her head and anchored it in place.

"Some brown-eyed Susans would add a touch of color. A cluster of them at the front would look pretty."

A wistful note shadowed her mother's voice. "No doubt. But I'm not interested in looking pretty, Mama." She adjusted the three tabs of fabric that fell like a flat cravat from the base of her high stand-up collar, then tugged the hem of her bodice down to straighten the row of buttons that marched from beneath the tabs to her narrow waist. *Plain and serviceable. Perfect.* She smoothed her hands over the front of the long skirt and turned from the mirror. "I'm a career woman. I want the men I encounter in my endeavors to take me seriously, not to court me." She left the rest unsaid.

"Not all men are like your father and brothers, Clarice."

The resignation in her mother's voice plucked at her heart. Yet the mention of her father and brothers chased any commiseration away. "I suppose not, Mama." It was the best she could do by way of capitulation.

The hardness in her heart would not yield to any appeal for softening. One look at her bedridden mother assured that. It also affirmed her determination to never marry and put herself under the grinding thumb of a man.

She pulled on her half gloves and walked to the bed. "Lean forward and I'll fluff your pillows before I leave." She pulled them from behind her mother, pummeled and replaced them. "Let's see, you have fresh water to drink… And Mrs. Duncan will come in throughout the day with meals and to help you with your private needs…"

"Stop fretting, Clarice. I'll be fine. I'm not used to being fussed over."

"Yes, I'm aware of that. But that's the reason I brought you here to live with me, Mama. So I could take care of you." She looked down at her mother's work-worn hands resting against the quilt that covered her legs and tried for her sake to swallow back the bitterness. A wasted effort. The resentment she held against her father for working her mother into a frail, bedridden woman was a part of her. Her brothers were as bad with their selfish demands. But her father's cruelty was the example they followed.

Her face drew taut, as it always did at the memories. Her father and brothers had treated her mother as their personal slave. And they'd tried to do the same to her.

God bless Miss Hartmore for rescuing her and making her education possible! If her teacher hadn't whisked her away from her father's tyrannical grasp, she would still be tending the garden and chickens and pigs and scrubbing piles of their filthy oil-coated work shirts and pants and socks with no hope of escape.

And for Miss Hartmore saving her mother all these years later. When she thought of her mother lying on the grass by a basket of wet laundry and unable to rise…and of her father declaring he had no use for a cripple and wanted no part of the burden of caring for one! His own *wife*, who had destroyed her health carrying out his demands.

She spun from the bed and walked through the archway to the desk in the small turret that formed the outside wall of her room, trembling from head to toe. She supposed she should be grateful for her father's callous attitude, as he'd made no objection when Miss Hartmore took her mother into her home. That had made it easy for her to go and bring her mother back here to the boardinghouse where she could care for her. If only she could have done so sooner! But the train fares had taken all she'd been able to set aside for the purpose and a bit more. Her stomach churned. How was she to manage her mother's care? How was she to pay for the increase in room and board?

She snatched her writing box off the desk and headed for the bedroom door, the short train of her skirt bouncing across the floor with her jerky stride.

"You need to let go of the anger, Clarice. You need to—"

"Please don't talk to me of forgiveness, Mama!" She whipped around and stepped to the bed. "You're lying there unable to walk because your husband and sons worked you to the point of crippling you. They are cold, cruel, *heartless* men. They don't deserve forgiveness!"

"If they deserved it, they wouldn't need it." The hard calluses on her mother's fingers and palms rasped against the soft skin of her hand. "It's not for their sake you need to forgive them, Clarice. It's for yours—and mine. I couldn't bear it if the anger you hold inside ruins your life."

"The way my father tried to?" She choked back a torrent of useless words. "The anger won't hurt me, Mama. It has driven me to succeed, to become a teacher, like Miss Hartmore." She took a calming breath and curved her lips into a smile. "And I truly enjoy writing articles for newsletters and magazines. I'm hoping that one of my articles will one day favorably impress the editor of a daily newspaper, and he will offer me a job as a journalist." Her smile faded. "Though that's not likely. It's a man's world—at present."

"And you believe this suffrage movement you talk about will change that? Women have been trying to gain equal rights for years with little success." Her mother shook her head. "Only God can change a man's heart, Clarice."

There was no point in trying to debate with her mother about God. "Well, perhaps He is using the suffragists to do so. Oh, I almost forgot…" She reached into her pocket, fingered the two coins she had left after paying the extra board for her mother then pulled out one of them. "Here, Mama, you may need something when I'm not here to go to the store. If so, I'm sure Mrs. Duncan will fetch it for you." She leaned down and kissed her mother's cheek. "I have to hurry or I'll miss the steamer for Fair Point. I'll be back tonight, Mama. Mrs. Duncan will look in on you." She relaxed her knuckle-aching grip on her writing case and hurried out the door.

Charles Thornberg buttoned the starched collar and cuffs onto his fresh white shirt then opened the small drawer in the center of his chestnut wardrobe. Light glinted on the silver pocket watch with its attached fob and the pair of silver-framed carnelian cuff links that rested there. The silver initials set into the brownish-red stones of the links gleamed up at him. *TJT. Thomas Jefferson Thornberg.*

Charles lifted the cuff links out of the drawer and stared down at them resting on his hand—all that he had left of his father, thanks to his mother's ambition and incompetence. She had lost everything else, including their house and furnishings, when she'd taken over the running of his father's prosperous investment business on his death and driven it into bankruptcy. Of course, he was already living in the boarding school by then. She'd sent him away the day after they buried his father.

His fingers curled over the cuff links, pressed them against his palm. He'd been so frightened when the strange man came to take him away he'd snuck into his father's dressing room and grabbed the cuff links to take with him. They were his father's favorites, and holding them had made him feel better—braver. He'd clutched them in his hand for the entire two-day-long journey to the boarding school.

His face tightened. Five years old and left all alone in a strange new place with no one to ease his fears or comfort him over his father's death, all because his mother wanted a *career* for which she was patently unsuited. As she had proven. He poked the studs through the small slits in his shirt cuffs, flipped crosswise the tiny bars to hold the treasured cuff links in place, then tucked his shirttails into his pants.

He hadn't had a home from that day—until he'd bought the *Jamestown Journal* newspaper and this house last month. He still remembered the bust of Shakespeare he'd stared at while the dean of the boarding school had given him the news that his bankrupt mother had remarried and gone to live with her new husband in Europe, along with the assurance that his schooling had been paid for, as if that made his mother's abandonment of him all right. He'd been unwanted, *discarded* to live in school dormitory rooms with pendulum clocks that ticked away the lonely years and then in rooms in boardinghouses wherever his work as a roving reporter took him. But he'd survived. Even prospered.

He swept a satisfied glance around his richly furnished bedroom then lifted a doubled strip of dark blue silk off a peg, wrapped it around his neck and secured it with a simple knot in the front. A smile touched his lips. That wandering life was over now.

In the end, he had inherited more than the cuff links. He'd had one more bit of communication from his mother—a letter she'd left with the dean to be given to him the day he finished school. It contained information about a trust fund his father had established for him that was to be his upon graduation. By making wise investments, he had turned the money from the trust into a small fortune. And in doing so, he'd discovered his father's talent for making advantageous business decisions ran in his blood. *That* was the best inheritance of all.

He buttoned on his vest, took the watch from the drawer and tucked it into his vest pocket letting the fob dangle, then shrugged into his suit coat and glanced in the mirror. *Uneven.* He frowned at the short ends of the blue silk tie resting against his white shirt, adjusted the knot until the ends hung even, then folded the stiff collar down over the blue silk encircling his neck.

The pendulum clock hanging between the two windows on the far bedroom wall gave a soft gong to announce the half hour. He tucked his steamer ticket and money into the inside pocket of his suit coat, grabbed his top hat and gloves, closed the wardrobe's double doors and hurried from the bedroom. He could hear Mrs. Hotchkiss working in the kitchen as he trotted down the stairs to the entrance hall and out the front door.

The balmy morning promised a lovely summer's day. He settled his hat on his head, tugged on his gloves and left the porch, rehearsing the finer points of the business offer he hoped to make to the leaders of the Chautauqua Sunday School Assembly held at Fair Point every August as his long strides ate up the distance to the dock. The deal was a good one, beneficial to both parties. He should have no difficulty getting an agreement from the Chautauqua leaders *if* he could meet with them today.

He frowned and joined the line to board the steamer. He hated doing things on the spur of the moment, but he'd been too busy until now with ordering equipment and moving the newspaper to the new building to act on his plan.

Today was his last chance of obtaining a meeting with the Chautauqua leaders before the assembly began tomorrow. They would be too busy to see him for the two weeks after that, overseeing the Bible studies, teacher training classes, musical entertainments, recreational activities and lectures the assembly offered. His frown deepened. And then it would be too late for him to do the work needed for this month—

"Ticket, sir?"

"I have mine." He pulled the ticket from his pocket, showed it to the collector and moved past those in line buying their tickets. Lake water flowed under the gangplank and lapped against the pilings of the dock. He boarded the *Griffith* and made his way forward through the crush of passengers milling about and talking, his reporter's senses on alert to pick up any tidbits of conversation that might lead to a story. Excitement was running high. Clearly, people were eager to attend the Chautauqua Assembly.

The steamer's whistle blew. The deck quivering beneath his feet lurched. He glanced down at the water and watched the gap between the ship and the dock widen. The hum of conversation swelled. He edged into an empty spot near one of the posts that supported the upper deck and looked over at the passengers occupying the benches on the open deck. A young woman, whose stylish gown matched the color of her blue eyes, smiled at him. He gave a polite nod in return and shifted his gaze to the crowded bench across from him.

Another young woman smiled, her bold glance clearly showing she was available for a little flirtation to while away the time aboard the steamer. His barely polite nod declined her invitation. He turned his head and stared down at the water, watched it foaming by and willed the steamer to put on more speed. He needed to have this meeting at Fair Point, then get back to Jamestown as soon as possible. He had a newspaper to get out.

He turned back to look at the passengers, the reporter in him seeking inspiration for a story. His gaze fell on a young woman perched on the end of the bench opposite him and a smile tugged at his mouth. She looked like a wren sitting among canaries and bluebirds and cardinals. His smile widened, the editor in him pleased by the apt description. The young woman was definitely plain as a wren, though her profile was more attractive than one as she stared out at the water. Her lack of color or adornment captured his attention. That and her posture. There was something alert about her, though she sat perfectly still—except for the tapping.

He lowered his gaze to the thin wood box resting on the young woman's lap, focused on her tapering fingers, which extended from a pair of half gloves. Their soft tapping on the box belied her quiet posture. And if the slight ripple occurring rhythmically at the hem of her long skirt was any indication, she was tapping her toe, as well. What had her so impatient? Or was it worry that— The ripples stopped. He lifted his gaze.

The young woman was looking at him, a small frown line between her arched brown brows. Obviously, she had sensed his interest and was not pleased by it. She turned her head back to look out over the water before he could catch more than a quick glimpse of her face. But even in that short moment, her eyes arrested his attention. They were light colored…perhaps blue or gray, and decidedly cool in their expression. Quite off-putting. And insulting. Had she thought him some lothario?

He glanced down and frowned. His dark blue suit, starched white shirt and simple matching tie should tell her he was a man of business. What made her so standoffish? The other young women surrounding her were all of a "holiday" frame of mind, as was displayed by their comportment. Hmm… He studied the passengers, forming an article about the excitement that was in the air in his mind.

The steamer lurched and then slowed. They were approaching Fair Point. He moved away from the post and edged his way to the rail to catch a first look at the campgrounds that housed the Chautauqua Assembly, nodded in response to the cheerful waves of people in dozens of rowboats and canoes that dotted the water closer to shore.

The *Griffith* blew its whistle. A bell ashore rang out an answering welcome, the sound mingling with the pounding of hammers. The construction going on would account for the pile of sawed lumber on the lower deck. He'd have to look into that, perhaps work it into another article for his paper.

The boat lurched again, steamed slowly toward the end of a wide dock.

He shifted his gaze to the grassy shore teeming with people then lifted it to the wooded hillside. Paths, lined with shingled rooftops interspersed among the trees, crisscrossed the hill in every direction. Here and there immense roofs showed in open glades. People swarmed on the paths, appearing and disappearing at breaks in the overarching cover of the branches of the trees. It put him in mind of a beehive. He'd heard several thousands of people attended the annual Chautauqua Assembly each August, but he hadn't really believed it until now.

Deckhands leaped to the weathered boards of the dock and snubbed the ends of the mooring ropes around the protruding ends of thick pilings, while others dropped the gangplank in place.

He turned from the rail, caught a glimpse of a plain brown dress with a small nondescript bustle near the gangway and glanced back toward the benches. The wren had left her perch. He moved forward with the other passengers lining up to disembark.

At the head of the line, the young lady with the thin wood box stepped onto the gangplank. He watched her cross the narrow span then walk the length of the dock, the short train of her gown trailing along behind her. She waved a hand to whoever was in the window at the gatehouse at the end and then kept right on going through the open gate.

So she was known to the gatekeeper. That she was familiar with the Chautauqua grounds was evident in her purposeful movements as she turned and threaded her way through the people on the shore. Not that she didn't look feminine. She did. Very.

He frowned at his preoccupation with a young woman he would likely never see again and stepped onto the gangplank. He was curious to know what was in that box the wren guarded so carefully, was all. He liked answers.

Clarice stood by the fence and eyed Dr. Austin's cottage. She'd spoken with the leader of the assembly a few times, but she'd never disturbed him at his home. Still, timidity never gained information for an article. She pushed through the gate, lifted her hem with her free hand and started up the porch steps shadowed by a striped canvas awning.

The cottage's door opened and closed. Footsteps sounded on the porch floor.

"Well, good morning!" The object of her quest smiled down at her from the top of the short flight of steps. "Miss Gordon, is it not?"

"Your memory serves you well, Dr. Austin." She returned his smile and backed down the two steps she'd climbed.

"As your articles about the assembly do you." Dr. Austin descended the steps and stopped in front of her. "You wished to see me, Miss Gordon?"

"I did, sir. But I see you are on your way out." She swallowed back her disappointment and smiled. "With your permission, I will return another time."

"Of course." He pulled the gate open and bowed her through. "I'm sorry to inconvenience you this way, Miss Gordon, but I've been summoned to a meeting I must attend." His brown eyes peered down at her. "Is this call about your annual article?"

"Yes, it is." She held back the frown itching to form. She didn't want to receive a no in answer to her idea because she didn't have time to present it properly. It was imperative that he agree. What would she do if he refused? She thrust the worry from her. He would agree. She'd convince him…someway.

"Then perhaps you would do me the honor of walking with me to the *Herald* office. We can talk on the way." He motioned her onto the path.

There was no choice. She couldn't say she had to

be elsewhere. She gripped her writing box and moved forward. He fell into step beside her and slanted a look down at her, the same sort of look she gave her students when they weren't forthcoming. She accepted the cue. "Dr. Austin, I have had the good fortune to have had a Chautauqua Experience article printed in the *Sunday School Journal* each year since you began the Chautauqua Assembly."

His nod set his beard whispering against his shirt-front. "And excellent articles they've been, Miss Gordon."

Warmth spread through her at his compliment. "Thank you, sir. But it is the article I will write for this year's Chautauqua edition of the *Sunday School Journal* I wish to discuss with you." She took a breath and glanced up at him. "The Chautauqua Experience articles I have written thus far have been from the viewpoint of an attendee. I would like to write this year's article from the viewpoint of the leaders, teachers, lecturers and entertainers who make the Chautauqua experience possible for the thousands of people who come here each August. To that end, I've come to request an interview with you."

"I see. This way, Miss Gordon."

Dr. Austin gestured toward an intersecting path, then lowered his head and stared at the ground as they walked. Her stomach tensed at the contemplative look on his face. She couldn't write the article as she envisioned it unless he agreed. She could pick and choose among the teachers, but Dr. Austin had to be included.

The readers would expect it. Would he agree to her idea for a new viewpoint?

The board-and-batten building with a painted sign that read Assembly Herald appeared ahead. She slowed her steps a bit to gain time. The tension in her stomach turned to knots. She had planned to write the article from the new perspective so she would be able to conduct interviews with the various teachers and entertainers over today and not have to return. She could not spend the next two weeks here at Chautauqua attending the classes and lectures to take notes for an article the way she had in the past. She had no money to pay Mrs. Duncan to care for her mother. With the increase in her weekly payment to Mrs. Smithfield for her mother, she barely had enough to pay for their room and board until the next school term began. And even then, her teacher's wage would not cover—

"I believe we need to discuss this further, Miss Gordon." Dr. Austin raised his head and glanced over at her. "Your articles have been very well received by our readers and I'm not certain changing them is a good idea. But I am willing to listen to your argument." He glanced at the *Assembly Herald* building and frowned. "I'm uncertain how long this impromptu meeting will take, but if you could possibly wait until I've finished, we could continue our discussion."

He hadn't said no. She might still convince him. "I will wait, Dr. Austin."

"Excellent. There is a bench over here."

She followed him along the short stone path that ran

parallel to the building, sat on a bench beside a door bearing a small sign that read Herald Office and rested her writing box on her lap. Her index finger searched out the small scratch in the smooth waxed surface and traced the indentation from end to end and back again in a tempo that matched the tapping of her foot. How would she care for her mother if he said no? She needed the money she would earn from the article to cover the increased room and board for September.

Her chest tightened, squeezed air from her lungs. She forced a breath and opened her box, pulled out paper and pencil and closed the lid. Worry would help nothing. And certainly prayer was of no avail. It was up to her to use her education and God-given talent— God-given? She thrust away that idea, narrowed her eyes and gazed around. Written words carried power. Much more than any argument she could present for the article would convey. She lowered her gaze to the blank piece of paper resting on the box and began to write the introduction she would use to convince Dr. Austin to agree.

> *The view from Dr. Austin's office at the* Assembly Herald *building is, at once, spectacular and calming. Maple, elm and oak trees paint dappled shadows on the paths and grass, and between their bark-roughened trunks one can see the water of Chautauqua Lake rippling in the sunshine. A warm breeze rustles through the tree branches and the leaf shadows dance...*

* * *

"It's a pleasure to meet you, Dr. Austin." Charles rose and extended his hand to the courtly older gentleman. "I am an admirer of your writings."

"You're too kind, Mr. Thornberg. And I'm quite certain you have not come to Chautauqua merely to compliment me. So why am I here? What is this meeting about?" Dr. Austin pinned him with a sharp look.

He smiled, stood by his chair and waited for the older man to take his seat. "I have submitted a business proposal to your partner, Dr. Austin. And Mr. Fuller graciously consented to summon you so that we might discuss it."

"Mr. Thornberg has recently purchased the *Jamestown Journal*, John. He has come here with a business plan that he believes will be advantageous to us both. I think he is right." William Fuller rose from the chair behind the cluttered desk and came to stand beside him. "So I will simply say, from a monetary perspective, that what he offers is, indeed, advantageous for us. And from that angle, I would recommend we accept the deal he brings. However, I know there are things about the *Assembly Herald* newsletter more important to you than profit. Therefore, I will leave you two to discuss those matters. A pleasure meeting you, Mr. Thornberg. I wish you well in your new endeavor."

"Thank you, Mr. Fuller." Charles shook the man's large work-scarred hand. "The pleasure was all mine, sir."

"I'll talk with you later to hear your decision, John."

William Fuller put on his top hat, tapped it into place and left the room.

"Well, it appears you have jumped one hurdle to your proposition, Mr. Thornberg. Let's see if you can clear the next." Dr. Austin stepped behind the desk, sat back in the chair William Fuller had vacated and folded his hands across his chest. "Have a seat and begin. And you can leave out the monetary details. That's William's decision. Mine is the content of the newsletter. What have you to say about that?"

"My proposition as to content is this, Dr. Austin." He sat in the chair facing the desk and leaned forward. "I will accept and edit any articles or columns you wish included in the *Assembly Herald*. I will lay out the newsletter with the regular columns on their designated pages, provide all 'filler' material, write an editorial if you wish and handle any correspondence that is not meant for a specifically named contributor. I will pass forward all such letters." He sat back, encouraged by the slow nodding of Dr. Austin's head. "All this plus the printing of the newsletter will be done at a cost less than you now expend. But the true value to you, sir, will be the time you will save for your other duties and callings."

Dr. Austin's gaze fastened on his. "You are a shrewd negotiator, Mr. Thornberg. You have pointed out all of the benefits to us here at the assembly. However, you have neglected to tell me what advantage this deal holds for you."

"A monetary one, sir. The *Jamestown Journal* is failing. The income earned from editing and printing your monthly newsletter will help to keep my newspaper afloat while I work to implement the changes I have planned and turn it into a profitable concern."

"I see. I like your honesty, Mr. Thornberg." Dr. Austin leaned forward, a smile peeking out from his beard. "If I understand you correctly, all of my present editorial duties will fall to you…including handling the correspondence."

"That is correct, sir."

"And I still have the final say over the content of our newsletter—the columns, articles and such?"

"Yes, sir."

"Then we have a deal, Mr. Thornberg. Unless you choose to back away."

He puzzled over the odd statement, could find no reason for it. "And why would I do that, sir? I'm the one who came to you with the offer."

"Look at the top of my desk, Mr. Thornberg, and tell me what you see."

He eyed the piles of letters spilling into one another, then glanced at the sudden twinkle in the Chautauqua leader's eyes. "I suppose it's too much to hope you are a very poor correspondent, sir?"

The older man let out a hoot. "You suppose right, Mr. Thornberg. These are this month's letters from the far-spread members of our nationwide Chautauqua Literary and Scientific Circle. And all of the questions they contain have to be answered in the monthly column in the newsletter. A few of the letters will be directed to specific teachers and those must be answered individually. So have we a deal, Mr. Thornberg?"

"We have, Dr. Austin." *Though I wish I had known about those letters and the time they will swallow preparing your monthly newsletter before I made my offer.* He rose, met the Chautauqua leader's hand over top of the letters littering the desk and shook it.

"There's one other thing, Mr. Thornberg—as long as you are here, I shall introduce you to the author of a new column I intend to include in the monthly newsletter."

"I shall be most pleased to meet him, Dr. Austin."

"Her, Mr. Thornberg."

Her? He jerked his gaze from the piles of letters and stared at Dr. Austin as he came around the desk, scowled after him as he walked toward the door. *A woman?*

"Would you please come in, Miss Gordon? I've someone here you need to meet."

He wiped the frown from his face and took a step toward the door.

"Of course, Dr. Austin."

A slender woman garbed in a plain brown dress and carrying a thin wood box appeared in the sunlit doorway. The wren! He jerked to a halt. *She* was the columnist? He wiped the astonishment from his face as she stepped into the room and glanced his way.

Dr. Austin closed the door and turned to face them. "Mr. Thornberg, may I present Miss Gordon. Miss Gordon, Mr. Thornberg."

"Miss Gordon." He dipped his head in polite acknowledgment.

"Mr. Thornberg."

You. She didn't speak the word, but it was clear from the cool look she gave him that she recognized him as the man she'd caught staring at her on the steamer. He clamped his jaw to keep from launching into an explanation.

"Well, this is a fortuitous meeting for all of us. Please be seated, Miss Gordon."

He moved to hold a chair for her as Dr. Austin strode behind his desk. She gave him a curt nod to acknowledge the politeness and sat, holding the box on her lap. He moved to sit in the other chair, eyed the polished wood and wondered at the contents.

"This morning has been full of pleasant surprises for me." Dr. Austin smiled at them and took his chair. "I hope it proves the same for both of you."

Charles swept his gaze from Dr. Austin to the piles of letters to Miss Gordon. He would not term these surprises pleasant. *Startling* would be a more apt description.

"Miss Gordon, I have given some thought to your idea for your next article for the Chautauqua edition of the *Sunday School Journal*."

He lifted his gaze to her plain felt hat, forced down the irritation percolating inside him then focused his attention back on Dr. Austin.

"I like the idea for your piece and will include it in the Chautauqua submission for the *Sunday School Journal*."

"Thank you, Dr. Austin."

Her voice sounded soft, a tiny bit husky and… relieved? He glanced her way.

"I also think the idea wonderfully suited for a monthly column in the *Assembly Herald*."

What? He jerked his gaze back to Dr. Austin but bit back the protest that sprang to his lips. The man had final say over the contents of the Chautauqua newsletter.

"You could feature one or two of the teachers or lecturers or entertainers here at Chautauqua each month, which will spur interest and excitement for next August. Should you agree, the stipend for the column will be the same as that you receive for your *Journal* articles. Would you care to take on the responsibility of the monthly column? I know you are a teacher and will have a large draw on your time come September."

The wren was a teacher? He cast a sideways glance at her and glanced again. The woman's face had transformed astonishingly, with an undeniable sweetness to her smile—a snare for the unwary.

"That will not be a problem, sir. I will be happy to write a monthly column for the Assembly Herald. To what address shall I submit it?"

"You will submit it to Mr. Thornberg. He will now be performing the editing and publication duties of the *Assembly Herald*."

The smile faded. She opened the box, took out a piece of paper and a pencil and turned her head and looked at him. *Gray eyes. Cool* gray eyes. Miss Gordon was no more pleased with the situation than he. Good.

"The address where you wish me to submit the column, Mr. Thornberg?"

He refrained from giving a mock shiver at the cold

tone of her voice. "That would be my newspaper office. The *Jamestown Journal* on West Second Street in Jamestown, New York."

She put the paper and pencil back in the box, met his questioning gaze with another cool look. "I've no need to write the direction. I'm familiar with the area and with your new *Journal* building. I live at Mrs. Smithfield's boardinghouse on East Second Street."

"How very convenient."

"Yes, isn't it?"

"Well, I must leave. There is an opening lecture I must give." Dr. Austin tucked his watch back in his vest pocket, leaned down, then straightened and placed a large burlap bag on the piles of letters. "Take the letters with you, Mr. Thornberg. You'll need time to read and answer them. And you'll have to make arrangements to get the others that will continue to come in. I'll see that they are placed in a sack for you." He rose and made a courtly bow. "Good day, Miss Gordon. I shall look forward to reading your new monthly Chautauqua Experience column in the newsletter."

Her new column…submitted to him. And all those letters with more to come! Charles cast a jaundiced eye at the piles, rose and picked up the bag. Miss Gordon clasped her box and stood. Well, that was one good thing. His curiosity had been answered. The box held writing supplies.

Sunlight slanted across the floor when Dr. Austin opened the door, disappeared when he closed it.

"Don't forget these." Miss Gordon put her box on the chair, stooped and picked up some letters that had slipped to the floor at the opposite end of the desk. "Why, these are all marked CLSC. That's the reading program…" Her voice trailed off. She rose and looked at the piles of letters, her eyes widened. "Oh, my." Her gaze lifted, met his. "Do you have to— I mean, are you going to—"

"Answer them in the *Herald*?" He opened the bag, grabbed a handful of the letters and shoved them into it. "Every one of them."

"Oh, my."

He slanted a look down at her. "You said that already."

Her chin lifted. "It bears repeating." She dropped the letters she held in the open bag, turned to the desk and snatched up those that had slid to the brink and were about to fall.

He studied her neat, no-nonsense appearance. She was a teacher. And a writer. Perhaps… He blew out a breath, examined the idea, decided he had no real choice. "Miss Gordon, could I interest you in a position answering correspondence at the *Journal*?"

Her left brow lifted. "Do you mean these *Assembly Herald* letters?"

"Yes."

She tossed the ones she held into the bag and reached for more.

Obviously, she was waiting to hear his offer before she expressed any interest. It galled him to yield to the tactic, but he had no choice. "I'd be willing to pay you—" he glanced at the high tottering piles "—two cents for each letter answered." That was too much.

He should have said a penny. No. He couldn't risk her turning him down. He couldn't handle this amount of correspondence and run the paper, too. It was worth the money to free his time. He sweetened the deal. "And you would be permitted to use the typewriter for writing your own articles in your off time."

She drew in an audible breath, straightened and looked at him. "A typewriter?"

Ah. He had her now. "Yes, the new Remington Standard model two." He smiled, appealed further to the writer in her. "They say once you grow proficient at using the machine, you can type eighty or more words a minute."

The corner of her mouth twitched. "I take it you have not reached such a proficiency—hence the offer?"

She was *laughing* at him! Brazen woman! He drew breath to rescind his offer. "Miss Gordon, I—" She dropped two overflowing handfuls of letters into the bag he held, gathered up more, dropped them on top of the others and gathered more. He watched her efficient movements, frowned and swallowed his words. "The typewriters and their desks have only just arrived. The machines are not yet uncrated."

"I see." More envelopes fluttered into the bag— more and more. Her plain brown hat bobbed with her curt nod. "I accept the position offered, Mr. Thornberg." She pushed the envelopes down to make room, gathered up the remaining letters, stuffed them on top of the others, leaned across the cleared desk and checked the floor on the other side. "Two more." She stepped around the desk, retrieved the letters from the floor and stuck them in the bag then looked up at him. "When do you wish me to start?"

Her gray eyes had blue flecks in them...

"Mr. Thornberg…"

"What? Oh!" He scowled down at the bag, drew the edges together, tossed it over his shoulder and moved toward the door. "Tomorrow morning at eight will be fine."

She nodded, picked up her writing box and sailed out the door he opened for her.

He watched her hurrying up the path toward the hill, then turned and headed for the dock to wait for the *Griffith*, wondering if he'd just made a mistake. Miss Gordon seemed a little too independent of spirit for his comfort.

Chapter Two

Clarice closed the door, hurried across the lamp-lit entrance hall and held herself from running up the stairs. Mr. Paul retired early, and he was grouchy enough to complain to Mrs. Smithfield if he was disturbed. The excitement she'd been suppressing ever since her morning meeting with Dr. Austin bubbled and churned with undeniable force, driving her upward. Her skirt hems whispered an accompaniment to the soft tap of her feet against the carpet runner as she rushed to the end of the upstairs hallway, opened and closed her door then leaned back against it hugging her writing box and grinning.

"Mama, I'm a journalist— Well, I'm not really a journalist for a real newspaper. But I'm now a columnist for the monthly *Chautauqua Assembly Herald* newsletter!" She spread her arms and whirled into the room, the writing box dangling from one hand.

"Clarice, how wonderful! I know how much you—" The words choked off on a sob.

She stopped twirling, dropped her box on the bed and grasped her mother's hands, gave a little tug to pull them away from her face. "What is it, Mama? What's wrong? Why are you crying? Is it the pain in your back?"

"N-no. It's only—I can't remember the l-last time I saw you h-happy."

"Oh, Mama, don't cry. I finally have you here with me and that makes me happy. And now I have an exciting new job."

"As a c-columnist?"

"Yes!"

Her mother tugged her hands free and wiped her cheeks and eyes. "You didn't tell me you were going to apply for a new position when you left this morning."

"I didn't. That is what is so amazing. It all happened quite by accident."

"Oh?"

She knew that tone. "It wasn't *God*, Mama. It was just…circumstances." She kissed her mother's moist cheek, whirled to the mirror over the dressing table and removed her hat. "Still, I have had the most astonishing day. It all started when I went to see Dr. Austin about an interview and—" She peered into the mirror, dropped her hat on the table and turned. "What is that in your lap?"

"It's a chemise." Her mother's chin lifted a tad. "I'm mending the torn lace on it for Mrs. Duncan."

"Mama, no! You don't have to work anymore." She rushed to the bed and reached for the undergarment. Her mother grabbed hold of her hands.

of the turret to the wardrobe. "Mr. Thornberg is going to edit and print the *Assembly Herald* from now on, and so I am to submit my articles to him."

"Here in town? Or must you still take the steamer to Fair Point?"

"Here in town." She gave a tug at the double doors, winced. "I *hate* opening this wardrobe. That squeak gives me shivers." She took her nightclothes off a hook on the inside of the door and stepped back into the small alcove formed between the wardrobe and the wall. "And there were all of these letters from CLSC members piled on the desk. *Hundreds* of them, which Mr. Thornberg now has to answer." A smile tugged at her. She stuck her head out beyond the wardrobe and grinned at her mother. "He looked so nonplussed I'm certain he didn't know about them. Anyway, he asked me if I would accept a position at his newspaper answering the correspondence for two cents a letter…"

"Two cents! And there are *hundreds* of letters?" Her mother's eyes widened.

"Maybe a thousand or more."

"Mercy me…"

She laughed at her mother's awed whisper. "I said yes, of course." How fortuitous it all was! Only this morning she had been so worried about how she was to pay the increased room and board. Now she would have money enough and to spare. She would be able to get a doctor to care for her mother.

Tears welled. So did the temptation to pray—to beg God to make her mother well. She blinked the tears away, looped her modest bustle and cotton petticoat over a hook along with her skirt and bodice, not allowing herself to even *think* that her mother might walk again. She had learned the futility of prayer as a child begging to be freed from her father's tyranny. Eleven years—

"How will you have time to answer all of those letters when you begin teaching?"

She shoved away the bitter memories. "I'm going to resign my position. I will earn more answering those letters every month than I would earn as a teacher. And more yet by writing my monthly column. And doing so will further my career."

Oh, how wonderful that sounded! She snatched up her wrapper, put it on and crossed to the dressing table to pull the pins from her hair. Soft, dull clinks accompanied their drop into a small pewter dish. "And he has a typewriter I will use!"

"A 'typewriter'?" Her mother's questioning gaze fastened on hers in the mirror. "What is a typewriter?"

"It's a machine that prints letters on a piece of paper when you depress a round button. I saw a picture of one once in an advertisement. Mr. Thornberg says that when a person becomes proficient in its use, they can write—type—up to eighty words a minute." She stared into the distance trying to imagine it, then ran her hands through her hair and set the long silky tresses rippling free. "And that is another bles—benefit. I am to be at the newspaper tomorrow morning at eight to begin my work." She ran her brush through her hair, looked at her mother and smiled. "The *Journal* building is close by, and unless Mr. Thornberg objects, I will be able to come home and see you at dinnertime. And I will be here with you for supper and every evening."

She slipped a length of ribbon between her neck and her hair, tied it and stepped over to the bed. "Lean forward and I will rub your back, Mama." She pulled the pillows out of her way, handed them to her mother, then massaged the muscles along her spine, frowning at the bony protrusions. Her mother was much too thin from all that hard work. Her face tightened. She thrust aside the infuriating memories. Her mother would never have to do such heavy lifting again. If only she could walk. But at least she was no longer in constant pain.

"That feels good, Clarice. It takes away the ache. Thank you."

"My pleasure, Mama." She lifted her hands and massaged her mother's bony shoulders and thin neck, wished it were her father beneath her hands. She would pummel him until he ached and be glad for doing it. She took a breath, reached for the pillows and punched them instead. "I'm sorry I had to leave you alone so soon after bringing you here, Mama. How was your day with Mrs. Duncan? Did she help with your personal needs all right? Did she bring you your meals?"

"Everything worked out fine, Clarice. Mrs. Duncan and I chatted like old friends. I enjoyed her company. I—"

She glanced at her mother's tightly pressed lips, tucked the pillows in place and finished the sentence for her. "You never had visitors on the farm. Father scared them all away, except for Miss Hartmore."

"Yes. God bless Miss Hartmore for her courage in rescuing you."

It was a prayer. She said it, too, every time she thought of her old teacher. The difference was her mother believed God heard and answered prayer—for her it was an expression of gratitude.

"And you, Mama."

"And me." Her mother shivered and smoothed the wrinkles from the quilt covering her legs. "What sort of man is Mr. Thornberg?"

The question caught her off guard. "I don't know, Mama. I only spoke with him for a few minutes." She thought about his handsome, strong-featured face. There was nothing soft about Mr. Thornberg, but he seemed eminently fair...even generous. Of course, he hadn't any choice. "He's strong, with decisive ways."

Her mother grabbed her arm. "Don't anger him, Clarice. If he does not want you to come home for dinner, I will be fine with Mrs. Duncan."

Her chest tightened. "You don't have to be afraid for me, Mama. Mr. Thornberg is a bit autocratic—as men are. But he's no despot. And I'm certainly in no physical danger." An image of Mr. Thornberg towering over her as she stuffed letters into the bag he held flashed into her head. He was a big man—like her father. Odd that she hadn't been frightened. Likely she'd been too focused on his job offer. She hid her shiver and smiled reassurance. "He's a businessman with socially acceptable manners. He would never hit a woman. It would ruin his reputation."

Her mother nodded and rested back against the

fluffed pillows, but the remnant of past fear shadowed her blue eyes. "Just be careful, and do as Mr. Thornberg says, Clarice. I can't protect you anymore."

She turned her mind from all the times her mother had stepped in and taken a blow meant for her from her father's hand, swallowed hard and pushed words out of her constricted throat. "There's no need, Mama. You and I are here together, and I will take care of us both. No man will ever hurt either of us again. I promise you. Not ever."

Charles tightened the screw in the wobbly table leg, tossed the screwdriver down and rose to shove the end of the table against the wall. "Ugh!" He ducked, rubbed the top of his head and shot a look upward. The three-lamp chandelier overhead was swinging. There were six of the traps for the tall and unwary hanging evenly spaced in two rows that ran the length of the room. One chandelier for each of the desks for the six reporters he hoped to need someday. So far he had one reporter—two counting himself—and a correspondence secretary acquired quite by accident. Well, accidental necessity. The deal he had made to edit and print the *Assembly Herald* newsletter was not quite as good as he had expected it to be, thanks to those letters. But he would still profit by it.

He tugged the chain to lift the weights and lower the light closer to the work surface, then glanced across the width of the room to the new black walnut typewriter desk sitting at a right angle to the outside wall. Miss Gordon would be out of the way there at the back of the editorial room. And the desk was handy to the shelves on the back wall that held reference books and supplies, and also to this table he had brought in to give her a place to sort those letters. She was going to need it.

He lifted the overstuffed burlap bag from where it leaned against the inside wall to the tabletop. Letters spilled out of the mouth of the bag onto the waxed wood when he let go. Curiosity reared. He picked up an envelope, broke the seal and scanned the contents.

Dear Chautauqua Literary and Scientific Circle teacher,
I have been doing my studying and reading and have come across these words I don't understand or know how to properly say. There is no library near me where I can look them up in a dictionary. Would you help me, please? The words are *phenomena* and *pantheists*.
     Also, please, how do you say these names correctly? Leucippus and Democritus.
Thank you for helping me.
Chautauqua Literary and Scientific Circle member Martha Hewitt, Burgessville, Iowa

He laid the letter on the table, lifted his hand and rubbed the muscles at the back of his neck. How would Miss Gordon ever manage to answer all of these letters in a column? It would take an entire page or more. He shook his head, strode to the door that opened into the composing room and continued on to the long, deep table that held the uncrated typewriters.

Miss Gordon had tried to hide her excitement at his mention that she would use a typewriter, but her eyes had betrayed her. Their gray color had warmed and those blue flecks had glowed with anticipation. And then she had challenged him.

He picked up one of the three typewriters and headed for her desk. How enthused and confident would Miss Gordon be when she saw the complex machine? Not to mention the thirteen-page brochure of directions on how to use and care for it. He would most likely have to help her in the beginning. Women weren't meant to work with machines. It wasn't their forte. They were best suited for caring for a home and a family. At least, most of them. His face went taut. He shoved away thoughts of his mother.

He settled the typewriter on the pullout shelf, tested it a couple of times to make certain it remained stable. Odd that Miss Gordon was yet unmarried. She wasn't unattractive. It was her plain manner of dress and that cool, standoffish attitude she manifested that made one think so. Still, when she smiled…

He shook his head to rid himself of the image, strode back to the composing room, picked up another of the new typewriters and carried it to Boyd Willard's desk in the front corner facing the stairwell. The reporter pounded up and down those stairs chasing after stories all day long and his comings and goings were less of a distraction with his desk in the front corner.

Boyd wasn't too keen on learning to use a type-writer, but he'd given him no choice. He wanted a modern, efficient newspaper and employees who would fit in with his plans. If Boyd continued to balk, he'd fire him and hire someone willing to learn modern ways.

One more. He carried the last typewriter to his desk, looked around and smiled. The new machines gave the editorial room a modern, businesslike look. He distributed the manuals that had come with the machines to the other desks, plopped down in his desk chair and opened his. He might as well get a head start so he'd have the answers when Miss Gordon came to him looking for help.

He scanned the information about setting the machines in place and skipped down the page. *Machines are packed and shipped, properly adjusted and ready for use.* Good to know. *Placing the Paper.* Ah, this was the information he needed.

He grabbed a piece of paper off the pile sitting on his desk and read the instructions. *Lay the paper upon the paper shelf (F) with the edge close down between the cylinder and the feed roll...*

Clarice turned onto the stone walkway and glanced again at the impressive building. The morning sun shone on the brick, warmed the gray stone that framed the doors and windows and formed the legend Jamestown Journal above the second-story windows. She worked here! Her dream come true. Almost. The word calmed her rush of nerves. It was true Mr. Thornberg had hired her, but her work was for the *Assembly Herald*, not for the *Journal*. Still, she would be working here at the newspaper building every day. The chance for her to prove herself as a journalist would come.

She took a deep breath, lifted the hem of her skirt and climbed the two steps to the large stoop. A long window in the wide paneled door reflected her image, the small white dots on the bodice of her midnight-blue day dress twinkling like stars in a night sky as she moved forward. She stole a quick glance to be sure every strand of hair was swept into the thick coil on the back of her head, then opened the door and stepped into a large entrance hall. There was a strange scent in the air—faintly metallic, rather…stale, though not like food. She sniffed, then sniffed again but couldn't identify it. She turned toward the open door on her left marked Office and stepped inside. The odd scent grew stronger.

A portly man with a bald spot and bushy gray eyebrows above eyes with squint lines at their corners turned from the counter he was leaning on and peered at her. She glanced at his ink-stained fingers and the black blotches smearing his leather apron. *Printer's ink. That's what that smell was.*

"May I help you, miss?"

"Yes, thank you. I'm looking for Mr. Thorn—"

"Here's the copy for that advertisement, Clicker." Charles Thornberg came striding out of what she took to be an inner office, glanced her way and stopped short. He handed the paper in his hand to the portly man. "Mr. Gustafson wants twenty posters. He'll send someone to pick them up this afternoon."

The printer nodded and hurried out the door beside her.

Her nose twitched as he passed by. It *was* the ink.

"You are prompt, Miss Gordon."

There was an underlying note in Charles Thornberg's voice that suggested he was surprised by the fact. Because she was a woman? What other reason would he have? She gave him a cool look. "It is my belief that tardiness shows a flagrant disregard for another's time. It has no place in the business world, Mr. Thornberg."

His left brow rose. "An admirable point of view, Miss Gordon." He came around the desk, gestured toward the door. "If you will come with me, I will show you to your desk so you are not delayed in your work."

Was he gibing her for having an opinion? She swallowed the desire to ask him if he would have addressed a man thus, lifted her chin and preceded him out of the door then waited for his direction.

"This way, please."

She followed him down the entrance room, through a door with a No Admittance sign and into a wide hallway. The odor of printer ink, much stronger in the smaller space, mingled with another somewhat rancid chemical smell.

"That is the…er…'necessary.'" Mr. Thornberg waved a hand toward a door opposite the one through which they had entered, then turned to the right and motioned to a door in the end wall. "Those chemicals you smell are from the photography room. It's located inside the printing room—Clicker's domain, which one enters at his peril."

His lips slanted in a wry grin that was utterly charming and impossible to withstand. She tried, but her traitorous lips curved in response.

He pivoted and strode toward the room then stopped at the base of a wide stairwell on his right. "We'll go upstairs." He moved to the far edge and waited.

A muted clicking came from the printing room. She shot a sidelong look toward the door, wishing he would take her in there to see how the printing was done. Perhaps if she were a man, he would have. Was that why he had warned her away? Because she was a woman? Her father had no such problem in assigning her man's work on the farm. Her face tightened. She took hold of the railing, lifted her hems with her left hand and started to climb, the whisper of the short train of her long skirt against the polished wood accompanied by the taunting clicking sound. Mr. Thornberg fell into step beside her. Her stomach tensed at his closeness. She forced herself to maintain a dignified pace instead of bolting ahead to put space between them.

"The stairway divides at the landing. The steps on the right go to the composing room. We'll take the left side that goes to the editorial room."

She nodded, crossed the landing to the left side and began to climb the second flight of stairs. Sunlight poured in a window on their right, making the polished oak treads glow. She stepped off the stairs onto the oak floor, turned toward the room and stared. "It's— it's huge."

"I built for the future. This town will grow and I expect to need the space for more reporters when the paper increases in circulation."

More reporters. Her heart skipped. *Oh, God, please, let me be—* She squelched the spontaneous prayer. Even after years of knowing it was simply a waste of time, the urge to pray rose from her heart during unguarded moments. She glanced at the morning sunlight pouring in the four large windows in the long side wall. "It's wonderfully bright in here."

"Yes. I wanted to capture all the natural light I could. There's little enough on stormy, rainy days or in the winter when it turns dark early. But I had chandeliers hung over each desk to take care of that problem—or for when there's an emergency of some sort and we have to work nights to get the story written and printed."

"That sounds challenging." She glanced up at the chandeliers hanging by loops of chain from the ceiling and took a step to the side. Not all men were cruel like her father and brothers, but being alone with one still unnerved her. It was a situation she tried to avoid. "It seems you've thought of everything."

"I've tried. But I'm sure there will come some point in the future when I'll discover something else was needed."

She stole a surprised glance at him through her lowered lashes. Where was the supercilious male attitude that had been so apparent?

He moved forward, gestured to the right, then to the left. "That is Boyd Willard's desk—he's my reporter. This is mine."

His? Didn't he have an office?

"This area is empty at the moment." His lips slanted

in another of those charming grins. "It will hold the desks for those reporters of the future."

"I'm sure it will, Mr. Thornberg." She wasn't sure why she uttered the reassuring words, or even if she meant them for him or for herself. It just seemed that somehow her dream of one day being a journalist blended with his dream of one day having a thriving newspaper. His patronizing attitude toward women in the workplace was a little daunting as far as her dream went, but biting her tongue when a retort sprang to her lips and working hard should change that. Her writing ability would speak for itself.

"Yes. Well… Through this doorway is the composing room." He motioned her ahead of him.

She stepped into the adjoining room, swept her gaze over three of the largest tables she had ever seen. On the opposite wall, between the windows, three hangers with serrated-edged cutters held wide, thick rolls of white paper. Supplies too numerous to take in and give name to filled floor-to-ceiling shelves that framed two windows on the back wall. She longed to go and peek in the boxes and small wood crates, to open the stoppered bottles and jars and find out what treasures they held. "This is where you design and lay out the pages the way you wish them to appear in the newspaper?" She moved forward to the center table and ran her hand over the smooth surface, imagining the process.

"Yes."

A small box filled with pieces of paper with writing on them sat at the end of the table. "What are these?"

"Fillers."

She looked up at him.

"They hold snippets of information, usually historical in nature—recipes, gardening hints, that sort of thing." He stepped to her side, reached into the basket and pulled out a few of the pieces. "As you can see, they are different widths and lengths." He glanced at her, then looked down at the papers he'd spread on the table. "Stories or articles or advertisements don't always fill a column or allotted block, and you don't want empty space on a newspaper page, so you choose one of these of the right length that will match the width of the column and use it to 'fill' that area."

"I see." She stared down at the filler pieces, touched the one touting "Indian Pudding." Her pulse quickened. "Who writes these?"

"There was an ample supply of them when I bought the paper, but they're running low. I've only enough for a few weeks left. I'll see about making more soon." He swept the pieces together and tossed them back in the box. "I'll show you to your desk."

Her desk. Her stomach flopped. She pressed her hand against it and followed him back into the editorial room.

"I put this table here for your use. I presumed you will need a place to sort through all of those letters."

She followed the sweep of Mr. Thornberg's hand and eyed the burlap bag with letters spilling out of it lying on its side on the table. "That was very thoughtful. Thank you."

He nodded and moved on, stopped.

Sunlight pouring in the last of four windows in

the outside wall shone on the polished wood of a low hooped-back chair with a red pad and a beautiful desk with six drawers. But it was the box on top that made her pulse race. Did it contain a typewriter?

"I placed your desk here close to the shelves of our research materials on the back wall, where it would be handy for you."

Another thoughtful gesture. She tugged her gaze from the box and looked at the shelves, stared in amazement at the treasure trove of rich leather-backed books.

"There is a dictionary and thesaurus, of course, along with other research books. Volumes of literature and poetry…books on history and the sciences… legal books…a Bible and concordance, of course… maps… There are also office and writing supplies. And now typewriter supplies, as well. You'll not need them to start, however."

Her heart sank. She promptly took herself to task for her attitude. So she wouldn't have a typewriter of her own. She had a job as a columnist, and she would work here in the editorial room of a newspaper, and she was free to use one of the other typewriters when—

"The machines come adjusted and ready for use."

Her heart all but stopped when he reached down and grasped the front of the box. He opened the hinged front sections out to the side like double doors and a typewriter sat there, sunlight gleaming on the metal, shining on the round white keys and warming the narrow wood bar at the bottom front. Her breath caught. It was the most beautiful thing she'd ever seen. Her fingers tingled to touch it.

"The shelf the machine sits on pulls out and locks in place when you wish to type—like this." He slid the shelf forward. "When you are finished with your work, you unlock the shelf and push it back, thus…" He demonstrated, then straightened and stepped back. "I believe that is all I need show you, Miss Gordon." His gaze fastened on hers. "I think it best if you learn how to use and care for the machine on your own. I will, of course, be ready to answer any questions you may have or give you any help you require. You may feel free to interrupt my work at any time—while you are learning about the typewriter. I trust it will not take more than a few days."

His tone said he expected there would be quite a few interruptions. She stiffened and lowered her gaze back to the typewriter. If a man could learn to use it, so could she!

"I placed the direction manual on the machine's use and care in the top right-hand drawer of your desk, along with paper for its use."

There were directions! She gave an inward sigh of relief.

"Any other writing supplies you might need are on the shelves. I felt it best if you arrange your desk as you wish."

"That is very considerate of you, Mr. Thornberg." And not at all autocratic. She shoved aside her surprise. He must have a reason. No doubt all of those letters! "Thank you…for everything."

"Not at all, Miss Gordon. I trust you will find all of the research material you need on the shelves. However, if you come upon a CLSC member's question you cannot find the answer to, you are to come to me. If necessary, I will purchase the needed resource material."

If necessary. The stiffness shot back into her spine. He might as well say straight out that he was certain he would be able to supply the answer to any question she found it necessary to bring to him. Well, she would wear her legs down to stubs walking to the public library to find any answer she might need before she would walk the few feet to Mr. high-and-mighty-superior-male Thornberg's desk!

"I shall leave you to your work now, Miss Gordon. I will be at my desk or in the composing room whe— should you need me."

She watched him walk away, then sat in the chair and slid the typewriter shelf toward her. The metal was cold to her touch, but, oh, how the feel of those round white keys warmed her. She pulled out the direction manual, cast a surreptitious look at the surprisingly thoughtful Mr. Thornberg and began to read.

Charles glanced toward Miss Gordon's desk, frowned and directed his gaze back down to the article he was editing. He scanned the words, looking for the spot where he'd been reading… *those who use science…spiritual existence…one truth can never contradict another…* Ah. There it was. …*accustom people to…* Now, what was she doing?

He scowled and put down his pen. The carriage on Miss Gordon's typewriter was lifted and she leaned forward peering down into the works, the manual in her hand. Why didn't she come to him with her questions? She had to have questions.

Her head lifted and their gazes met. His gut tightened. She gave him a tentative smile and went back to whatever she was doing with the typewriter, but the look in her eyes had said more clearly than words that she was uncomfortable with his attention. It was the same look she'd given him when she'd caught him looking at her aboard the *Griffith*. The woman made him feel like some *lecher*, and that would end right now! He sucked in air, shoved his chair back and rose. "Miss Gordon…" Her head lifted again and her unusual, expressive gray eyes fastened on him, uneasiness shadowing their depths.

"Yes, Mr. Thornberg?"

His remonstrance died unspoken. It was the woman's first day and he was her boss. No doubt his presence made her uncomfortable. He should have thought of that. "I will be in the composing room, should you need my assistance." He stepped toward the connecting door, paused at the pound of shoes against the stair treads.

Boyd Willard burst into the room headed for his desk, glanced his way and changed directions. "Hey, boss. I—" The reporter's gaze shot to the back of the room and a roguish grin tilted his lips. "Who is this?"

Charles stepped forward, annoyed by the predatory look in Boyd's eyes. He'd heard the reporter's claims of his many conquests. "Miss Gordon is the *Journal*'s correspondence secretary." He led the way to her desk. "Miss Gordon, this is Mr. Willard, the *Journal*'s reporter."

Boyd Willard whipped off his hat, stepped close to her desk and smiled. "Correspondence secretary? I wouldn't mind getting a letter from you, Miss Gordon."

"That's enough, Willard."

The reporter stiffened, jerked his gaze to him.

"This is a workplace, and Miss Gordon is an employee. You will treat her with respect." From the corner of his eye he saw Miss Gordon turn her head and look up at him. Those gray eyes held what... incredulity? Irritation surged. He gestured Boyd Willard to his desk with a flick of his hand, then strode back to his own. So much for leaving the room to make Miss Gordon more comfortable. He would stay at his desk until Willard left to rove about town in the search for stories...or whatever he did with his time.

He pulled the article he'd been editing toward him then glanced toward the back of the room. His gaze crashed against Miss Gordon's and she quickly looked back down at the pages in her hand, but not before he'd seen the relief in her eyes and felt the power of her tenuous smile.

"It's the most marvelous thing you've ever seen, Mama!" Clarice lifted her supper tray from her lap and rose from her chair. "It really does print out words on paper. You push down the key with the letter you want printed on it, and this skinny metal rod they call a 'type bar' comes up and strikes the underneath of the cylinder, and there's the letter on the paper!"

She put her tray on the table by the bed, glanced at her mother's tray and frowned. "You need to eat more,

Mama. You're too thin. Would you like me to spread preserves on your biscuit for you?"

"I've had enough, Clarice. I don't get very hungry being in bed all day long."

"Half a biscuit, then. Mama, you told me last night that you need something to do with your days..." She slathered preserves on the top half of the biscuit.

"You're not going to scold me again for mending Mrs. Duncan's chemise, are you?"

"I wasn't scolding, Mama. I just don't want you to—" She glanced at her mother, spotted her smile, grinned and handed her the biscuit top. "Stop teasing. Or I'll make you eat the other half of this biscuit."

"That's better. You fret about me too much, Clarice. I know it's hard for you to see me this way, but—"

"I wasn't fretting, Mama. I was about to ask if you would help me with some work."

"*Help* you?" Her mother cast a suspicious glance up at her. "How?"

"By writing down some of your recipes for me." She slipped her mother's tray away so she had no place to put the biscuit. "And perhaps some of the ways you've found to save time or do a better job of cleaning or gardening."

"Oh, Clarice..." Tears glistened in her mother's eyes. "I *am* a burden to you. You've spent all day thinking about how to help me stay busy."

"I did *not*. And don't ever say that again, Mama!" She piled the supper trays and started for the door.

"Then tell me how my recipes and household tips can possibly help you."

"I'm going to make them into fillers."

"Fillers?"

"Yes." She balanced the trays and opened the door. "They're short items of general interest that Mr. Thornberg uses to take up blank space when he composes the pages for the newspaper. He's running out of them, and I intend to keep him supplied. I'll explain after I take these supper trays downstairs." She stepped into the hall and pulled the door closed.

"Clarice, come back! You forgot this biscuit!"

No, Mama. You did. She grinned and hurried down the hall to the stairs.

Charles laid his book aside and stepped out onto the small balcony that overlooked the street. Captain Nemo and his adventures held no interest for him this evening. He rubbed the back of his neck, blew out a breath and stared into the distance. Miss Gordon had gotten into his head. There was no denying it. It was her smile. It was so soft and warm, the exact opposite of her prickly disposition. And rare. He found himself waiting for her to smile, like some schoolboy hoping to catch a favorable glance from his secret crush. He scowled, raked his fingers through his hair and rocked back on his heels. It was the surprise of her smiles, of course. And the way her eyes changed…

A breeze rose and cooled his face, the skin exposed by the unbuttoned neck of his shirt and his bare forearms protruding from his rolled-up sleeves. The flow of air carried the scent of rain. Hopefully, he wouldn't have to close the door. He liked sleeping with it open. It helped to cool the accumulated heat of the day.

He leaned back against the stone wall of the house and gazed up at the night sky. No stars. Rain clouds must be closing in. Her hair was as black as that sky. So were her eyelashes. And they were long. They looked like shadows against her fair skin as she sat reading the directions for operating the typewriter.

He pushed away from the wall, stepped to the railing and shoved his hands in his pockets. Why hadn't she come to him with her questions? She had to have had some. That section on changing the rubber bands and the one on adjusting the spacing dogs were quite technical. Not to mention the one on cleaning and oiling the machine.

Perhaps she hadn't read that far yet. His lips skewed into a lopsided grin. He was quite certain the prickly Miss Gordon didn't know the tiniest bit of the tip of her tongue showed at the corner of her lips when she was concentrating. It was most distracting. Every time he'd seen it, he'd wanted to go and help her.

And he wasn't the only one who had noticed Miss Gordon's winsome way. Willard had stolen glances at her all day long. One more reason it wasn't good to have a woman in the workplace. Men lost their focus. He had. But that lapse of self-discipline on his part was understandable. Miss Gordon was a new employee. It was his responsibility to give her the help she needed— when she asked.

And that was the crux of the matter. The woman had plagued his thoughts all day because she hadn't asked for his help when he knew full well she needed it. Any woman would. Well, he'd not give her a thought tomorrow. He had a newspaper to run.

He banished Miss Gordon from his thoughts, pulled his hands from his pockets, went inside and picked up the book.

"It's apparent from Mr. Thornberg's thinly veiled contempt that he shares the prevailing viewpoint that men are superior and women have no business being in the workplace." *But he is still thoughtful...* Clarice frowned at the dichotomy, swirled her dressing gown on over her nightdress and slammed the wardrobe doors so hard they didn't squeak.

"But he hired you, Clarice."

"Yes, because Dr. Austin asked me to write the monthly column right there in front of him. *And* because he needed someone to free him from having to respond to all of those letters." She yanked the ties at the neck of her dressing gown so tight she almost choked herself. She coughed, slid her fingers beneath the twisted ribbon and loosened the bow. "But he does not think I can learn how to use the typing machine on my own. He thinks I will have to run to him with questions. He even gave me a few days!" She shot her mother a look. "*And* he said if I found one of the CLSC members' questions too difficult to answer, I am to go to him. As if he—being a *man*—will, of course, know the answer my poor, inferior woman's brain cannot supply."

"Clarice..."

"Well, it's true, Mama!" She marched to the desk in the turret, the sides of her dressing gown flying out behind her. "And I intend to prove Mr. Thornberg wrong. I am going to become *indispensable* to him. And I'm going to start by writing those fillers he needs—without being asked to do so." She glanced over at the bed. "Will you help me write them, Mama?"

"Of course I will, Clarice. I think it's an excellent idea. And it will give me something useful to do. But you can hardly blame an older man like Mr. Thornberg for being uncomfortable with having a woman in his employ. It simply wasn't done until recent years."

"He's not that old, Mama." She removed the ink, lest it leak onto Mrs. Smithfield's quilt, then snatched her writing box off the desk and carried it to the bed. "Everything you need is in here. Pencils…paper…"

"How old *is* Mr. Thornberg?"

"I don't know, Mama." She thought about it, pictured him looking down at her. "Perhaps five or six years older than me."

"That *young*?"

She nodded and placed the box on the covers over her mother's extended legs.

"What does he look like?"

"A prosperous businessman."

"Clarice…"

"What does it *matter*, Mama?"

Her mother shook her head, sighed. "It doesn't *mat-*

ter. I'd just like to be able to picture you at work while I'm sitting here. I get restless with nothing to do."

She looked at her mother's legs stretched out beneath the quilt and guilt smote her for her lack of understanding and compassion. "I'm sorry, Mama. Mr. Thornberg is tall and very neat in appearance. He has wavy brown hair, cut short, and—"

"Wavy?"

Now, why did that make her mother smile? "Yes, wavy…as if it would curl if it were longer. And dark, rather heavy eyebrows…and blue eyes. A strong chin and a—" his image flashed before her "—a charming smile. No. It's more of a grin…sort of crooked and self-deprecating, you know, like a boy that has been caught at some mischief."

Her mother's eyes widened. "Charming…"

"Did I say that?"

"You did." Her mother's gaze narrowed on her. "You said Mr. Thornberg has a charming smile."

She snorted, waved the description away. "I suppose it is—given the right circumstances." She turned her attention back to the work. "Now…you can write on the box—be mindful of this scratch—then put the finished work inside it. But don't do too much. I don't want you to tire yourself."

"Clarice, have your forgotten I fed and cared for a flock of chickens, cleaned their coop, slopped and mucked out pens for over a dozen hogs and took care of the garden and the house and—" her mother shook her head, picked up a pencil and smiled "—and made lots of preserves. I'll start with your favorite."

Rhubarb Jam
Select fresh red rhubarb in pieces one inch long,
take sugar pound for pound. Cook together and
let stand all night. In the morning pour off the
syrup and boil it until it begins to thicken. Put
in the rhubarb and heat...

She left her mother to her work, walked to the desk
and opened the directions manual for the typewriter
she'd brought home with her. Her mouth firmed as she
read the words across the top of the length of the last
page. *Diagram of Key-board of the No. 2 Remington*
Typewriter (Actual Size).

She laid the page down on the desk, tugged her chair
close and placed the fingers of her left hand on the *A-*
S-D-F keys on the paper, closed her eyes and repeated
the names of the letters over and over, tapping the corresponding finger on the paper key. Her index finger
she used for the *G* key, also. When she was satisfied
she had them memorized, she moved to the right side
of the key-board and did the same with her right hand.
"*J-K-L* colon and semicolon. And also the *H*."

"What are you doing, Clarice?"

"I'm learning to use the typewriter, Mama. See…"
She rose and carried the manual to the bed, showed
the key-board to her mother. "I put my fingers on the
keys, thus…" She placed them as the manual advised.
"And now to write—type—a word I just push down
the right keys. Watch me do your name…*h*…" She
pushed down her right index finger. "Oh, no, that's

wrong. I must push down this key that says Upper Case first." She pushed the key on the left side of the bottom row above the space bar then pushed down with her right index finger again. "Capital *H*... Now I push the upper-case key down again to disengage it. And then I press the rest of the letters..." She peered down at the key-board and found them. "*e...l...e...n*. There! I have typed your name. If I were using the typewriter, your name would be printed on a piece of paper beneath the...the roller thing. See. Here it is." She opened the manual to the picture of the typewriter with all of the parts named.

"You have to learn all of that just to write my name?" Her mother shook her head, laughed and lifted the pencil she held into the air. "I'll use this, thank you."

"Well, I am going to learn how to use this typewriter. And I am going to learn it without Mr. Thornberg's help. And you can help me, Mama." She carried the manual back to the desk. "When I have all of these keys memorized, and I have practiced enough that my fingers don't trip all over each other trying to find them, I will sit over there by the bed and you can call out words for me to type. I will keep my eyes closed, and you can watch my fingers and tell me if I hit the right keys. I am going to type better and faster than anyone else at the *Journal*—including Mr. Thornberg. That will show him my value as an employee."

She placed her fingers over the center row on the paper key-board and studied the top row on the left side. *Q-W-E-R-T.* Now, which fingers should she use...

* * *

The letters were blurring too much for her to practice any longer. Clarice blinked her eyes and glanced at her open locket watch she'd placed in the light cast by the oil lamp. One o'clock. She looked over at the bed and smiled. Her mother had set the writing box aside and succumbed to sleep close to two hours ago. And she was sleeping well. She hadn't once moaned with pain.

Could the surcease of pain mean that her mother might walk again? Hope sprang to her heart. She would arrange for a doctor to come and see her mother as soon as she had the money. And that meant she had to stop practicing with the typewriter at work and concentrate on answering those letters. She wasn't being paid to learn how to use the typewriter. And her mother's care came first, even before her ambition to be a columnist for a real newspaper.

She closed the manual and slipped from her chair to take the writing box off the bed. Her mother's Bible was open beside it, a verse marked with a small star in the margin. She averted her eyes. How could her mother still believe in God after all she had suffered? She picked up the writing box and placed it on the seat of the chair by the bed, where her mother could reach it, and glanced back at the Bible. The marked verse drew her eye. *For my thoughts are not your thoughts, neither are your ways my ways, saith the Lord.*

Well, that was certainly true. She would never have let her mother be crippled!

Trust me.

The thought was so clear it might have been spoken. She spun about and hurried back to the turret area, turned down the wick to dim the lamp and shrugged out of her dressing gown. The night was warm, but shivers prickled her flesh. She slipped beneath the blanket on the window seat and pulled it up around her neck, seeking the comfort of its softness and warmth. All was dark outside the windows. There were no stars to look at—nothing.

The silence of the night settled around her. Her heart ached with a longing she didn't understand and refused to acknowledge. She turned onto her other side and stared at the dim spot of light, the lowered wick glowing against the darkness.

Chapter Three

Muted voices came from the office. Clarice paused, uncertain as to whether she should seek out Mr. Thornberg or go upstairs on her own. The door ahead beckoned. No Admittance. A smile curved her lips. That sign no longer applied to her. She had gone to the school and turned in her resignation. She stepped through the door and hurried to the stairs.

The editorial room was empty, but the chandelier over Mr. Thornberg's desk glowed against the overcast morning. So did hers. And the one over the table with the burlap bag of letters on it. Consideration? Or a subtle message for her to start working on the letters? She fought back a spurt of irritation and strode to her desk. The man was her boss. He had every right to tell her what to do and when to do it. But it took away her chance to show him that she had initiative and was responsible and reliable. And he obviously thought her lacking in those virtues. He hadn't lit Mr. Willard's chandelier.

She unpinned her hat and tossed it into the bottom drawer, turned her back on the enticing sight of the wood box covering her typewriter and crossed to the table. The burlap bag was too heavy for her to easily lift. She dragged a pile of letters out of it, then rolled it to the side of the table and eased it to the floor.

An open letter rested on the table. She read it, catalogued the questions as a request for the definition and pronunciation of words, placed the letter at the top right corner of the table and opened another. A science-experiment question. That letter started a stack for science-related questions at the top center of the table. The next was added to the first pile, and the next started a stack for grammar queries. Questions having to do with mathematics, she placed at the extreme-left top corner.

She sailed through the pile, defining the topics and placing the opened letters in the corresponding stack, then grabbed more letters from the bag, tossed them into a big heap in the middle of the table and began again. The second letter from that heap was directed to Dr. Austin. She set it aside in a personal-correspondence pile and snatched up another.

"Well, what have we here?"

She jumped, jerked her gaze to the man standing at the top of the stairs. Her stomach knotted. "Good morning, Mr. Willard."

"It is now." The reporter grinned, tossed his hat on his desk and strode down the room toward her. He swept his gaze over the stacks of letters covering the table. "What's all this?"

She held her uneasiness in check and answered in a calm, polite tone. "The CLSC letters I'm going to answer."

"All of *those*?"

She noted his shocked expression and nodded. "And many more. This whole bag, in fact." She indicated the bag leaning against the wall.

He let out a long, low whistle. "It looks like you're going to need a lot of help to get all of those letters answered." He gave her a wolfish grin. "I'd be happy to volunteer."

She gave him a cool look to discourage his flirting and cast another look toward the stairs. They were all alone. A shiver slipped down her spine. "Thank you for your considerate offer, Mr. Willard. But I am managing fine by myself. Now, if you'll excuse me, I've a great deal of work to do." She scanned a letter, added it to the grammar stack and picked up another.

"Ah, don't be like that, cu—"

"Is there something you needed from the reference shelf, Willard?"

Mr. Thornberg. The tension left her spine and shoulders.

"Just saying good morning to Miss Gordon, boss."

"We still need a lead story for tomorrow's edition, Willard. Have you one?"

"Not yet."

"The annual Chautauqua Assembly is important to the economy of this city, and I've heard rumors of a substantial amount of construction going on. Why don't you go to Fair Point and see what you can find out?"

It was clearly an order, given in a tone that left no doubt of Mr. Thornberg's opinion over the reporter's waste of time. She looked up, stared at her boss's taut face. The reporter wasn't the only one Mr. Thornberg was displeased with. Surely, he didn't think she had *invited* Mr. Willard's attention? The knots in her stomach twisted tighter. She plunked the letter in her hand on top of the definition-of-words stack and grabbed another from the heap.

Boyd Willard walked away, the strike of his shoe heels against the wood floor loud in the silence. Mr. Thornberg took the reporter's place across the table from her. She pressed her lips together to hold back the urge to explain. She'd done nothing wrong. She slapped the letter she held onto the mathematics pile and snatched up another.

"What are you doing, Miss Gordon? What are these different piles?"

She glanced up. There was a slight frown line between Mr. Thornberg's straight dark brows and a glint of curiosity in his brown eyes. The discomfort in her stomach eased a bit. "I am sorting the letters into different classifications. These—" she indicated the first stack on her right "—have questions about words… their pronunciation or definition. And these—" she moved her hand to the next pile "—have queries about science. And then there are grammar and mathematics stacks. And those—" she gestured toward the smallest stack at the edge of the table "—are the ones directed to Dr. Austin or specific teachers at the Chautauqua Assembly.

"When I'm finished sorting, I will answer one stack of letters at a time. As they will all deal with the same subject, I won't have to keep switching reference material *if* I don't know the answers." She couldn't stop herself from putting a slight emphasis on the word *if*. He didn't seem to notice. He picked up and scanned letters from each stack, his head nodding slowly.

"This is an excellent idea, Miss Gordon." He put the letter he held back on its stack and smiled. "Your work is most efficient."

The smile took her aback. Her lips curved in response. "Thank you, Mr. Thornberg."

"Yes. Well…" He coughed, cleared his throat. "I'll leave you to your work. Don't hesitate to ask for my help—though you seem to have things well in hand." He dipped his head and walked back into the composing room.

She tamped down her pleasure at his compliment of her work and returned to her task.

"I appreciate your zealous approach to your work, Miss Gordon, but it's time for your afternoon meal break."

Clarice jumped, looked from the letter in her hand to Mr. Thornberg standing on the other side of the table and blinked to adjust her vision. "Thank you, sir. I didn't realize—" The splatter of rain against the windows burst upon her consciousness. "It's raining!"

"Yes, for over an hour now."

"Oh, dear." She breathed the words, placed the letter on the science pile and stared at the water coursing down the windows.

"Is there a problem, Miss Gordon?"

"What? Oh. No. Well…" She moved to her desk, opened the bottom drawer, pulled out her hat and gave a rueful little laugh. "I suppose under the circumstances *this* qualifies as a problem." She lifted the small felt hat to her head, snatched the pin from where she'd tossed it on her desk and jammed it into place. Her imagination was already making her shiver as she started for the stairs.

"You're going out in this rain with no waterproof or umbrella?"

His tone was one of utter disbelief. He obviously thought her either insane or foolish in the extreme. She stopped and turned to face him. "There are times when we are left with no choice in matters, Mr. Thornberg. For me, this is one of those times. My mother is bedridden and depends upon me for her needs. When I came to work this morning, I did not know it would rain today and thus did not wear my waterproof. Nor did I make other arrangements for my mother's care." She gave an eloquent little shrug of her shoulders. "Thus…no choice." She started again for the stairs.

"Wait!"

The command in his voice raised her hackles. She'd had enough of that from her father and brothers. But this was her boss. She made her feet stop walking, tensed when he strode up beside her.

"Come with me, Miss Gordon. I've an umbrella in the office."

* * *

The rain beat on the umbrella, hit the walkway with such force it splashed almost as high as her knees. The hem of her long skirt was sodden, the short train so heavy it felt as if she were dragging one of the large baskets of wet laundry from her childhood behind her. The wind gusted, blew the rain straight at them. She shivered, thankful Mr. Thornberg held the umbrella. She was having difficulty enough making progress against the wind.

"Stop!" He leaned down to put his mouth near her ear. "Hold the umbrella."

She didn't question his command. It was his umbrella. She took it into her two hands and raised her arms to hold it high enough to clear his head, tried to keep it from shaking from her shivering. "What are you d-doing?" She gaped as he shrugged out of his suit coat. *Now who was insane?*

"What I should have done before. You're shivering. Lower your arms." He draped his jacket around her shoulders, held it there with one hand, took the umbrella into his other and straightened.

The warmth from his body clinging to the suit coat seeped into her. She stared up at him too astounded to speak, let alone protest.

"The jacket is much too large for you. Hold it tight or the wind will whip it away."

"But you—"

"No argument, Miss Gordon."

She nodded, grabbed the edges of his jacket, twisted her hands to the inside and held it close against her. A gust of wind swept down the street and she staggered backward. His hand slipped to her lower back, steadied her against the force of the wind as they moved forward.

The blowing rain formed large wet blotches on his shirt. *He must be icy cold.* She looked down at his suit coat enfolding her in its dry warmth and a band of tightness squeezed her throat and chest. She stared down at the splashing rain and fought back the unexplainable urge to cry.

Main Street was deserted in the storm. The unimpeded wind whipped her skirts into a frenzy. His arm tightened. She could feel its strength angling down her back to where his hand supported her as they crossed to the walkway at East Second Street and continued down the block. She fought the tightness in her chest for breath and watched the houses they passed, slowed her steps then unlatched a gate bearing a sign that read Smithfield Boardinghouse. "This is where I live."

He escorted her up the stone walk to the deep porch. Large rhododendron bushes growing in front of the railing blocked the wind and rain. She stepped behind their protection and slipped off his suit coat, shivering in the cold, damp air. "Thank you for seeing me home in the storm, Mr. Thornberg. I'm sorry you have gotten soaked and cold. I would ask you in to get warm, but—" She could manage no more. The constriction of her throat choked off her words. She looked down at his suit coat in her hands.

"But boardinghouses do not lend themselves to such amenities. I quite understand, Miss Gordon. I'm no stranger to boardinghouses. I lived in my share when I was a roving reporter." He took his suit coat from her, shrugged to settle it on his shoulders and picked up his umbrella. "Please do not try to return to work in this storm. My regards to your mother. I hope her health improves soon. Good afternoon, Miss Gordon." He dipped his head, trotted down the steps and hurried out through the gate.

She wrapped her arms about herself and stared after him until he disappeared into the rain, waiting for that strange urge to cry to go away so she could go inside.

Charles scooped the last spoonful of soup from his bowl, picked up his coffee and walked into his study. The clink of dishes and clatter of flatware followed him as Mrs. Hotchkiss cleared the dining room. He scowled and closed the door, unreasonably irritated by the normal sounds of his daily life.

It had been a mistake. One he couldn't avoid—he could hardly have let Miss Gordon walk home in the storm with no protection whatsoever—but a mistake nonetheless. He had hated leaving her standing there on the porch when she looked so defenseless and—

Thunderation! How was he to get the picture of her out of his head! And why, in the name of all that was *sane*, should it make him feel lonely? The new house he'd found such comfort in suddenly felt like an empty tomb.

He slammed his cup down on the mantel and wished there were a fire on the hearth so he had a log he could kick. He hadn't felt so—so *alone* since his mother had shipped him off to boarding school when he was five years old.

He shook his head, jammed his hands into his pockets and stared out at the rain. He'd thought he was over all those old, worthless emotions. There was nothing more useless than self-pity.

He frowned, buttoned the coat of the suit he'd changed into and headed for the entrance hall. Getting out a newspaper couldn't wait for good weather.

She was caring for a bedridden mother. No wonder Miss Gordon was prickly. That was a heavy load for a young woman to shoulder. The shadow of it had been in her eyes when she'd looked up at him. And surprise. No, something more than surprise…shock had filled them when he'd put his suit coat around her. As if no one had ever taken care of her.

Something twisted deep in his gut. He pulled on his mackintosh and hat, grabbed the wet umbrella from its stand and stepped out onto the porch. Taking Miss Gordon home had been a mistake…one that, in spite of his better sense, he would willingly make again.

The radiant warmth of the late-afternoon sun chased the damp chill from the editorial room. Clarice leaned the umbrella she had brought with her in the corner by her desk and removed her wrap.

"I didn't expect you to return today, Miss Gordon."

She spun about. Charles Thornberg stood in the doorway to the composing room a sheet of paper in his hand. She took a breath to calm her racing pulse.

"There is still almost two hours until quitting time and the storm has passed."

He nodded, glanced toward the umbrella. "I see you don't intend to be caught unprepared by a rainstorm again."

Was he displeased with losing work time by walking her home? Had she ruined her hope of being employed as a columnist on the Journal? She hastened to assure him it would not happen again. "Once was forgivable. Twice would be shoddy carelessness."

"And you would not be guilty of such a thing."

Father's quick hand taught me the folly of that. She turned and draped her wrap over the chair. "I learned when very young it was not wise to make the same mistake twice."

"Mr. Thornberg, sir!" Footsteps pounded on the stairs. A young boy burst into the room, braced his hands on his knees and sucked in a long breath.

Charles Thornberg pivoted and hurried toward the boy. "What is it, son?"

"Fire…sir…"

The breathy gasps drew her forward. Perhaps—

"Fire! Where? What is burning?"

"Steamers…at the dock…"

"Carry on, Miss Gordon!" Charles threw the paper he held toward his desk and clattered down the stairs, the boy close on his heels.

She ran to the front window, peered down—Charles Thornberg and the boy burst from the building and ran down the street. She clenched her hands and started back toward the table holding the piles of letters. *Carry on, Miss Gordon.* Charles Thornberg would probably have had her come along if she were a *man*. Carry on, indeed!

The paper Charles had thrown had missed his desk. She scooped it up off the floor and scanned the report beneath Boyd Willard's name. It was about a proposed public water system the city council had discussed at their last meeting. A dull, colorless report. Some descriptions of the councilmen's attitudes would have brought it alive...

She sighed, carried the paper into the composing room and glanced over the partially finished layout for the next edition resting on the tables. Where was he going to— There. No. The report was too small for the empty space on the large piece of white paper. There was a sizable gap left. She glanced over her shoulder at the page layout on the table behind her. It couldn't go there. That page was finished.

Fillers!

She riffled through the items in the basket, frowned and sorted through them again. None of them were large enough to fill the gaping space. Perhaps two... Yes. If she slid the paper holding the report on the council meeting down a bit and added a filler at the top and another at the bottom. Or she could move the item at the top of the page over, put the report in its place and change that filler... Her fingers flew over the piece of white paper, rearranging the layout. A smile curved her lips. Perfect! But she'd best put them back as they had been and get to work, lest Mr. Thornberg find out she had—

"Miss Gordon? Where are you?"

She gave a guilty start at the impatient hail and hurried into the editorial room. The clerk from the office downstairs stood on the stairs peering over the railing. He looked irritated. "What is it, Mr. Warren?"

"I need you to come down to the office." The man turned and headed back down the stairs.

"Wait, Mr. Warren! What—" She swallowed the rest of the question as he disappeared from view, shot a look at the composing tables, then lifted her hems and followed after him to the office. She'd arrange the page back the way it had been when she returned.

"Mr. Warren, I've work to—" A wave of his arm directed her gaze across the room. A small, well-dressed boy of perhaps two, at the most three, years old, sat huddled on a wooden chair. There were tears in his eyes and on his cheeks, and his lips were trembling, but he didn't make a sound beyond soft, shuddering intakes of breath that clutched at her heart.

"The boy can't stay here. You have to take him."

"Take him!" She jerked her gaze from the boy, gaped at Mr. Warren. "What are you talking about?" She swept her gaze around the room, lowered her voice. "Where are his mother and father?"

The office clerk shrugged his thin shoulders, picked up an envelope and handed it to her. *Mr. Charles Thornberg.* She frowned and offered it back to him. "This isn't for me. It—"

"It goes with the boy." The clerk shot a look in the tot's direction then fixed his gaze on her. "Here's the way of it, Miss Gordon. A man come in here with

the boy and asked for Mr. Thornberg. I told him Mr.
Thornberg wasn't here, that he'd have to wait or come
back another time, and he said that was impossible,
that he had a train to catch. He said he'd been hired to
deliver the boy and the envelope to Mr. Thornberg and
that his job was done." A scowl drew the clerk's brows
down. "I tried to stop him, but he walked out and kept
going. So you have to take the boy."

"Me?"

"Well, he can't stay here! And you're a woman and
all…"

She stiffened and gave him a cool look. "Being a
woman doesn't come with instructions for caring for
children, Mr. Warren." She looked over at the huddled-
up little boy and her heart melted. He looked so afraid.
"What is his name?"

"The man only called him 'the lad.' Those are his
things."

The lad. As if he were no more important than the
large leather grip sitting on the floor! She shoved the
letter in her skirt pocket and walked over to kneel down
in front of the chair. The boy pressed back and stared at
her out of fear-filled eyes. She tamped down a surge of
anger at whoever had treated the boy so callously and
smiled. "I hear you've had a journey on a train. That
must have been exciting!" There was no response, only
those blue eyes staring at her. "But riding on the train
can be tiring. And you can get very hungry, too." The
boy's eyes flickered, and another surge of anger shook
her. Had the man not *fed* the child? Concern pounced.
How would she—

"Mr. Thornberg's housekeeper will feed him."

Mr. Thornberg had a housekeeper! Relief eased her concern for the toddler's welfare. She looked over her shoulder at Mr. Warren. "Do you know where Mr. Thornberg lives?"

The outer door opened and closed. Footsteps approached the office. "One block left. The stone house on the corner. Now get the boy out of here!" The clerk hissed the words, resumed his place behind the counter and faced the customer at the doorway. "Good afternoon, sir. How may I help you?"

She rose and leaned down to pick up the little boy. "This is a busy place. Let's go to Mr. Thornberg's house and get you something to eat." The boy stiffened, but he did not burst into tears or fight her, for which she was grateful. She settled him in her arms, eyed the large leather valise and left it on the floor. The boy was enough for her to carry.

Clarice sat on the edge of the settee and removed the sleeping tot's shoes. Her chest tightened at the sight of his small feet. He was so young. So *helpless*. And scared. Too scared to speak. Though he seemed an intelligent child, the best she'd been able to coax from him while he was eating his bread and jam was a nod or a shake of his head. Poor little fellow. What had he been through? She pulled in a breath at the thought of the way the man had simply left the boy at the newspaper office like some piece of *luggage*. She'd have told the man what she thought of his treating a child in such a heartless manner! No wonder the boy was afraid! How long had he been in that thoughtless man's care?

She covered the toddler with a throw from a nearby chair, tucked the soft woven wool close around his stocking-clad feet and rose. The letter in her pocket crackled as she straightened. She withdrew it and stared down at her employer's name written in ornate flowing letters across the front. It was a woman's handwriting. The child's mother? The thoughts held at bay while she'd cared for the toddler crowded into her head.

Was the boy Charles Thornberg's son? He had the look of him with his curly dark hair and blue eyes. And what other possible reason could there be for a woman to send the boy to him accompanied by a letter and a valise full of his things? The woman obviously expected—

No. She jerked her thoughts from the speculation. Charles Thornberg's private life was none of her business. And neither was the boy. She would be done with him as soon as Mr. Thornberg came home. Hopefully that would be soon.

Silence pressed in on her, broken only by the steady ticktock of the longcase clock in the corner. She frowned and walked to the fireplace, leaned the letter against a pewter candlestick on the mantel then looked around the large, well-furnished room, uneasy at being alone in the house. Mr. Warren had been wrong. There was no housekeeper. The house was empty when she arrived. She'd felt like a snoop hunting out the kitchen then poking through the cupboards to find something for the boy to eat.

The clock gonged. She jumped, glanced over at the sleeping toddler. He hadn't stirred. The poor little tot was exhausted. What was she to do? Her mother would be expecting her home shortly after the clock struck the hour. If Mr. Thornberg hadn't come home by then, she would have to wake the boy, take him home with her and then bring him back after she had cared for her mother.

The thought gave her pause. Who would care for the boy? What would happen to him? Would Mr. Thornberg keep him? She eyed the envelope, itching to open it and find out the answers, then sighed and turned away from the private missive. The boy was Mr. Thornberg's concern, not hers.

Where was he? The fire must be a bad one. She wrapped her arms about herself and listened to the clock ticking away the minutes. Mr. Warren would be closing the office and going home on the hour. There would be no one to tell— *He was here!*

Footsteps pounded across the porch. The door opened, closed. Quick footsteps sounded in the hall, changed tempo. He was going upstairs. She ran for the doorway. "We're in the sitting room, Mr. Thornberg!"

He came to a dead halt, twisted about and stared down at her. "Miss Gordon! What are you doing— *We're?*"

"Yes. The boy and I. I didn't want to take the liberty of going upstairs."

"Boy?" A frown creased his forehead. He descended the stairs into the lamp-lit hallway and scowled down at her. "What boy?"

"The one who was left—" She stopped, stared at the black-rimmed holes that peppered his shirt then lifted her gaze. His face was covered with black smudges and there was a large blister on the side of his neck above his opened collar. "You've been fighting the fire."

"Yes. The dock went ablaze and everyone pitched in to fight the fire, lest it spread to the nearby buildings. What boy?"

She drew her gaze from the angry blister and gathered her thoughts. "You haven't been to the newspaper, then?"

"No. I came directly home to wash and change into a clean shirt." His scowl deepened. "What *boy*?"

"The one who was delivered to you at the newspaper office."

"*Delivered* to me. A *boy*?"

He looked astounded—which for some reason made her feel better about the whole strange situation. She nodded and plunged into an explanation. "Yes. A man came to the office with the boy and a large valise. He told Mr. Warren he'd been hired to deliver the boy to you and—".

"What man? Who hired him? Why me?"

His questions came at her in rapid succession. She shook her head. "I can't answer your questions, Mr. Thornberg. The man simply left the boy, his valise and a letter directed to you with Mr. Warren and hurried off to catch a train. Mr. Warren bade me bring the boy here to your house, where your housekeeper could care for him. When I arrived, there was no one here, so I stayed with the boy. That's all I know. Now, as you are here, I'll be on my way." She headed for the front door. "The letter is on the mantel. And the boy is asleep on your settee."

"Wait, Miss Gordon!"

She turned back, looked up at him.

He lifted his hand and rubbed the back of his neck, winced when his fingertips touched the blister above his collar. "If you would give me a minute to take this all in and collect my thoughts, please…"

"Of course."

She followed him into the sitting room, watched him stride over to the settee and look down. He spun back to face her, shock written all over his features.

"He's a *baby*."

"A toddler of two or three years, I would guess."

"And someone brought him to the newspaper office and left him there for *me*?"

"Yes."

"Unconscionable!" His face darkened. The muscle along his jaw twitched. "What kind of person would simply leave—" He sucked in a breath and strode to the mantel, snatched up the envelope, broke the seal and scanned the letter. His face tightened. "So, Mother, you've done it again."

Mother? No. His words had been choked, barely audible. She'd misunderstood.

He crushed the letter in his hand and apprehension tingled along her nerves. She'd never seen such cold fury in a man's eyes. Anger, yes—many, many times— but this… He moved toward the settee and she rushed forward to protect the child, stopped as her employer bent and scooped the boy into his arms.

"It's all right, Jonathan, everything is all right. You have a home now. No one will ever discard you again. I give you my word on it."

Discard him? What was in that letter? Charles Thornberg cleared his throat, and she lifted her gaze from the crushed letter to his face. Her breath caught at the fierce, protective look in his eyes.

"I know nothing about caring for a young child, Miss Gordon. And I am a stranger to Jonathan. Will you please come with me while I put my little brother to bed? I don't want him to be frightened should he awaken."

Chapter Four

I'll be home as soon as I can, Mama. Clarice drew her gaze from the clock, sighed and hurried out of the sitting room after Charles Thornberg. But for the boy's tender age, she would have refused her employer's request for her help. Still, it would take only a few minutes to settle the exhausted child, and then she would be on her way. She had no desire to become involved in Mr. Thornberg's private problems.

She gripped the banister, lifted her skirt hems with her free hand and followed him up the stairs to a wide hallway. The dim light of dusk filtered through slatted shutters on windows at either end.

"This way, Miss Gordon." Her employer strode down the hallway on the right and stopped. "If you would open the door, please?"

She moved in front of him, twisted the knob and pushed the door open. A bed loomed in the darkness against the far wall of a large, well-appointed bedroom. She hurried forward, her hems brushing against an Oriental rug, Charles Thornberg's footfalls a dull thud behind her. The richness of soft wool caressed her fingers as she turned back the woven coverlet and blankets.

Her curiosity grew as Charles laid his brother on the readied bed, straightened and stared down at him. He looked…stunned was the only description she could come up with.

"He's awfully small, isn't he?"

She was trying not to notice that. "It's a large bed."

"Hmm."

Her employer didn't sound comforted by her observation. He didn't look it, either. He was frowning. She leaned forward and began undoing the buttons on the sleeping toddler's outfit.

"His suit coat is stained. Is that bits of *food* dried on it?"

It was an outraged whisper. Not surprising considering Charles Thornberg's own normally impeccable appearance. "At least he was fed."

His eyes flashed. Obviously, he took no comfort from that observation, either. "There is no reason for such neglect. I'm certain the man was well paid for his services!"

Her own anger over the man's treatment of the toddler surged at the hissed words. What had this boy been through? She took a breath to calm herself. Anger served no good purpose. "There's no nightshirt to put on him, but he should be comfortable enough without his jacket and vest." *His hands are so little…* She eased the boy's unresisting arms out of the sleeves, slipped her hand beneath his small back and raised him enough to tug his garments free.

"Is he all right? He's not moving or anything. Should I go for the doctor?"

She laid the boy back against the pillow and glanced across the bed. The muscle along Charles Thornberg's jaw was twitching. "I think he's fine. Children sleep very soundly, and he's exhausted. He must have had an arduous journey on the train."

"And ship." Charles Thornberg's eyes darkened, his mouth and jaw tightened, and that small muscle jumped. The letter, still clutched in his hand, crackled as he shoved it in his pocket. "Who knows what my brother has endured these last few weeks. *And* before…"

Ship? Weeks? She stole a glance at the bit of white paper peeking out of her employer's suit-coat pocket. What was in that letter? She looked down, fumbled with the unfamiliar knot in the small tie, uncomfortable with Charles's angry presence. "I'm afraid I'm more familiar with bows…"

"I'll do it."

His fingers brushed against hers, warm and strong but gentle in their touch, even in his anger. That odd sensation she'd experienced when he'd given her his suit coat during the rainstorm washed over her again. She was used to a hard grip or a quick slap from men's hands.

She drew back and studied his face while he undid the knot and removed the boy's tie. That fierce, protective look had leaped to the fore. She took a deep breath to ease a sudden tightness in her chest and folded the boy's clothes, determined to keep her emotions uninvolved. "Have you a towel?"

"A towel?" He tossed the small tie on the boy's folded clothes and gave her a quizzical look.

"To place under him. He's very young and very tired and I don't know if he will wake should he need to…" Heat climbed into her cheeks at having to mention the indelicate subject. She lowered her gaze, made a vague gesture toward the boy. "A towel will protect the sheet and mattress."

"Oh." It was a low, perplexed growl. "I never would have thought of that." He shook his head, turned and headed for a door in the right-hand wall. "There are towels in the dressing room. I'll be right back."

Discarded. The word slithered through her mind. She loosened the buttons and removed the toddler's starched collar, placed it at the foot of the bed with his jacket, then, unable to stop herself, touched his soft dark curls. *You have a home now. No one will ever discard you again. I give you my word on it.*

"Here you are."

She started, jerked her gaze and her hand from the boy.

"Do you want me to lift Jonathan while you spread the towel?"

"That would be helpful." She took the towel, folded it into a pad and placed it on the bed. "I'm finished." She watched Charles lower Jonathan back to the bed then pulled the covers up over him, leaned down and tucked the blanket edges beneath the mattress.

"Why are you doing that?"

"He probably still sleeps in a crib. I don't want him to roll out of the bed."

"Oh. Another thing I would not have thought of…" The mumbled words drifted across the bed as Charles bent and copied her actions on the opposite side.

What if Jonathan woke? She straightened and looked down at the sleeping toddler. He would be so frightened waking in a strange room with a strange man to tend him. Tears stung her eyes. She blinked them away, smoothed her palms down the front of her skirt. "That's all I know to do for him, Mr. Thornberg. I'll be going now."

"Wait!"

The hissed word stopped her in her tracks. "Mr. Thornberg, I must go." She clenched her hands, tried to keep her exasperation from slipping into her quiet response. "My mother—"

"I realize your mother needs your care, Miss Gordon. But I'm in an untenable situation here." He came around the bed toward her, shoved his hand through his already mussed hair. "I can't leave my brother alone, but I *have* to get to the *Journal* office. I *have* to write the story of the fire, finish composing the pages and—" His words ended on another frustrated hiss.

"I understand your problem, Mr. Thornberg, but—" *The composing page!* Her stomach sank.

"So here's my solution." He clasped his hands behind his back and looked down at her. "Surely there is someone at your boardinghouse willing to care for your mother for a fair recompense?"

An easy solution for him. He had money! She did not. "Well, yes. Mrs. Duncan sometimes—"

"Ah! Mrs. Duncan!"

"Yes, but—"

"No buts, Miss Gordon. If you will stay with Jonathan, I will go straight to your boardinghouse, explain the situation to your mother and arrange for her care until you are able to go home. I will pay any expense involved, of course, and also pay you for your time."

The offer was generous but not fair. She glanced at the toddler, wanting to refuse and knowing she couldn't. There were too many reasons why she should agree—to save her job not the least among them. Not that it would be fair of him to terminate her employment at the paper because of his personal problem. But when were men ever fair? "Very well, Mr. Thornberg, I'll stay. But you *must* hurry to the boardinghouse. My mother has been expecting me for some time now."

"I'll wash and change and then run all the way, Miss Gordon! Thank you!"

She watched him pivot and run out the door, heard his rushing footsteps in the hallway and the opening and closing of a nearby door. Hopefully, he would keep his word and hurry. It was almost supper time and her mother needed care. Worry gnawed at her, but there was nothing more she could do. She let out a long sigh and looked around for a lamp. It would be full dark soon, and she had no desire to sit in a strange house with no light.

Sit. She made a slow turn, spotted a chair beside a dresser and carried it over close to the small one-drawer stand against the wall at the head of the bed. There was a lamp and a small wood chest on the stand. Would she find matches in the chest? She rubbed her hands down her skirt, reluctant to open someone else's possession.

A door opened, closed. Light flared in the hallway. She hurried toward the open door, stopped when Charles Thornberg appeared holding a hand oil lamp and two books.

"I thought these might help you pass the time. Now I'm off to see to your mother's care."

He handed her the lamp and books, pivoted and disappeared into the hallway. A moment later his footsteps were pounding down the stairs. A door slammed.

I thought these might help you pass the time. She stared down at the lamp and books in her hand trying to make sense of Charles Thornberg's thoughtfulness in light of the selfish cruelty she'd experienced of men. It was impossible. She took a breath, shook her head and hurried toward the bed.

"I apologize for the inconvenience I'm causing you, Mrs. Gordon, but there is simply no choice." Charles lowered his gaze from the older woman sitting propped up in bed to the writing box resting on the quilt covering her legs. Guilt soured his empty stomach. "And that sounds completely selfish and heartless. I—" Mrs. Gordon's lifted hand halted his words.

"Not at all, Mr. Thornberg. A small child is helpless and needs constant attention. I may be crippled, but I'm not helpless."

The curve of the older woman's lips brought an image of her daughter's smile flashing into his head. Not that Clarice Gordon's warm, sweet smile had been in evidence tonight.

"Clarice bought me a bell so I can summon help should the need arise. And Mrs. Duncan will take good care of me." Mrs. Gordon lowered her hand back down to cover the piece of paper she'd been writing on when he entered the room.

His sharp gaze caught the first line before she hid it. *How to Keep a Cookstove Shiny and Clean.* That would make a good filler. He shrugged off the errant thought. "As I said, your daughter has agreed, though she is not at all happy with the arrangement."

A shadow darkened Mrs. Gordon's blue eyes. "Clarice worries about me overmuch."

The guilt cut deeper. His fingers tightened on his hat brim. How could Clarice Gordon feel otherwise? In spite of her protestations to the opposite, Mrs. Gordon *was* helpless. His thoughts swirled, but he could find no other solution to his problem. He frowned, laid out the rest of what he'd come to say. "I'm afraid, if your daughter agrees, the situation may extend for a few days—until my housekeeper returns or I can think of another way to care for Jonathan."

"I understand." Mrs. Gordon tipped her head and peered up at him, a look in her eyes he couldn't decipher. "Clarice's concern for me will override her head and her heart, Mr. Thornberg. You tell her I said the child comes first, and that I want her to care for him."

He dipped his head. "Thank you. You are a very kind and gracious woman, Mrs. Gordon."

"I'm simply a mother, Mr. Thornberg."

The door behind him opened and a short plump woman bustled into the room carrying a tray laden with food. "Here's your supper, Helen. Nice and hot."

The interruption stopped him from having to answer her enigmatic reply. He stepped aside, made a polite bow. "I must hurry to the newspaper, Mrs. Gordon. Thank you again for your understanding. And thank you for your help, Mrs. Duncan." He stepped out of the bedroom, reached to pull the door closed.

"What a nice young man Clarice works for, Helen. And very handsome, too."

He paused, scowled at the innuendo in Mrs. Duncan's words and tone. Had he done harm to Clarice Gordon's reputation by coming here?

"Mr. Thornberg is *very* nice, Dora. And most considerate. Not many *employers* would concern themselves with the crippled mother of an employee that must *work* beyond quitting time. Is that shepherd's pie I smell?"

A smile touched his lips. There was nothing to worry about. Mrs. Gordon had set the situation straight. And her tone said clearly she would not tolerate any gossip about her daughter and her daughter's employer.

He eased the door closed, hurried down the hall to the stairs, trotted down and rushed out the front door. The smell of wood smoke drifting on the evening breeze erased thought of everything but the fire and the story he had to write. He shoved through the gate at the end of the walkway and broke into a run.

Was that crying?

Clarice held her breath and listened. The boy *was* crying. Sobbing, in an unnatural, quiet way she could barely hear. She turned from the window and hurried to the bed, stood in the dim light of the oil lamp and hoped the toddler would remember her and not be afraid. The lamplight glittered on the tears pooled in the boy's eyes and running down his temples to dampen his hair. His lips were pressed tight and his little chin quivered with his effort to be quiet. Had he been told not to cry?

Her eyes stung. She blinked hard and smiled reassurance. Charles Thornberg's words tumbled from her mouth. "You're all right, Jonathan. Your long journey is at an end. You're home now."

He stared up at her, the blankets covering him rising and falling slightly with his uneven indrawn breaths.

"I'm Miss Gordon and I'm here to take care of you. Do you need something? Are you hungry or—?"

"Me g-go potty."

"Oh." Now what? She had no dry clothes for him. And where would she find another sheet if one was needed? She pulled the covers back, glanced down and let out a sigh. The boy's clothes were dry. She smiled and held out her arms. "I'll take you. Let's hurry…"

He looked at her a long moment, then pushed himself to a sitting position and raised his arms. She lifted him and gathered him close. His little body was soft and warm, his hair silky against her cheek. Emotions she didn't want to experience rushed through her. She snatched up the hand lamp and hurried to the dressing room.

"Me do it myself."

There was determination in the toddler's sleepy voice and in the set of his chin. He looked remarkably like Charles Thornberg. She nodded and lowered him to the floor, then paused, reluctant to leave him. He looked so small and helpless standing there in his shirt and socks. "I'll be outside the door, if you need me." She stepped back into the bedroom, leaving the door open a crack so she could hear if he called, grateful the night was warm so he wouldn't get too chilled. There was a small scrape, the sort of sound a stool made when it was pushed along the floor. She curled her fingers tight into her palms, resisting the urge to open the door and go in to help him.

"Me done now."

His soft voice grabbed at her heart. She opened the door and scooped him up into her arms. His head lolled against her shoulder. His warm breath puffed against her neck as soft as a feather. She moved toward the bed, fighting the impulse to cuddle him close, to turn her head and kiss his soft cheek. His body went lax.

She lowered him to the bed and tucked the covers close around him, then went back for the hand lamp. The house was so silent she could hear the ticking of a clock in another room. She started when it gonged, counted as it struck the hour. Eleven o'clock. How much longer would Charles Thornberg be?

The opening of the front door downstairs answered her question. She released a long sigh, smoothed back the strands of hair that had fallen free of her tightly constrained bun and hurried out into the hallway.

Light flared on the stairs. Heels struck against the oak treads. She stopped and waited, watched as a man's shadow grew larger and spread up the wall.

"Miss Gordon!" Charles Thornberg stopped, glanced toward the bedroom door behind her. "Is something wrong? Is Jonathan ill or—"

"No. He's fine. He woke a while ago and used the… necessary…then immediately fell back to sleep. He's so tired I think he will sleep through until morning." She took a step toward the stairs, stopped when he didn't move. "It's time for me to leave. I'll wish you a good evening, Mr. Thornberg."

"In a moment, Miss Gordon. I have a proposition to discuss with you."

Not again! She stiffened, determined to withstand whatever he proposed. She had her career to build. She could not afford to lay it aside and care for the boy, no matter how she sympathized with—

She drew in a breath, stared at Charles Thornberg standing at the top of the stairs with the boy's valise gripped in his hand. For a moment she had forgotten the man was her employer. "Very well."

She spun about and retraced her steps to the boy's bedroom. Why waste her time and breath? No argument would change his mind. Men cared about *their* problems…no one else's—unless they interfered with their comfort or wishes. She stepped to the wardrobe and opened the carved double doors then marched over to where Charles Thornberg stood looking down at his little brother. "Mr. Thornberg, I don't mean to be rude, but I really must get home. If you will give me the valise, I'll put your brother's clothes away in the wardrobe."

His gaze shifted, met hers. "I'll hold the valise. It's too heavy for you."

She clenched her hands, fought to keep her exasperation out of her voice. "That's not necessary. I was slopping hogs and cleaning the chicken coop on my father's farm when I was five years old. I can manage the valise." Silence. She held out her hand for the leather bag, recognized her error when his knuckles whitened on the grips.

"This is my home, not your father's farm, Miss Gordon. I will hold the valise."

His voice was quiet, firm. She glanced up and met his gaze. It was unfathomable and…unsettling. "As you wish." She grabbed the lamp and walked back to the wardrobe, aware of him behind her, annoyed by her unease in his presence. She set the lamp on one of the shelves, jumped when he cleared his throat.

"I wanted to speak to you about this situation I find myself in, Miss Gordon. But first let me assure you I have arranged for your safe transportation home. There is a carriage and driver waiting outside."

"A *carriage.*" She spun to face him, unable to hide her astonishment. "Whatever for? I've only to walk a few blocks."

"Nonetheless, the hour is late and I promised your

mother I would see you safely home. Obviously, I can't escort you, so I made other arrangements." His gaze narrowed on her. "Are you always so prickly when someone tries to take care of you?"

I wouldn't know. No other man has ever done so. She swallowed the retort that sprang readily to her lips and formed a more judicious reply. "Forgive me, Mr. Thornberg—my response was inappropriate. I'm grateful for your thoughtfulness." She reached to undo the buckled straps on the valise he had balanced on his extended forearms to avoid his gaze. She knew how to react to a slap or a curse, but his kindness left her at a loss.

"My housekeeper left today for a weeklong visit with her daughter. That's the reason the house was empty when you brought Jonathan here."

Ah, the real, self-serving reason for his "kindness." Her uncertainty fled. She was on familiar ground again. "How unfortunate." She snatched a small dark blue sailor suit from the clothes stuffed in the boy's valise, examined it in the light of the lamp, smoothed and folded it then placed it on a shelf.

"I'm glad you grasp my predicament."

A lot better than you grasp mine! She grabbed a small brown suit from the bag, frowned at the stains on it and dropped it on the floor to begin a wash pile. There was no doubt that she'd be looking after the boy. It would likely cost her her job to say no. And she certainly couldn't afford that. At least his baby clothes weren't stained with crude oil, as her father's and brothers' work clothes had been.

"I know it's an imposition, but, as is apparent, I've no idea of how to care for a baby."

He's a toddler. He walks and talks and feeds himself. She grasped the underthings in the bag. They had all been worn. She tossed them onto the wash pile, frowned and rooted deeper in the bag, pulled out a nightshirt and three pair of socks…all dirty.

"I have a newspaper to run. You know the work that involves."

Yes, she did. And it was unfair of him to use her knowledge of the workings of the newspaper to undermine her resolve. She threw down the socks and braced herself for what was coming.

"I've no choice but to ask that you please come tomorrow morning to care for Jonathan, Miss Gordon. I will pay you for your time, of course."

And what of my career? How can I advance that if I'm not working at the newspaper? "Very well." She clamped her jaw against the agreement she was forced to utter, pulled a coat and matching hat from the bag and hung them in the right side of the wardrobe then straightened the small sleeves.

"These boots and this tie are all that are left in the valise."

He sounded angry. She stole a glance at him. He scowled, shoved the boots on a shelf in the almost-empty wardrobe, then scooped up the pile of clothes on the floor and jammed them back in the valise, muttering beneath his breath. "If they didn't keep him clean, what else did they neglect to do for him?"

They? Only one man had brought Jonathan to the

newspaper office. She closed the wardrobe and carried the hand lamp back to the table by the bed. The soft light fell on the sleeping toddler, made smudges of the dark lashes resting on cheeks pink with warmth, shadowed the sweet slightly open lips of the small mouth above the little round chin burrowed into the blankets covering him.

"You said he woke earlier. Was he frightened?"

The whisper brought the memory of Jonathan's quiet sobs flowing into her head. "At first."

"What did you do to alleviate his fright?"

She drew her gaze from the toddler, moved to the end of the bed where Charles Thornberg stood. "I stood in the light so he could see me and told him I was here to take care of him. I think he remembered that I brought him here and gave him bread and jam. I believe that reassured him."

He nodded, stuffed the clothes she had taken off Jonathan into the valise and motioned her toward the door. "I think you are right, Miss Gordon. I think your care will help Jonathan to feel safe here. And by the time Mrs. Hotchkiss returns—"

She halted, turned. "Mrs. Hotchkiss?"

"My housekeeper."

She stiffened, took a breath to control a rush of frustration. "Mr. Thornberg, I agreed to come and care for your brother tomorrow. But then I must return to my work at the newspaper. That is my livelihood. And, as you know, I must take care of my mother. I am sorry, but you will have to find someone else to care for Jonathan." Something crackled. She glanced down, stared at the letter he pulled from his pocket.

"I am not unsympathetic to your concern for your mother, Miss Gordon. But she assured me she will be fine with Mrs. Duncan caring for her. And Jonathan is so young and—" he frowned, stared down at the letter "—and he has suffered the care of strangers long enough." He thrust the letter at her. "Read this, Miss Gordon, and then give me your answer. I'll go tell the carriage driver you will be out shortly."

She watched him start down the stairs then stepped close to the wall sconce and unfolded the letter.

Dear Charles,
The boy that has been delivered to you is your half brother. His name is Jonathan David Thornberg. He was born in Paris, France, the 18th day of December, 1875.

The child is the result of an illicit liaison, hence the name Thornberg. His father is a married man of social prominence and, of course, wants no part of the boy or any scandal. Nor do I. My elderly husband threatened upon our marriage that if he were ever to learn of any indiscretion on my part, he would immediately procure a writ of divorcement and throw me into the street with no provision. He has the power to do so, and should the boy's existence be discovered, my life of luxury and ease will cease. I birthed the boy during an extended vacation in Paris I told my husband was for the purpose of buying new gowns, and I have been boarding him with various strangers until he reached sufficient age to survive the trip to you in America. That time has now come and when he is gone from Europe, I will be safe.

I am enclosing a bank draft of an amount sufficient to pay for the boy's living in a boarding school until he graduates. I realize you owe me no filial allegiance, but you are the only person in America with sufficient interest in this information not becoming known to keep it secret. And once you enroll the boy in a boarding school, he will be of no further bother to either of us.

I do not wish to affix my name to this document so will simply sign as,
Your mother

Discarded. She knew what Charles Thornberg meant now. Clarice stared at the letter, Jonathan's sweet, innocent face imposed against it. Her hands trembled with the desire to rip it to shreds so that he would never know his mother had thought of him not as a child to love but as an inconvenience to be hidden and gotten rid of at the earliest opportunity for her own selfish gain. Not even her father was that coldhearted.

She grasped the banister and started down the stairs, the letter crunched in her hand. Her shoes tapped against the treads. Her short train bounced from step to step. She strode to the front door, handed Charles Thornberg the letter and took a breath to control the tightness in her throat. "I will care for Jonathan until

Mrs. Hotchkiss returns, Mr. Thornberg. In return, I ask that you will permit me to work on the CLSC letters at home."

"That is not necessary, Miss Gordon. I will compensate you for—"

She shook her head, raised her chin. "I have a job, Mr. Thornberg. I intend to do it."

He studied her for a long moment, then dipped his head and reached to open the door. "I will bring the letters home for you tomorrow at dinnertime."

"Then I shall be here early in the morning." She snatched up the valise sitting on the floor beside the door.

"What are you doing?"

She tightened her grip and looked up at him. "I'm taking Jonathan's clothes home to launder. Wasn't that your intent?" His eyes clouded. Well, too bad. She was too angry to play polite games.

"It was not!" He gripped the valise, stared down at her.

The touch of his hand against hers sent warmth flowing through her. She jerked her hands from the handles and took a step back, her heart pounding.

"I placed the valise here so I would not forget to take Jonathan's things to the laundry tomorrow." He threw the bag to the floor and pulled open the door. "You, Miss Gordon, are to care for my brother, not act as a maid or washerwoman! Is that clear?"

Not in her experience. But then nothing about Charles Thornberg fit with her experience. Unnerved, wanting only to flee his presence, to escape the confusion that overwhelmed her when he looked at her, she nodded, rushed by him and hurried to the carriage that sat waiting at the edge of the road.

Chapter Five

Charles stared into the darkness, tense, straining against the silence. Miss Gordon thought Jonathan was so tired he would sleep through until morning, but what if he didn't? What if he fell out of that big bed? He was so little he could break an arm or leg or something. It could happen. And he might not hear anything. He was a sound sleeper.

He surged from his bed, shrugged into his dressing gown and strode down the hallway to Jonathan's bedroom in his slippers, the robe flopping around his legs.

Silence. He blew out a breath and walked to the bed. The boy was sound asleep, one small arm raised to curve above his head. He stared down at him, an odd sensation filling his chest. *He* slept like that. He studied the dark curls and the small almost straight-across brows, the mouth with a suggestion of a dimple on the right side, and the small pugnacious chin. It was like looking at a miniature of himself. His chest swelled, trapped air in his lungs. Jonathan was his *brother*. The truth of it settled into his heart. After twenty-one years of being alone, he had a family.

I realize you owe me no filial allegiance, but you are the only person in America with sufficient interest in this information not becoming known to keep it secret.

Secret? His mouth quirked. His mother had discarded Jonathan just as she had discarded him all those years ago. And in so doing, she had, inadvertently, given him the best gift he could ever receive. Place his brother in a boarding school? Never! He had lived that life. He would never subject Jonathan to that loneliness, that need to belong somewhere, to someone. He huffed out a breath, ran his hand over the back of his neck, winced when he accidentally touched the blister. Jonathan would stay right here, with him. But he had to manage that in a way that would keep Jonathan from being hurt by their mother's abandonment.

He lifted the chair from where Clarice Gordon had placed it beside the stand, set it close to the bed, sat and closed his eyes to work out a story. He didn't lie, so it would take some finesse. At least he had Jonathan's immediate needs taken care of—for a week. Not that Clarice Gordon was happy about that. Well, neither was he; he certainly wouldn't choose a career woman to care for his young brother. Jonathan needed someone warm and loving and caring after the unfeeling way he'd been treated—not a coolly efficient suffragist.

Clarice Gordon's face floated before him, her eyes challenging, her small rounded chin lifted. It was a major battle to try and do something for the woman! He frowned and opened his eyes, stared into the darkness wondering what made her so independent and prickly. Though she wasn't like that when she spoke of her mother. Her face softened and her voice warmed when that happened. But even so, there was an anger that burned in the depths of her eyes.

He placed his elbows on the chair arms, slid forward on the seat until he could rest his head against the chair back, then laced his fingers over his stomach. She had very telling eyes. And beautiful. Startlingly so. Gray with blue flecks. And long, thick lashes as black as her hair. Her eyes were the first thing he'd noticed—once he'd gotten a good look at her face. Before that it was the plain, unadorned way she dressed, as if she wanted not to be noticed, and the thin wood box she carried. She'd clutched that box as if her life depended on it. And, of course, as it turned out, her livelihood did.

His lips twitched, lifted into a wry grin. She'd been plenty prickly that day. And frosty. Whoo! She could have frozen a pond with the looks she'd sent his way. But she was too smart to let her feelings, whatever they were at the time, influence her judgment when he offered her a job. And the way she'd stayed silent and merely kept shoving those letters into the bag he held until he laid out his offer… He smothered a chuckle and shook his head. He might not approve of career women, but he had to admit Clarice Gordon was intelligent, efficient and clever. None of which would help Jonathan. He needed the love and warmth of a caring heart.

He lifted his hand and scrubbed at the stubble forming on his chin, drew his thoughts back to the present. He needed a cover story…

* * *

Clarice tiptoed up the stairs, turned toward her room and caught her breath. A sliver of light showed beneath the door. Guilt settled like a rock in her heart. She ran on tiptoe, her skirt train bouncing along the hall runner, slipped into the bedroom and hurried toward her mother's bed. "What's wrong, Mama? Are you in pain? I'm sorry I wasn't here to massage your back to help you sleep. I'll do it—"

"Hush, Clarice. You'll wake Mr. Grumpy down the hall. I'm fine." Her mother waved a hand toward the windows in the turret. "There's no moonlight to speak of, and I was a little worried about you walking home, is all."

The clamp around her heart eased. "I didn't walk, Mama. Mr. Thornberg sent me home in a carriage."

"A *carriage*!" Her mother's brows shot skyward. "Why?"

She moved to the dressing table and sank onto the bench, chiding herself for her foolishness. She had to get over this nagging fear that when she left, she would find her mother's condition worse when she returned. She leaned down to unlace her shoes and hide her face. Her mother had good eyes and sharp intuition. "He said he promised you he would see me home safe."

"Well, yes. He did say that. But I never thought…"

"And as he couldn't escort me, he arranged for the carriage."

"Gracious me…"

Her mother sounded as astonished as she had been—still was. She looked up and forced a grin. "He doesn't know after years of chasing chickens and run-away pigs on the farm, I can likely outrun any man or beast that would intend me harm." She wiggled her toes, rose and began undoing the buttons on her gown to keep from thinking about how she had felt riding home in that carriage.

"I've been waiting to hear about that little boy." Her mother squinted at her through the dim light. "You're going to take care of him, aren't you? Poor little mite, being left at the newspaper office for Mr. Thornberg like that. He was right shocked, I'll tell you. I could see it in his eyes. I had to bite my tongue to keep from asking how a body doesn't know they have a brother."

"It's because Jonathan was born in Paris, France, Mama." She swirled her dressing gown on over her nightdress and braced herself against the screech when she closed the wardrobe.

"That little boy has come all the way across the *ocean*?"

"Yes. And he's not yet three years old." She crossed to her mother's bed table and raised the wick on the lamp. She could afford a bit of extra oil now.

"What happened to his mother and father?"

His father is a married man of social prominence and, of course, wants no part of the boy or any scandal. Nor do I.

Anger drew her face taut.

"Clarice…"

"Jonathan is the 'result' of an illicit tryst between two married people, Mama. And neither of them want him. His mother has been hiding him from her wealthy husband. She sent him to Mr. Thornberg here in America to protect her marriage."

Air hissed through her mother's teeth. "Well, I never! I, who never wanted to let you go, had to send you away to protect you. And this woman throws her child away for her own comfort and ease! She has no heart. She should be—" Her mother gripped her arm, the strength of years of hard work in her hand. "Clarice, did you agree to take care of that little boy?"

"Yes, I did, Mama. Until Mr. Thornberg's housekeeper returns." She frowned and sat on the edge of the bed as the worries came flooding back. "But it's not like working at the newspaper. I don't know how long I will be gone each day. I may not be home in time to rub your back at night or—"

"That doesn't matter, Clarice. That little boy needs love."

"I know, Mama. I'll manage." *And likely lose my heart to him in the process.* She sighed, rose and reached for the pillows. "Lean forward, and I'll rub your back now. It's past time for us to be asleep." Tears stung her eyes. Anger lent strength to her fingers kneading the spare flesh over her mother's protruding hip bones.

"My, my…"

"What is it, Mama?" She massaged along the bony spine, then raised her hands to knead the muscles across her mother's thin shoulders.

"I was just thinking about Mr. Thornberg hiring that carriage to bring you home."

She stiffened, refused to recall that odd feeling she'd

experienced when he'd *looked* at her. She'd been unable to shake her reaction during the ride.

"He's a nice young man. Honorable, too, keeping his word like that."

He had his own selfish reason, Mama. Men always do. She worked her way back down her mother's spine then smoothed her nightgown. "There. Let me fluff your pillows and you can go to sleep."

"He will make some woman a good husband."

If there was such a thing. "Have a good night, Mama. I'll see you in the morning." She kissed her mother's cheek and lowered the wick on the lamp, turned then paused when her mother took hold of her hand.

"Clarice, please don't let your father and brothers sour you on marriage. Please don't rob yourself of the joy of children of your own because of the way your father treated us. There are good men who love their wives and children and treat them well."

"I know. But I prefer to be a career woman and take care of myself and you, Mama." She ignored her mother's sigh, walked through the archway to the wide window seat in the turret and made up her bed. The rumbling of her stomach reminded her she had missed supper.

This is my home, not your father's farm, Miss Gordon. I will hold the valise. Charles Thornberg's words pressed through her resistance, as insistent as the man himself. She slipped beneath the blankets, turned onto her side and stared out into the darkness, refusing to remember the way he had looked at her...the unsettled feeling his presence caused her.

I placed the valise here so I would not forget to take Jonathan's things to the laundry tomorrow. You, Miss Gordon, are to care for my brother, not act as a maid or washerwoman! Is that clear? Her stomach rumbled again. She pressed her hand against it, puzzled over his words. His attitude was so different from her father's. But did he truly mean what he said? She had to feed Jonathan. And that meant she had to cook and clean the kitchen. Who was to do the shopping for supplies? Clearly, she had to discuss her duties with Mr. Thornberg tomorrow morning.

She closed her eyes to make a mental list of questions she needed answered, but Jonathan's sweet face formed in her head. Would he sleep all night? What would Charles Thornberg do if the toddler woke? The soft, ragged sobs that had torn at her heart pierced her memory. It was unnatural for a child to be so quiet when he cried. Had he been punished for disturbing someone's sleep? With how many strangers, in how many countries, had he been boarded? Small wonder he was afraid.

It's all right, Jonathan, everything is all right. You have a home now. No one will ever discard you again. I give you my word on it.

The image of Charles Thornberg holding his brother, looking fierce and protective as he spoke those words, shaped itself against the dark window. Her concern that Jonathan would wake and be afraid eased. There was no reason for it to—nothing in her life suggested that a man would be careful or tender with a child—but against all she knew, she believed Charles Thornberg would keep that promise. It didn't make sense—but neither did his providing the carriage for her. Or walking her home beneath his umbrella in the rainstorm. Or wrapping his suit coat around her. None of it made sense.

She yawned and pulled the blanket close around her. Her eyelashes fluttered down. He was bigger than her father or brothers, but his touch had been gentle.

The jacket is much too large for you. Hold it tight or the wind will whip it away.

She'd felt so…different wrapped in his coat… She'd felt…warm…outside and inside…and somehow…safe. It made…no sense…at all… How could a…coat…make you…safe…

The oil lamp on the table in the corner cast a golden glow into the entrance hall. Clarice closed the front door and paused, listened. Silence. Had she come too early? She eyed the stairs, gnawed at the corner of her lip. She couldn't go up there. What if Charles Thornberg was still abed? Or came walking into Jonathan's room in his nightclothes!

That thought drove her down the short hallway to the kitchen she'd explored briefly yesterday when she'd been trying to find something to feed Jonathan. She moved into the room and looked around. The set-back cupboard held dishes and flatware on its shelves. Most likely there were serving dishes hidden in the cupboards on the bottom.

The gray light of dawn filtered through the small panes of the window in the top of the back door. She peered out, looked beyond a deep porch to a sizable yard with a stable at the back. If the stable was empty, as she suspected it was, it could be an interesting and fun place for Jonathan to play. But that would come after he had settled in and learned to know them. No, after he learned to know Mr. Thornberg. *She* would be back working at the newspaper by then.

The floor overhead squeaked. She glanced up. That had to be Charles Thornberg moving around. Jonathan was too small to make a floorboard squeak. Was the toddler awake? It didn't matter. She couldn't go up there. Another squeak added to the tension across her shoulders. She turned her attention to the stove.

The fire was out. A quick search won her paper and kindling from one end of the wood box and matches from a shelf above it. She shook down the cold ashes, opened the dampers in the chimney and fire door and laid the fire. The match flared and the paper she'd crumpled caught afire on her second try. A minute later the kindling burst into tiny flames. She chose a few of the smallest pieces of wood, added them to the fire, careful not to smother the flames, then walked to the refrigerator that sat against the opposite wall. A large bowl sitting on top held apples. Sheep's nose, by the look of them.

She leaned down and opened the top door on the left to check the state of the ice. There was a large chunk, only slightly melted around the edges. A recent delivery, then. The smaller door below the ice compartment held several paper-wrapped parcels. Grease stains on one implied bacon. Did two-year-olds eat bacon? She stared at the package, then closed the door, depressed the handle to unlatch the compartment on the right and gave a tentative sniff. No spoiled food or stale odor. Mrs. Hotchkiss was a good housekeeper. The butter and milk she needed were on the top shelf beside a bowl of eggs.

The stovepipe crackled. She carried the items to the work table in the center of the room then stepped to the stove and adjusted the damper and draft to slow the burn. Footfalls sounded overhead. She glanced at the ceiling, lifted a small pan down from a rack then paused. An enamel coffeepot sat on the stove's warming shelf. She stared at it a moment, then shrugged and carried the pan to the sink cupboard, pumped water into it and returned to the stove. Now to find some oats…

She lifted covers and peered into various-sized crocks clustered on the work table. Flour…sugar…oats… Ah. She filled the scoop, snatched a wood spoon from a bunch of utensils standing in a gray crock and stirred them into the water in the pan and set it over the fire. Another board above her head creaked. That must be how Mrs. Hotchkiss knew to start breakfast. She turned and stared at the refrigerator…

Chapter Six

Charles braced himself for the sting of alcohol on his shaved face, splashed on the cologne and stared in the mirror. The blister on his neck was puffed, the flesh around it red and ugly. It would be impossible for him to wear a high starched collar and tie today. He grabbed his comb, ran it through his still-damp hair and scowled at the deepening waves. He needed a trim or his hair would start curling. But there was no time to go to the barber today. He had a newspaper to run. And a little brother to take care of.

A smile chased the scowl from his face. Time to check on Jonathan again.

He left his dressing room, strode to his wardrobe, pulled a shirt of soft blue cotton off the shelf and slipped it on then closed the wardrobe doors. It was not a good day for a man who prided himself on his professional appearance. He buttoned the shirt, left the collar open then shoved the shirttails into his pants and walked down the hallway to his brother's bedroom. *Jonathan sure slept—*

He froze, stared as his little brother padded out of the dressing room, his dark curls mussed, his shirt wrinkled and his socks sagging down around his ankles. He'd been waiting for the boy to wake up, but now that he had, panic struck. His heart thumped. What should he say? What should he do? He didn't know how to take care of a *baby*! *Where was Miss Gordon?*

"Me go potty. Me done now."

There was something bordering on defiance in the soft child voice. And fear. He looked at the blue eyes gazing steadily at him, the little lips pressed together and the slightly jutted chin then glanced over at the bed. The blankets were hanging over the edge into a pile on the floor. So that was why he hadn't heard him. His stomach flopped. What if he'd gotten hurt getting out of bed by himself? He drew breath to issue a warning then swallowed it back. Had Jonathan been scolded or punished for doing that? Was that why the defiance and fear were there? Anger burned away his sense of incompetence. He nodded and smiled. "Good man. Are you hungry?"

Jonathan stared at him a moment, then nodded. A black curl flopped forward onto his forehead. The blue eyes studied him, wary, frightened.

Lord, help me to show him it's all right. That he's safe with me. He stifled his uneasiness, crossed to the wardrobe and pulled out the one clean outfit they had found in the valise. "Well, then, Skipper, let's get you washed and brushed. And then we'll go downstairs and find something to eat."

"Me Jonathan."

His lips slanted into a proud grin. His chest filled. The little guy had courage. "So you are."

"What skipper?"

So he was curious and liked to learn. His pride swelled. "Do you remember the big ship you were on?" He moved forward and squatted on his heels to allay any fear that might be caused by his moving close.

Jonathan's smooth brow furrowed. He looked straight at him and nodded. "It made my stomach hurted."

He squelched a chuckle. "That happens sometimes. Anyway, the important man on the boat is called a skipper. And I think you're important. And you have a sailor suit—" he held up the outfit in his hands "—so—"

"Me Skipper."

"Yes."

"Who you?"

The pressure in his chest swelled. "I'm Charles. I'm your brother." He held his breath, looked at Jonathan's frown and waited.

"What brover?"

Help me, Lord. Give me the words so he'll understand. "It means we're a family." There was no change in Jonathan's expression. Clearly, that word meant nothing to him. Anger surged. He tamped it down, searched for the right words. "And being a *family* means I belong to you, and you belong to me." That truth hit him hard. Saying it aloud made it…real. He

cleared the lump from his throat. "And since I'm the…
biggest, and I have this house, you are going to stay
here with me always, and I'm going to take care of
you." The blue eyes, so like his own, studied him. The
furrows in Jonathan's little forehead deepened. *Please,
Lord. Help him understand.*

"Me be here?"

He nodded, curved his lips into a smile. "Every day.
From now on. For always."

There was a soft exhalation. Jonathan's blue eyes
shifted to the bed, came back to rest on him. His small
right arm lifted and one pudgy little finger pointed at
the bed. "It too big. Me fall."

The breath trapped in his lungs released. It was
going to be all right. Jonathan might not have understood the family concept, but he knew what staying
in one place meant. The rest would come. He nodded,
held back the smile tugging at his lips and treated the
information with all seriousness. "I'll take care of that
today. Now, shall we get you washed and dressed and
go get some breakfast?" He rose, waited, unsure of
what to do if the little guy said no.

Jonathan nodded, reached up and grabbed hold of
his hand.

The touch was like nothing he'd ever experienced.
His heart swelled, pushed the air from his lungs. His
throat constricted. It wasn't the clutch of the little
fingers or the smallness of the hand in his; it was
the absolute trust. He blinked hard, scooped his little
brother into his arms and carried him into the dressing room.

* * *

"Hmm, coffee. Smells good."

"Mr. Thornberg!" Clarice gasped and whirled, pressed her hand to her chest. "I didn't hear you coming."

"Obviously." His mouth slanted in a lopsided, teasing grin. "Be careful or you'll stab yourself with that fork."

He looked so different... "Hardly." She shifted her gaze to the toddler riding on her employer's arm and her heart melted. His baby face was clean and shiny, his curls were combed, and he was dressed in the blue sailor suit. The socks that covered his chunky little legs to his dimpled knees left a little to be desired in cleanliness, but the buckled shoes she'd removed last night had a new gloss to them. Mr. Thornberg had been busy. No wonder she'd heard him moving around upstairs. "Good morning, Jonathan."

"Me Skipper. Me 'portant."

"Oh?"

"The outfit." She looked up and her gaze clashed with the proud, albeit amused one of her employer. Her stomach quivered to life. "I explained about captains on ocean liners."

"Oh."

"You said that already."

The words and the wry look that accompanied them brought the memory of the day he'd employed her to answer the CLSC letters sweeping into her head. She took refuge in thoughts of her work. Would he remember to bring home the letters for her to work on, as he'd promised? Was he even going to work? He didn't look it. Not in that blue shirt. Without his starched white shirt and high stiff collar and tie, he looked relaxed... handsome. Heat stole across her cheekbones.

"Him my brover. Me be here." Jonathan's blue eyes studied her. "Who you?"

Brover. Mr. Thornberg had done some explaining. She smiled, ignored the tug on her heart to step close and touch the toddler, to hold him again. It was better to stay uninvolved. She was here for only a few days. "I'm the lady who cooked your breakfast."

She turned back and slid the sizzling bacon to the cooler part of the stove. "I have Jonathan's porridge ready, Mr. Thornberg. If you would please take him into the dining room, I'll bring it right in."

She lifted the pan of cooked oats staying warm at the back of the stove, scooped them into the bowl she had waiting on the work table and added a pat of butter and a drizzle of the molasses she'd found in the pantry.

"I'd rather he eat here in the kitchen, where he won't be alone." A chair scraped along the floor.

"But I've—"

"Yes?" Charles sat Jonathan on a chair, turned from the small eating table against the wall and looked at her.

She'd made a mistake. Well, she'd know better tomorrow. "I've set a place for you in the dining room, as well."

"For *me*?"

She nodded, wiped her palms down the skirt of the apron she'd found hanging on a peg by the stove. "You needn't sound incredulous. It was a perfectly understandable mistake given the situation. We've not yet discussed my duties."

His eyes took on that dark, clouded look she was beginning to recognize as a prelude to full-blown annoyance. "I told you last night you are to take care of Jonathan, not act as a maid or washerwoman."

She splashed a bit of milk on the prepared oats. "And that is what I am doing. I thought, perhaps, Jonathan would like your company at his meals. But since that offends your stated wishes—"

"Me hungry."

She snatched up the bowl and hurried to the table. "Here you are, Jonathan. Just let me get the pad I made for you to sit on from the dining room and then—"

"I'll get it."

She opened her mouth to protest, but Charles had pivoted and headed for the dining room before she could speak. She lifted Jonathan into her arms. He leaned against her as if he belonged there. "It will only be a minute—"

Charles returned with the folded throw she had covered with a dish towel, placed it on the chair and fastened his gaze on her. "The pad is very clever."

His gaze, his praise were disconcerting. "It's necessary." She settled Jonathan on the pad and handed him a spoon. "He's too small to sit on a chair."

"Or to get out of that bed upstairs by himself. I intend to buy him a crib today."

"Or you could get him a set of bed steps." The suggestion was out before she thought better of making it. His raised eyebrows spurred her on. He'd asked for her help; she would give it. "He will soon outgrow a crib. And he is able to take care of his…personal needs himself. The steps would allow him to do so safely." She sniffed the air and hurried back to the stove. The bacon was nicely crisp, not that it mattered. She slid the pan aside.

"That looks good."

She froze, glanced over her shoulder. He was standing behind her, a cup in each hand.

"The coffee smells too good to resist." He set the cups on the table, snagged the coffeepot and poured them full.

She stared, pressed her lips together but couldn't hold the words back. "You're giving Jonathan a cup of *coffee*?"

He chuckled and put the coffeepot down. "Even I know better than that." His long fingers tapped a cup. "This one is yours."

Her jaw dropped. She stared at the dark brew in the cup, grappling with the idea that he had poured it for her.

"Do you fry eggs? I like your idea, and I've decided to have breakfast with Jonathan." His smile made it an apology.

She nodded, pulled the griddle back over the hot plate at the front of the stove, slid the bacon to one side and reached for the bowl of eggs she had waiting. "How many do you want?"

"Two. And one for Skipper."

Could his tenderness with Jonathan be real? She stared at Charles Thornberg trying to believe it was so.

"And fry some eggs for yourself, Miss Gordon." His gaze swung back to her. She looked down at the bowl of eggs. "We'll discuss what Jonathan needs while we eat."

While we eat? No. That was a family thing. She shook her head, broke three eggs into the hot bacon grease and set the rest aside. "Thank you, but I'm not hungry."

He frowned, swept a hand toward the windows over the sink cupboard at the end of the room. "It's not yet fully light, Miss Gordon. And I lived in boarding-houses long enough to know you eat when the meals are scheduled and at no other time. You have not yet eaten." He shoved the bowl of eggs back toward her. "Fry yourself an egg. And plan to eat all of your meals here with Jonathan. That will be part of your care of him. You know that, as a newspaperman, my hours are dictated by events. I may have to miss a few meals, and I don't want him eating alone."

The clock in the sitting room gonged. He'd be leaving for the newspaper soon, and she had to find out exactly what her care of Jonathan entailed before he left. She didn't want any more mistakes like this one. She pushed aside her uneasiness, broke another egg into the grease and watched him carry the two steaming cups of coffee to the table.

"Him squirrel." Jonathan pointed up at the mass of gray fur sitting in the tree with its bushy tail twitching.

"Yes." Clarice picked up an acorn and tossed it at the branch the squirrel was on. "Hear him chatter?"

"What that?"

"Chatter is the way squirrels talk."

"What him say?"

How eager he was to learn. She loved answering his innocent questions. "I think he is telling us he would like us to move along so he can come down and gather acorns to eat." She bent, picked one up and showed it to him. "This is an acorn. Squirrels like them, but they're not good for little boys, so you mustn't eat them. They'll make your tummy hurt."

He thought that over a moment. "Me won't." He pointed again. "Bird."

"Yes. A blue jay." His little brow furrowed, and she hastened to explain. "That's his own special name— because of his color. See, his feathers are blue like your sailor suit."

"What he special name?"

She looked in the direction of Jonathan's pointing finger. "That is a goldfinch. And that friendly little bird on the bush is a chickadee. You can sometimes coax them to say their own name. Listen…" She imitated the bird's call: "Chick-a-dee-dee… Chick-a-dee-dee…"

The tiny black-and-white bird hopped along a twig of the bush, tipped its head and answered her.

"Him did it!"

She laughed at Jonathan's delight and called again, but the bird flew off.

"Him go away."

The disappointment on his face pierced her heart. "I think that was a mama chickadee and she is returning to her nest to feed her babies."

"See nest?"

She smiled and, unable to resist, rumpled his curls. "The birds build their nests high up in the trees, and they are hard to find."

He looked up at the branches over their head. "Me fall down. Birdies fall down?"

"No. The babies stay safe in the nest until they grow up and can fly." She clamped her lips closed on a promise that he would be safe in Mr. Thornberg's home until he was grown. She hoped it was so. But she didn't know.

"What that?"

She glanced where Jonathan's pudgy finger pointed. "That's a stable. I don't think Mr. Thornberg has a horse in the stable now, Jonathan. But, if he permits, it may be a nice place to play. Let's go see."

She rose and took his hand, led him to one side of the double doors. "You stand here until I see if everything is all right." She lifted the latch, opened one of the doors a crack, peered inside then pushed the door wide. Sunlight streaked across a plank floor littered with what she fervently hoped was dirt and bits of hay. Her heart sank. Jonathan had only one outfit to wear. The rest of his clothes Mr. Thornberg had taken to the laundry. She would have to keep his exploration short.

"Come along." He ran to her. She took his small hand in hers and stepped inside. Though it bore the stale odor of horse and hay, the stall was empty, as she suspected. "Oh, look, Jonathan! A carriage."

"Me drive it!" He tugged free of her grasp, ran to the

open two-seat buggy standing with the shafts resting on upended chunks of log and pulled at the iron step.

"Wait, Jonathan! Don't pull on it." She rushed over and scooped him into her arms. "Let me help you." She scanned the front seat for telltale droppings or rips and tears that could provide a home for a mouse. It looked safe enough—only dusty. She balanced Jonathan on her hip, grabbed a rag hanging over the stall wall and wiped the leather clean. "Now you may drive the buggy." She smiled and lifted him to the seat. "Where are you going, sir?"

He scowled down at her. "Me not sir. Me Jonathan."

She looked at his serious little face and her throat tightened. "So you are. Where are you going, *Jonathan*?"

A smile curved his mouth, deepened the dimple at its edge. "Me go get brover."

The words struck straight at her heart. She watched the toddler, his black curls bobbing as he bounced on the seat laughing and calling to a pretend horse, and fear for him rose in a choking wave. He was all alone. He had no mother to protect him as she'd had. *Don't let Mr. Thornberg hurt him, Lord. He's only a baby and men are cruel. Please don't let Mr. Thornberg hurt him.*

Her face tightened. Begging God had never stopped her father from striking her. It had not protected her mother from her father's cruelty. But even though she didn't believe it would do any good, she couldn't stop the prayer.

* * *

Charles finished the sentence, tapped the period key and rolled the cylinder to free the paper. A quick glance showed abundant mistakes. More than before. He wadded the paper, threw it in his wastebasket with the others and shoved to his feet. Using the typewriter was harder than it ought to be. Especially when he couldn't concentrate.

He could *feel* her absence. Odd how quickly Clarice Gordon had become a part of the editorial room. Though why that should be, he couldn't say. She just read and sorted the CLSC letters until it was time for her to go home and eat her dinner with her mother—then she returned and did the same. She'd even demanded he bring those letters to his house for her to work on. A real *career* woman. How did she expect to care for Jonathan and do the work required to answer those letters, too? At least he'd been able to take the care of her crippled mother off her for the week.

That had been a surprise. When Miss Gordon had told him her mother was bedridden, he'd assumed it was a temporary condition due to illness. It had brought him up short to see the frail-looking woman propped up in bed with Miss Gordon's writing case resting on the quilt spread over her outstretched legs. And they'd never moved a bit…not even a twitch while he'd talked to her. It was sad. Yet she was a charming, intelligent woman. Caring, too. It had shown in her eyes when he'd explained about Jonathan. And she'd been quick to say she would be fine, that her daughter should care for his brother. A pity Clarice didn't share her compassion.

He shoved the fingers of his free hand through his hair and walked toward the back of the room. He'd put her desk there where she wouldn't disturb him or Boyd. He gave a disgusted snort. That had worked well—he couldn't stop thinking about her. It was probably because she was at his home caring for his brother. Yes, that was it. Her absence was disturbing because he knew she was with Jonathan.

He checked the clock on the wall. It was almost time for dinner. Now he'd be able to see how Jonathan was doing under the cool and prickly Miss "Career Woman" Gordon's care. Though to be fair, the woman seemed to know what to do to care for a young child. It was her help that had gotten him through last night. And she knew how to cook. An image of her standing at the stove wearing pink cheeks and Mrs. Hotchkiss's too-large apron over her brown dress flashed into his head. She'd looked—

No, looks could be deceiving. Miss Gordon was a career woman through and through.

Dictionary…thesaurus…lexicon… He put the reference books she might need in the bottom of the bag then carefully placed the first stack of letters on top. A Bible? No. He had two of them at the house, and Mrs. Gordon had one. He'd seen it on the table by her bed. A concordance? She might not have one of those. He laid the heavy book atop the letters, twisted the bag down snug to hold everything in place and headed for the stairs.

Chapter Seven

A faint smell teased his nose. Charles closed the door and walked to the staircase, set the bag down and headed for the murmur of voices coming from the kitchen. The smell grew stronger. He sniffed. Beef... and something else... He sniffed again. Biscuits? His stomach welcomed the idea with a quiet rumble.

"Him am green."

Jonathan's voice stopped him in his tracks. He sounded different...contented.

"That's right. And do you remember what color this one is?"

And the prickly Miss Gordon sounded different, too. He could hear a smile, a softness in her voice.

"Him am red."

"Yes! *Very* good, Jonathan. Be careful..."

Be careful? What was he doing? He hurried down the short hallway and edged up to the door, halted at the sight before him. Jonathan, his little brow furrowed in concentration, was kneeling on the braided rug in front of the step-back cupboard placing a toy building block atop a short, unsteady tower of them. Clarice Gordon was kneeling in front of him in a puff of her long skirts with one hand poised to help and a soft smile curving her lips. The tension that had been building all morning eased. The emergency plan for Jonathan's care he'd put in place was working out, even if Miss Gordon *was* a reluctant participant. He rolled his shoulders and exhaled a long breath. He could stop worrying.

"And this one?"

Jonathan reached over his shaky tower for the one Miss Gordon held. "Him am yellow."

"That's *right*."

Pride surged. Charles grinned and stepped into the room. "It looks like someone is learning his colors. Good work, Skipper."

"Brover!" Jonathan beamed up at him. "Me gots blocks."

"I see that. Why don't I show you how to build them up high?" He moved to stand beside him.

"Excuse me. I think the biscuits are done." Clarice Gordon gathered her skirts to rise.

A perceptive woman. He smiled his gratitude to her for removing herself so he could spend time with Jonathan and offered her his hand. She froze, stared at it. Had he gotten ink from the typewriter ribbon on it? He looked down to check.

She drew an audible breath, placed her hand in his and rose. "Thank you." She slipped her hand from his and hurried to the stove.

He curled his fingers over his palm then opened them again.

"Him fall down!"

He shoved away thoughts of the warm softness of Miss Gordon's hand and glanced down. Jonathan was staring at his toppled tower, his little lower lip quivering. The sight of it wrenched his heart. He squatted and touched his small shoulder. "Don't cry, Skipper. I'll show you how to stack the bricks so they won't wobble and fall." His brother's brow furrowed.

"What wobble?"

"This." He jumped to rigid attention, then rolled his feet, bent his knees and shook his legs, swaying from side to side.

Jonathan giggled and scrambled to his feet. "Me do it!" He bent his dimpled knees and wiggled his chunky little legs, lost his balance and plopped down on the rug, giggling. "Me fall like blocks."

"Just so." He dropped to his knees and tickled him. Jonathan squealed and curled into a giggling ball. "Oh, no you don't!" He laughed and continued the gentle assault, his chest swelling at Jonathan's giggle.

A spoon clicked against china. He glanced up. Clarice Gordon stood watching them, her expression guarded. But the warmth in her smile took his breath. His gaze met hers and he sank back on his heels, his hands stilled.

"Dinner is ready." She looked down at the tureen she held and hurried to the table.

Jonathan's little hand grabbed his and tugged. "You do more."

Pleasure spurted through him. He grinned and shook his head. "Not now, Skipper. It's time to eat. We'll play later." He grabbed Jonathan beneath his arms, straightened and tossed him into the air, laughed at his squeal, caught him as he fell and did it again then held him close against his chest.

"Me want more! Me want more!"

"Whoa, stop bouncing, Skipper, or we'll both fall." He tightened his hold and turned toward the table. There were three place settings, as he'd requested. He eyed a narrow chair with sides and long legs. "I see Jonathan's chair is here." He sought Clarice Gordon's gaze with his, wanting to recapture that earlier moment, to explore what had been in her eyes, but she was moving about.

"Yes. Things have been arriving all morning." She set a towel-covered bowl on the table, stepped back and glanced his way. "Everything is ready, if you want to settle Jonathan, Mr. Thornberg."

"Who Fornberg?"

The question sobered him. He glanced at Jonathan, then laughed, settled him in his high chair and slid it up to the table. "Does he miss anything?"

"Not that I've found."

She stepped close, and a hint of lavender rose from her hair. He made a manly effort not to lower his head and breathe in the fragrance.

"Hold still, Jonathan. I'm going to fasten this around your neck to keep your sailor suit clean." She shook out a towel, tucked it beneath his chin and fastened it at the back with a clothespin.

"Ah!" He snapped his fingers. "That reminds me. I arranged for his laundry to be delivered this afternoon." He grinned at Jonathan's efforts to snap his pudgy little fingers, moved over and pulled out her chair. "Given his question, I think it will be less confusing for Jonathan if we use our given names, Miss Gordon. Call me Charles."

"If you wish." She looked at his hands on the chair rail, smoothed her skirt and sank onto the chair.

He frowned, made another quick check of his hands, then took his seat at the other end of the table. "Bow your head and fold your hands while I say grace, Skipper." He demonstrated. Jonathan imitated his movements. "That's a good boy." He cleared his throat and closed his eyes. "Heavenly Father, I thank You for this food. Bless it to our use, I pray. Amen." He glanced over at Clarice and grinned. "I thought it best to keep it simple, or we'd be answering questions instead of eating."

"I think you're right."

Her soft laughter made his gut clench. He removed the lid from the tureen, watched her place before Jonathan a small bowl of stew she had set aside to cool earlier. Clarice Gordon was as efficient here as she was in her work at the newspaper. She seemed to think of everything. "This stew smells delicious. If you will hand me your plate—" He stopped and looked at her. "You didn't answer me before. Have I your permission to call you Clarice?"

"If it is best for Jonathan."

Her voice had cooled. A subtle but effective reminder that he was her employer, and she had no choice? He nodded, ladled out the stew, returned her plate and filled his own. The first bite drew his thoughts to his meal.

"Me gots steps."

"You do?" He stabbed another bite of beef and watched Clarice butter a biscuit, add a bit of apple butter and hand half to Jonathan. The boy took a bite. Apple butter rimmed his little mouth. He glanced at his own heavily endowed biscuit with the missing bite, picked up his napkin and wiped his mouth—just in case.

"Me climbed 'em."

"Several times." The smile was back in Clarice's voice. "And you will climb them again when you are through eating."

He forked up some turnip and carrot and glanced across the table at her.

"Small children nap after dinner."

"Ah." He nodded understanding, took another bite of his biscuit, then speared a piece of potato and dipped it in the gravy pooled on his plate. He followed it with another bite of the tender meat.

"I intend to work on the CLSC letters while he sleeps." She fastened her gaze on him. "You did bring them home with you?"

So the situation was not as good as he'd hoped. Clarice was caring for Jonathan, but she was still focused on her career. Not that that was surprising. He really hadn't any right to expect otherwise. "Yes, one pile of them. And some reference books that you might need."

"That was thoughtful of you. Thank you."

Now, why had that made her all prickly again? He took the last bite of carrot, stuck a bit of onion on his fork with the last bite of beef and swiped them through his remaining gravy. "The meal was as delicious as it smelled, Clarice. Your mother must be an excellent cook." He put the last bite in his mouth, then crossed his knife and fork on his plate.

"My mother is crippled."

Bitterness colored the words. He looked at her taut face, hurried to cover his insensitive blunder. "I didn't mean now. I meant she must have taught you to cook when you were young."

She gave a curt nod. "Until I was eleven."

"Is that when she became disabled?" She looked down, but not before he saw the flash of anger in her eyes.

"No. That is when I…left…home. I learned my skills cooking for my room and board."

The shock held him mute.

She jerked to her feet. "Jonathan has fallen asleep. If you will excuse me, I will put him down for his nap and then return to serve your dessert." She untied the towel, slipped it from under Jonathan's small chin, dipped a corner of it in his water and gently wiped the apple butter from his face. A smile touched her lips, warmed her eyes. The tenderness of it made his heart hurt. She eased the spoon from Jonathan's pudgy hand then looked over at him. "I'll be right back. The coffee is hot."

He shook his head and pushed a whisper from his

constricted throat. "I'll carry him. He's heavy for you." He rose and lifted Jonathan into his arms, looked down at the silky black curls, the little arms hanging limp and swallowed hard. *I don't know how to be a family. What if I fail him? Dear Jesus, please don't let me fail him.*

"I'll go and turn down his bed."

Her whisper added to the sweet agony of the moment. He nodded and followed her from the kitchen, holding Jonathan close, listening to the soft puffs of breath that feathered against his neck as they walked to the stairs. "Leave the bag. I'll get it after I put him in bed." His whisper carried a command.

She glanced his way then lifted her hems and climbed the stairs.

He followed her neat, trim figure, garbed in the same brown gown she'd been wearing the day he met her, down the hallway and into Jonathan's room. The new toy chest he'd ordered was a splash of red under the window. The new steps were in place against the bed.

Me climbed 'em.

He looked down at Jonathan and smiled. *Not this time, Skipper. You are sound asleep.*

He watched Clarice move, lithe and graceful, to the bed and fold back the coverlet then lift the blankets. The sunlight filtering in through the slatted shutters gleamed on the thick coil of black hair on the back of her head, shadowed her gray eyes and dusted her high cheekbones with gold when she straightened and glanced at him. He blinked, stared. How had he ever thought her plain?

He laid his brother on the bed, stood back and watched her tuck him in. The sight brought a stab of loneliness he hadn't known was in him.

She looked up, turned and walked from the room. "Where do you wish me to do my work?"

Her factual, businesslike tone brought him back to reality. "In this bedroom." He stepped across the hallway, pushed open the door and stepped back. "There is a table, small but, I believe, adequate, straight in from the door against the outside wall. You will be able to hear Jonathan from there."

"I'm certain it will do fine." She headed for the stairs.

"I'll get the bag for you." His long strides overtook her.

"Yes, I know. I'm going down to serve your dessert. I have pudding in the refrigerator." She gripped the railing and started down the stairs.

"There's no need. I'll forego the pudding." He trotted by her, stopped on the step below and turned to look at her. "I've already lingered longer over dinner than I normally do. I wasn't prepared for—" He stopped, looked into her eyes, now almost on a level with his, and mentally deleted what he'd been about to say. "That is, I haven't had any family since I was five years old. And Jonathan's a charmer." Her eyes widened—an expression he couldn't identify flickered in their gray depths. He lost his train of thought.

"Yes, he is."

He dragged his thoughts back from the path they'd started down and cleared his throat. "Well, let me get that bag for you. I have to be getting back to the newspaper. I still have my editorial to write and the final page to compose before tonight's printing." He trotted down two steps then turned back. "I meant to tell you I saw the composing work you did on the second page yesterday."

Oh, no! She had forgotten about that. She stiffened, moistened her lips with the tip of her tongue. "I assure you, I didn't mean to overstep my place, Mr. Thornberg. I picked up Mr. Boyd's report that you had dropped and carried it back into the composing room. And I *know* I should have just left it there on the table, but when I saw the space on the paper—" She lifted her hand and smoothed back hair that was already perfectly in place. "It... Well, it tempted me and I gave in. And then the report was too small, and the fillers didn't work, so I changed the articles around. I meant to put it back as you had it, but then Mr. Warren called me to come to the office and Jonathan was there and—" she gave a tense little shrug "—the rest you know."

"Well, it was fortuitous for me that you were interrupted." He smiled to put her at ease. "Not only are you taking excellent care of Jonathan—but your rearrangement of the page worked perfectly. You have an eye for spacing and layout."

She stared at him, her face a picture of disbelief. And then she smiled.

He almost toppled backward down the stairs.

"Did you have a nice dinner, Mama?" Clarice pulled the pins from the bun at the back of her mother's head, tossed them onto the night table and ran her fingers through the dark, gray-streaked strands to loosen them.

"I did. Dora brought her meal and ate with me. She's really a very nice lady. We're becoming friends."

"I'm glad you enjoy her company, Mama. You deserve to have friends. Father chased away any woman you liked because friendship interfered with the farm work he demanded of you!" She snatched up a spoon and whipped baking soda into the pint jar she'd filled with warm water.

"Clarice, you're going to crack that jar if you're not careful."

"What? Oh. I guess I am being a little vigorous."

"Well, I'd appreciate it if you'd get rid of that anger before you start scrubbing on my scalp."

She stared at the smile on her mother's face then put the jar down and picked up the washbowl. "I don't know how you can smile about what he did to you, Mama. It makes me furious!"

"Would you rather I sit here all day with a scowl on my face?"

She laughed at her mother's comic attempt at a fierce scowl and pushed thoughts of her father away. "That's lovely, Mama. Here, hold the washbowl on your lap."

"I only wish I could—" Her mother sighed, leaned forward and wrapped her arms around the large bowl.

"What, Mama? *Walk? Move your legs?*" She draped a towel around her mother's neck, brushed her long hair forward, picked up the jar and poured the baking soda water over her head, scrubbing gently with her other hand.

"No. I wish I could take away your anger before it ruins your life."

She glanced at the towel covering her mother's useless legs and blew out a breath. "The anger doesn't harm me, Mama—it protects me. It reminds me never to marry and put myself under the grinding thumb of some *man*!"

Her mother gave another sigh, arched her neck and turned her head slightly. "Tell me about your day, Clarice. Was… Jonathan…difficult?"

"Not at all. He's very well behaved. And eager to learn. No one seems to have bothered to teach him anything, which is a pity. But I suppose it's understandable since he was moved from place to place—even country to country."

"Poor little boy. He must have been terribly confused."

"Yes." She stopped scrubbing and picked up the vinegar water. "Here comes the rinse…" She emptied the jar over her mother's clean hair, working it through the long strands as she poured. "I taught him his colors today." *Him am red.* She smiled, put the jar down, picked up the pitcher of warm water and finished the rinse. "All right, Mama. You can dry your hair now." She lifted the bowl of water off the bed and emptied it into a bucket.

"He's a fortunate little boy to have you to care for him, Clarice." The words came muffled by the towel.

"Only until Mr. Thornberg's housekeeper comes back, Mama. I'll be going back to work at the newspaper then." *Would Mrs. Hotchkiss teach Jonathan things? Would she take him outside to play in the backyard?*

"Yes, I know." Her mother lowered the towel. Their gazes locked, communicated without words.

"Mr. Thornberg is kind to him, Mama. I think it will be all right." The image of Jonathan asleep in Charles Thornberg's arms swept into her head. She would never forget the expression on Charles's face in that moment, though she had a hard time believing the tenderness, the love she had seen there was real.

"I thought he might be. He seems a kind, thoughtful man."

"Yes." *I haven't had any family since I was five years old.* She drew a breath, poured clean hot water into the bowl and dropped in a wash cloth. That was likely the reason for Charles Thornberg's attitude toward Jonathan. It was all new to him. Jonathan was like a new toy. How would he treat him when the newness wore off? When Jonathan got willful or irritable or ill? *Please don't let him hurt Jonathan.*

And just who was she talking to? The God who had let her father cripple her mother? She stiffened, pulled the dish with the soap on it to the edge of the bedside table where her mother could easily reach it and snatched up her own bag full of bathing needs and a towel. "I'll leave you to bathe, Mama. Your clean shift is here on the bed. I'll braid your hair when I come back from my bath."

She grabbed her nightclothes and walked to the dressing room down the hall. Chances were good that she would be able to wash her hair and bathe at her leisure with the other tenants retired for the night. Would Charles think to bathe Jonathan? Would— No. No more questions about Jonathan. He was not her concern. And he was already too dear to her. She had to protect her heart.

She slid the bolt lock on the dressing room door in place, set the bag on the washstand and draped her nightclothes over a towel rail. She would be back at the newspaper where she belonged soon. And then there would be no more interruptions in her work.

She yanked the pins from her coiled hair. No more thoughts of Jonathan. She had her mother to care for and a career to build.

Chapter Eight

Clarice hitched Jonathan into a more secure position on her hip and scanned the produce on the cart, her childhood on the farm coming to the fore. "How often do you come around, Mr. Porter?"

"Twice a week, miss. I'll stop by again on Friday so's things are fresh for the weekend."

"I think Mrs. Hotchkiss will have returned by then." She drew her gaze back to the farmer standing by the end of his cart. "I'm only here temporarily. Will it be all right if Mrs. Hotchkiss pays for my order when she returns?"

"No need to fret about paying, miss. Mr. Thornberg settles up the end of the month."

"I see. Well, in that case…" She lifted an ear of corn, checked the silk and pressed lightly to feel the size of the kernels. "I'll take a dozen of the corn…"

"Me have corn." Jonathan bent from the hips, reaching down.

"Oh! Jonathan, be careful!" She pulled the toddler

back and slipped her hand around his waist. "I have to cook the corn or it will make your tummy hurt. Now, you need to sit still so you don't fall. All right?"

A chuckle rumbled from the farmer. He stepped close, an empty basket in his hands. "Looks like you've got a lively one there, miss."

Jonathan stared at the farmer, pressed back against her and laid his head on her shoulder. Was he afraid of strangers? Her throat tightened. Why wouldn't he be, after the way he had been moved around? She laid her cheek against his soft, silky curls and patted his small back, furious with his selfish, uncaring mother. "It's all right, Jonathan. I've got you…"

"I'm sorry, miss. I didn't mean to frighten your boy."

Her boy? She stared at her hand patting Jonathan, heard her crooned words of comfort echoing in her head. It was exactly what she didn't want. She took a breath, lifted her head and turned her attention back to selecting vegetables. "I'll take two bunches of carrots…and a braid of onions…a dozen potatoes and a cabbage. Oh, and a rutabaga and six of those tomatoes."

She eyed the basket the farmer filled as she spoke, thinking of dinners for the next few days. "That will be all."

She led the way around to the back porch, tried her best not to feel proprietary as she opened the door to the kitchen. "You can leave the produce there on the table."

"Yes, miss." The farmer's boots clumped against the floor. He plopped the basket on the table, pulled the vegetables out with his large, work-scarred hands.

"M-me no g-go." Jonathan twisted and threw his little arms around her neck, burrowed his head against her shoulder and sobbed.

"Jonathan!" Understanding struck. He thought— Tears stung her eyes, clogged her throat. "Oh, no, Jonathan, *no*. No one is going to take you away. Shh… shh… Look, the man is going. He delivered our vegetables." His arms tightened. She held his trembling little body tight against her, fighting back tears as she swayed back and forth, trying to reassure him by her touch that he was not going to be taken to yet more strangers in another strange home.

"Be back Friday, miss." The farmer's boots clumped against the floor. The door closed.

"Look, the man is gone, Jonathan." He clung tighter, pushed his little face hard against her neck. She spun about, hurried down the short hall, across the entrance and stood in front of the window. "Look, Jonathan. Look *outside*. The man is driving his horse and cart away."

His head rolled against her shoulder. She looked down, sighed with relief when one blue eye peeked out, blinked then closed. A quiet, ragged sob shook him and his small body relaxed in her arms. She laid her cheek against his soft curls and walked back to the kitchen. She had to put the vegetables away and start dinner or Mr. Thornb—no, *Charles*—would be home before it was ready.

"Do you want to play with your blocks, Jonathan?"

His head rolled side to side. He took a ragged breath. She glanced at the rocker in the corner, sat and settled him close in her arms. The rockers whispered against the floor. The ticktock of the clock in the sitting room floated on the silence. She hummed softly, looked down and straightened his stocking. His little shoes had been shined, the buckles gleaming. "One, two, buckle my shoe…" She murmured the words of the rhyme, tried to visualize Charles Thornberg polishing the toddler's shoes but couldn't imagine it.

"Me gots b-buckles."

Her breath caught. She kept rocking. "Yes, you do—silver ones. Your brother polished them for you. He takes good care of you."

"Brover do blocks."

"Yes. He showed you how to build them so they wouldn't fall down, didn't he?"

He nodded, stirred in her arms, pushed back and looked up at her. "Him wobble."

She smiled. "And so did you."

"Me fall down."

"And he tickled you." The clock in the sitting room gonged. She stopped rocking. "Do you hear that, Jonathan? That is the clock telling me your brother will soon be here to eat dinner with you." Inspiration struck. "Do you want to help me fix dinner?"

He studied her for a minute then nodded.

"Good! But first we have to take care of those vegetables." She carried him to the work table, slid a crock to the middle and sat him down beside it. "Help me put these potatoes in here, please. We'll play a counting game as we put them in the crock." She handed him a potato. "Put it away, please."

He grabbed it with both of his pudgy hands and dropped it the crock.

"That's one. Can you say 'one'?"

"Him one."

She smiled and handed him another. "Two…"

He dropped it in the crock—"Two"—and reached for the next one.

"Three…"

The door was open. Charles stopped, rapped his knuckles against the door frame.

"Who is it?"

"It's Charles Thornberg, Mrs. Gordon. May I come in?"

"Yes, of course."

He stepped into the bedroom, looked toward the bed and met Mrs. Gordon's worried gaze.

"Is there something wrong, Mr. Thornberg? Is Clarice—"

He shook his head. "Clarice is fine, Mrs. Gordon. I stopped by to see how you are doing. If there is anything you need. And to bring you these." He moved to the bedside, held out a bouquet of straw flowers.

"*Flowers!* Oh, my…" She blinked, blinked again, took the bouquet into her hands. "How thoughtful of you, Mr. Thornberg. Autumn is my favorite time of the year, and I so miss—" She stopped, inhaled a quick little breath. "Thank you. The flowers are lovely. You're most kind."

"I think it's more guilt than kindness, if the truth be known." He gave her a lopsided grin. "I have stolen your daughter from you, and my conscience keeps reminding me of it."

"Then you must tell your conscience to hush. Your motive was pure." A frown creased her forehead. "I'm afraid I can't offer you refreshments, Mr. Thornberg, but won't you sit down? And if you would be so kind as to fetch me that small pitcher off the dressing table? How is your little brother getting on?"

"Well, I think. I don't know enough about little children to truly say, but he seems happy. He's very smart. And inquisitive. He asks a lot of questions."

Her smile faded. Her face drew taut. "I hope you don't mind that. He has a lot to learn."

What had brought about that change in demeanor? Clarice did the same thing. "I don't mind at all. I enjoy answering him. When I can, that is." He smiled and handed her the pitcher then moved to the chair on the other side of the bed. He glanced at the open writing case on the bedside table and froze, his gaze locked on the titles of the top papers on piles of various sizes. *To Mend Cracks in Stovepipes... How to Clean Mica... How to Keep the Lamp Chimneys Clean... Secret to Salt Rising Bread...*

"Oh, dear."

He glanced at Clarice's mother. She looked…guilty.

"I forgot that case was open."

He frowned, looked back at the piles of papers. "Those look like the fillers I use at the newspaper."

"I don't suppose you could pretend you didn't see them?"

He grinned at her wry tone and fastened a suspicious gaze on her. "And why would I do that?"

Her thin shoulders lifted in a small, eloquent shrug. "Mrs. Gordon…"

She sighed, met his gaze. "I don't know if Clarice really wants to give them to you—or if she was only trying to give me something to do so I would feel… *useful* again." She looked down, rearranged one of the flowers she had placed in the pitcher. "It does help."

The last quiet words ripped at his heart. He sank onto the chair and leaned toward her, encouraging her to talk. "How did this come about?"

She gave him a sidelong look. "Does that mean you're not going to simply forget you saw those papers?"

"I'm afraid so."

"I thought not." She breathed another sigh, then rested back against the pillows propped against the headboard. "Clarice's first day at the newspaper—when you showed her around—you showed her how you put the pages together. She said you used these things called 'fillers' and that you were running low on them. She said she was going to make you some, and she asked me if I would help her."

"And so you've been making fillers for me."

She nodded then looked down at the flowers. "Unless Clarice was only trying to give me something to do with my days."

There was an uncomplaining acceptance of her condition in the soft words. His heart hurt for her. "May I look at what you've written?"

She looked up her lips curved in a resigned little smile. "You might as well. They're no secret now."

He rose and thumbed through the piles. "These are really good. I can certainly use these, Mrs. Gordon."

Her eyes widened. She stared up at him, took a breath. "Truly?"

"Truly."

"Well, I never…"

He grinned down at her. "I will pay you, of course."

"For writing down how to keep a chimney lamp clean?"

He chuckled and turned back to the writing case, pleased at the unexpected turn his visit had taken. "Let me count how many fillers you have here, Mrs. Gordon. And then we'll discuss a fair recompense for your work."

She shook her head. "I thank you for your kindness, Mr. Thornberg. But you didn't ask me to do the fillers. Clarice said she would do them as part of her job. They're included in what you already pay her."

"But I—" Her chin jutted. He'd seen that particular little gesture before. Clarice Gordon was very like her mother in her mannerisms. "Very well, Mrs. Thornberg. I'll just take these with me. And I would appreciate it if you would make me more." He stuffed the papers into his pockets and then looked down at her. "But I want it clearly understood that I am now commissioning you to write fillers for me, and you *will* be paid for your work. Is that understood?"

"It is."

That had been a little too easy. "And agreed?" He held out his hand.

"And agreed."

She smiled and slipped her small hand in his. It was rough and calloused—work worn. Mrs. Gordon had not been crippled for long. He tucked the information away and smiled. "Good. I am not accustomed to losing at negotiations."

"I'd think not." She laughed, a light musical ripple that made him wonder if her daughter's laughter would be the same.

"I have to be going, Mrs. Gordon. Would you like me to set the flowers on the nightstand for you?"

"No, thank you, anyway, but…I want to hold them." She smiled up at him. "Thank you again for bringing me the flowers. It's—" She shook her head, took a little breath. "Please come again, Mr. Thornberg. I like knowing the people in my daughter's life. It's…been a while. And please, leave the door open when you leave. It makes the room seem less…confining."

Charles finished the last of his cold sliced beef then spooned up the last bit of his soup. "This tomato soup is delicious, Clarice. And judging from the look of his face, Jonathan shares my opinion."

"Thank you. But I'm afraid you can't judge Jonathan's likes or dislikes by his appearance." She smiled and rose, using the protective towel to wash off the soup smeared around the boy's mouth. "It's a matter of skill, not approval, isn't it, Jonathan?"

His breath caught. There was something different…

She'd been gentle before, but now... She looked up and caught him studying her, straightened and laid the towel beside Jonathan's dish.

"I'm afraid I hadn't time enough to make dessert."

All warmth was gone. The cool career woman had returned. He tossed his napkin on the table and rose.

She stepped back.

He looked at her suddenly taut face and held back a frown. Did she think he would dismiss her from the newspaper because she didn't cater to him? "I've told you you're not here to cook for me, Clarice. Though I'd be lying if I said I didn't appreciate the excellent meals." He lifted Jonathan from his high chair. "Nap time, Skipper."

"Me play blocks."

"When you wake up." He settled Jonathan in his arms and followed Clarice up the stairs, irritated by her preoccupation with her career. It was none of his business, but— He jerked his thoughts from that direction and carried Jonathan to his bed. "If I get home early enough, we'll go for a walk, Skipper. Would—"

"Me no go! Me no *go*!"

Jonathan twisted his body and threw himself out of his arms onto the bed before he could restrain him. He watched in astonishment as the toddler scrambled to the other side, wrapped his arms about Clarice and buried his face in her skirt, gasping out ragged, heart-wrenching sobs.

"What—"

"Hush, Jonathan, hush. It's all right. You're not going anywhere... Shh...shh..." His throat tightened as Clarice lifted Jonathan into her arms and swayed side to side, holding his head tucked beneath her bowed head, murmuring…soothing… She lifted her head and looked over at him. Anger burned in the depth of her eyes. "Mr. Porter came this morning, and for some reason, Jonathan thought he was here to take him away. I tried to—"

"Take him *away*? I don't—" *I have been boarding him with various strangers…* Pain stabbed into his heart. The poor little guy, being carried off from place to place by people he didn't know. His face went taut; he clenched his hands. He strode around the bed, stopped at Clarice's side, his throat so constricted he could barely force out words. "Jonathan, look at me. Who am I?"

Jonathan rolled his head to the side, peered at him from beneath his black curls. "B-brover."

"That's right." He fought to stay calm, to hold the anger from his voice. "And do you remember what that means? It means we are family. That I belong to you, and you belong to me." He pulled in a breath, unclenched his hands and braced them on his knees, bending down until his face was level with his brother's. "And do you remember that I told you that since I'm the biggest and I have this house, you are going to stay here with me always, and I'm going to take care of you?"

The sobs quieted. Jonathan's blue eyes studied him. *Help me, Jesus. Give me the right words so he can understand.* "That was a promise, Jonathan. Do you know what a promise is? It means I have to do what I said. I'm going to take care of you always, Jonathan.

I'm your brother. I will *never* let anyone take you away from me."

"Brover."

"Yes." He held out his arms, swallowed hard when Jonathan reached for him. He pulled him close, cleared his throat, walked to the wardrobe and opened the doors. "See those clothes, Jonathan? Those are *your* clothes." He slapped his hand against the wood. "This is *your* wardrobe." He strode to the dresser and slapped his hand down on the top. "This is *your* dresser."

Jonathan leaned out and slapped his small hand on the wood. "Him me dresser."

"That's right!" He carried him to the window, squatted and slapped his hand on the red chest. "This is *your* toy chest. These are *your* toys!"

Jonathan's little hand slapped the red wood. "Him me toys!"

He nodded, rose and pointed out the window. "And that is *your* yard to play in."

"Him *me* yard." Jonathan pressed his nose against the window, turned back. "Me tree?"

"Yes, it's *your* tree." He turned, swept his hand through the air in an all-encompassing gesture. "This is *your* room! This is *your* place." He stepped to the bed, slapped a corner post. "And this is *your* bed."

Jonathan slapped the post. "Him *me* bed!" He twisted around and slapped his little hand against his shoulder. "You *me* brover!"

He laughed, blinked and hugged him tight. "I sure am, Skipper. I'm your brother, and you will be right here with me always. No one is ever going to take you away from me. Do you understand, Skipper? You are *safe* here. This is *your* home, and I won't let anyone take you away."

"Me be here?"

He cleared the lump from his throat. "Yes. You will be here with me for always." He sank down on the bed, leaned back against the pillow, stretched out his legs and flipped the folded-back covers over them both. Jonathan wiggled himself comfortable against his chest, sighed and closed his eyes.

He heard a whisper of sound, looked up and saw a swish of blue hems disappear around the door frame. Clarice…

The idea came out of nowhere. He closed his eyes, smiled and let it develop until it formed into a plan.

Chapter Nine

The floor overhead creaked. Clarice strained against the silence and faint footfalls on the stairs met her ears. He was coming. The footsteps grew louder. She stiffened, snatched up another of the washed dishes from the wood drainboard. She wasn't ready to see Charles Thornberg. She was too shaken. Too...*confused*.

"Jonathan is sound asleep."

She nodded, grabbed another bowl to dry to keep her back to him. *Let him leave now. Please let him leave.*

"I want to talk to you, Clarice. Will you join me for a cup of coffee?"

His deep voice was quiet, pleasant, but he might as well have snarled an order. He was her employer. Did he think she would dare to say no? China clinked. The coffeepot scraped against the stove plate.

He was pouring her coffee again! She took a breath, swiped the towel around the bowl. Why didn't he just tell her what he wanted her to do, instead of playing these games?

"You take your coffee with a bit of cream, right? Looks like you've already put it away. I'll just—"

"I'll get it." Anything to make him *stop*. "Just let me put these bowls away first." She threw down the towel, stacked the bowl on top of the other dried ones and turned, stopped. Charles was standing at the work table, two steaming cups of coffee in front of him. *Wonderful.* She had to pass him to get to the step-back cupboard where the bowls were kept. He'd be sure to notice her red, puffy eyes. "Or I can put them away later."

She set the bowls back on the sink cupboard, hurried to the refrigerator and snatched up the small pitcher of cream. If she kept her head down… She poured cream in her coffee and returned the pitcher to the refrigerator. There was nothing else to do to keep her distance from him. She placed her fingertips against the cold pitcher, held them to her puffy eyes for a moment then closed the door and turned. "You wanted to speak with me?"

"I wanted to *talk* with you, yes. But upstairs. I promised Jonathan I would be there when he woke."

Her throat tightened. She blinked her eyes and pressed her lips together to keep from shouting at him to stop pretending. That Jonathan's little heart would be crushed when he tired of playing his game of protective big brother, for whatever his reason. The letter from Jonathan's mother with the enclosed bank draft flashed into her mind again. Her stomach soured. It was the only reason she could think of that Charles might be keeping Jonathan. Brothers weren't *protective*—they were mean and selfish. She should know. It had to be the money.

She nodded, ducked her head, reached around and yanked the ties of Mrs. Hotchkiss's too-large apron, frowned and yanked again. *Knotted.* Perfect. Just what she needed. She probed with her fingers, tugged.

"Need some help?"

No! "I can manage, thank—"

"Turn around."

His shoes appeared in her vision. She froze. *Don't—* His hands grasped her shoulders. She went stiff as a board, bit down on her lip to hold back a demand that he not touch her. He gave a gentle nudge, and she turned on wooden legs. The apron drew taut around her waist. She held her breath at the touch of his fingers and knuckles against her dress, tried not to remember how her father had grabbed the ties on her aprons and yanked her to him when she tried to escape his punishing hand.

"That's got it."

The apron loosened, hung in deep folds. She listened to him move away.

"I'll carry the coffee."

Good. Because if she had it in her hands right now, she'd throw it at him. She slipped the neck loop over her head and removed the apron, hung it on a chair back and led the way into the entrance hall and up the stairs.

"We can talk in the bedroom where you are working. You can sit down in there."

She shook her head, moved to stand close to Jonathan's bedroom door. "I prefer to stay here in the hall-

BUSINESS REPLY MAIL
FIRST-CLASS MAIL   PERMIT NO. 717   BUFFALO, NY

POSTAGE WILL BE PAID BY ADDRESSEE

READER SERVICE
PO BOX 1867
BUFFALO NY 14240-9952

NO POSTAGE
NECESSARY
IF MAILED
IN THE
UNITED STATES

Send For
2 FREE BOOKS
Today!

I accept your offer!

Please send me two
free novels and two mystery
gifts (gifts worth about $10).
I understand that these books
are completely free—even
the shipping and handling will
be paid—and I am under no
obligation to purchase anything,
ever, as explained on the back
of this card.

102/302 IDL GHP3

Please Print

FIRST NAME

LAST NAME

ADDRESS

APT.#   CITY

STATE/PROV.   ZIP/POSTAL CODE

Visit us online at
www.ReaderService.com

HLI-815-GF15

(side text, left margin) ® and ™ are trademarks owned and used by the trademark owner and/or its licensee. Printed in the U.S.A.

▲ © 2015 HARLEQUIN ENTERPRISES LIMITED ▲ Detach card and mail today. No stamp needed. ▲

way. Jonathan was very frightened this morning, and I want to be sure we'll hear him if he stirs."

He nodded, handed her the cup of milk-laced coffee. "I know you would prefer to be working at your job at the newspaper, Clarice. But I thank you for the excellent care you are giving Jonathan. The way you comforted him—" He broke off, took a swallow of his coffee.

His praise was meaningless…hollow. He wanted something more from her. She took a sip of her coffee and waited.

"It's obvious that Jonathan trusts you."

"He has no choice." Her throat thickened. "I'm the one looking after him—at the moment." *Poor baby, being passed around like unwanted clothing.*

"There's more to it than that, Clarice." Charles took another swallow of coffee, looked down and swirled the hot brew in his cup. "I want him to trust me that way—to know he's safe with me. So I've decided to stay home from the newspaper tomorrow and spend the day with him."

She jerked her gaze to his face. "Stay home from the *newspaper*?"

"Yes." His brow furrowed. "It will take some doing, but I can manage it. The next issue isn't for two days." He glanced into the bedroom. "Do you think Jonathan would like that? That it would help him to know that he can depend on me…that I will take care of him?"

Her mind balked. She stared at him. Men didn't take care of children. At least, not her father or the other men she'd known in her life. And Jonathan didn't have to trust him in order for him to keep the money. Did he? She held back a frown. He was looking at her…waiting for an answer. "I'm sure he would like to spend more time with you. And that it would build his trust." His smile added to her confusion.

"I thought he might like to go for a steamer ride on the lake."

She nodded, picturing Jonathan's excitement. "That's a wonderful idea. I'm sure he will love the steamers." She ignored the wrench the thought of being separated from the toddler, of not knowing if he was all right, brought and glanced toward the bedroom across the hall. The first stack of letters were answered. She would be able to go to the newspaper and bring back another pile to—

"And then have a picnic dinner at Chautauqua." Charles drained his coffee cup and sat it on the small table along the wall. "I saw some tables and benches in the trees along the shore area when I was there."

"A picnic?" A smile touched her lips. Jonathan would have a wonderful time exploring—

"I thought, perhaps, you could make us up a meal? There must be a suitable basket around the kitchen somewhere. If not, I will buy one."

So that was what he wanted of her. She nodded and set her cup down beside his, mentally revising the supper she had planned to one that would provide cold food for a picnic. Perhaps chicken…

"Whatever you and Jonathan would like is fine—"

"Me?" The new menu flew from her mind.

"Why, yes." He frowned, fastened his gaze on hers.

"I thought you understood that you would be coming along. I'm afraid Jonathan would think I was taking him away if I went off with him alone. You must come so he is comfortable on our expedition."

"I see." Unfortunately, she did. What he said made sense—and eased her mind about Jonathan being on a steamer without her there to watch over him. She took a breath, nodded. "Very well."

"Good. That's settled, then." The clock downstairs in the sitting room gonged. He glanced back into Jonathan's bedroom. "How long does he sleep? I told Robert Tyner I'd stop into the bank today with that bank draft."

It *was* the money. Her stomach sank, churned. "You've no need for concern. Jonathan will be awake long before the bank closes. Now, if you will excuse me, since you are staying with Jonathan, I have dishes to finish." She snatched the coffee cups off the table and hurried down the stairs.

Charles frowned at the gathering clouds and stepped into the bank. He nodded to the tellers conducting business at their cubicles on his way to the offices and removed his hat.

"Good afternoon, Miss Paul. Is Mr. Tyner in?"

The blond-haired secretary smiled and nodded. "He said you were to go right in, Mr. Thornberg."

"Thank you." The door on the left bore a discreet sign that read Robert Tyner, President. He rapped and waited.

"Come in."

The door whispered open and closed with a gentle

push. His footsteps on the plush Oriental rug barely disturbed the hushed atmosphere of the elegant office.

"Good afternoon, Charles." Robert Tyner rose and extended his hand in welcome. "I've been expecting you. How is the newspaper doing?"

"We're keeping our head above water." Charles met the bank president's firm grip with his own. "And circulation is improving every week. I expect to turn the *Jamestown Journal* into a daily paper by the end of the year."

"Well, I'm all for that. This town needs a strong newspaper to help build our businesses and keep the politicians honest."

"Well, I can't promise to do that—" his lips slanted in a wry grin "—but I'll do my level best."

"That's all the people of Jamestown can ask." Robert Tyner waved a hand in the direction of the pair of leather chairs in front of his desk. "Have a seat. What can I do for you?"

He pulled the bank draft out of his pocket and handed it to the banker. "First you can tell me if this is real."

Robert Tyner adjusted his glasses, peered at the document in his hand. "Hmm, an international bank draft written on the Bank of England." He glanced up at him over the top of his glasses. "It's real, all right." He looked back down. "And made out to you." His eyebrow quirked. "This is a sizable amount." He laid the draft on his desk and lowered his glasses. "Did you want to deposit this in your savings account?"

"No. I want to use it to open a trust account in the name of Jonathan Thornberg."

"*Jonathan* Thornberg?"

"He's my brother."

"I wasn't aware you had a brother."

"Neither was I. He's a toddler, not yet three years old and just arrived from England." He sat back in the chair to finish his story with the ambiguous truth he'd decided on to protect Jonathan from the harsh fact of his mother's abandonment of him. "My mother is, of course, an older woman now, and there were complications surrounding Jonathan's birth. There is doubt she will ever recover from them, so she sent him to me." He fought to keep the anger from showing on his face or coloring his voice. "The draft is for his care. But I am more than capable of caring for him. Thus, I want the money from the draft set up as a trust for him."

"Most generous of you, Charles." The banker opened a drawer, pulled out a form, perched his glasses back on his nose and picked up his pen. "Donor… Charles— Have you a middle name?"

"Jefferson."

"Thank you. And the boy's full name?"

"Jonathan David Thornberg."

"Place and date of birth."

"Paris, France, the eighteenth day of December, eighteen hundred seventy-five."

He watched Robert Tyner fill out the information, listened to the clock on the wall ticking out the minutes and shifted in his chair. He had to get to the newspaper. He had a lot to—

"And when do you wish Jonathan to come into this trust?"

"Upon graduation from school or when he is twenty-one—whichever comes first."

"Very good. Now, if you will just sign here…" The banker pointed to a line on the paper and handed him the pen.

He signed the document and handed the pen back. "There's one more thing…"

Robert Tyner lifted his head, glanced across the desk at him. "Whatever you need, Charles. I'm here to serve."

"I want all of my savings and other assets used for Jonathan's care should something happen to me. I'll get Thad Fox to draw up the legal papers, but that takes time and I wanted to know if there is anything I can do to assure that my wishes in the matter are met *now*. I want to know if I step outside and get struck by lightning or run down by a carriage, Jonathan will be all right. Can I give you a note to that effect? Or is there anything that you would recommend?"

"You can set that up as a nonspecific open-ended trust to include *all* of your savings, as you will have no idea as to the actual amount that will be in your savings account at the time the trust would go into effect. Then as assets are liquidated, the monies can be deposited in the savings trust. Would that suit?"

"That sounds fine."

"And do you wish to sign the form and put that trust into effect today?"

"Yes. I want to know if something happens to me, Jonathan will be taken care of."

The banker pulled out another form and started filling in the information.

He watched him writing and the worry he'd been carrying since Jonathan arrived lifted. His brother would be—

"And who will be the administrator of the savings trust?"

"Administrator?" He stared, taken aback by the question.

"Yes." Robert Tyner peered at him over the top of his glasses. "If the boy is young when the savings trust goes into effect, you must have someone who will make certain it is used wisely for the boy's benefit. It's usually another family member, the person whom you appoint as guardian in your stead."

"I don't *have* any other family here. That's what all this is about." He jerked to his feet, shoved his fingers through his hair and started pacing. *Who, Lord? You, who knows all things—*

"Someone you trust, then…"

Clarice. The name froze him in his tracks. *No.* Images swarmed. He blinked, shook his head, but the picture of Clarice comforting Jonathan would not be dislodged. *No. It was a crazy idea.* He started pacing again. The image clung. *No! Of all the people—no! She is a career woman!* He mentally listed his employees, thought of old teachers, his lawyer. The image stayed firmly in place.

I sure hope this is You leading me, Lord. He took

a breath, plowed his fingers through his hair, walked back and sank down onto the chair, telling himself he had lost his mind.

"You've decided on someone?"

"Yes. Miss Clarice Gordon."

It was *insane*. *He* was insane. Charles frowned, flopped down on his bed and laced his hands behind his neck. Images had been swarming him ever since he'd left the bank and he couldn't make them stop. *Clarice* seated at the table in the editorial room reading and stacking CLSC letters. *Clarice* holding the instruction manual and peering into the workings of her typewriter. *Clarice* running her hand over the composing table and asking questions about the procedure. She was a *career* woman through and through. And he was a madman to entrust Jonathan to her care. *Insane*.

He jerked to his feet, yanked open the door beside his bed and stepped out onto the balcony. A raindrop splatted against his forehead. Dark blotches formed on the floor. He ducked back to the doorway, scowled and leaned against the frame. Would the rain pass, or would it ruin his plans for the outing with Jonathan tomorrow? And with Clarice.

He jammed his hands in his pockets and hunched his shoulders, watched the tree branches beginning to stir before a rising wind. He should have told her. As soon as he returned home, he should have told her. In spite of the late hour. In spite of her declaration that she had to hurry home to her mother, he should have told her. Instead, he'd grabbed onto the excuse to put off telling her and let her go. *Coward.*

White light flickered against the distant sky. Thunder grumbled. The wind blew the rain in his direction. It looked as if the storm was coming their way. Lightning flashed again. Thunder clapped.

He glanced over his shoulder. Would the storm disturb Jonathan's sleep? Some kids in the boarding schools he'd lived in had been frightened of rainstorms. He could remember some of them ducking under their blankets and crying.

He stepped back, closed the door and headed down the hallway. He'd sit in Jonathan's room until the storm passed—just in case.

The answer to your question is William Shakespeare. Clarice tapped the words out on the paper keyboard as fast as she thought them. A smile touched her lips. She had not hesitated at all—not even once. She could type! She would be able to type out the CLSC answer column in a few hours once she returned to work at the newspaper. Of course, that meant she would no longer be caring for Jonathan.

She thrust the disturbing thought away, lifted her hands from the paper keyboard, yawned and rubbed her tired eyes. She had lost a few hours sleep each night practicing, but it was worth it. She would be able to type her Chautauqua Experience article as she thought it, instead of writing it down and then typing it. Only imagine the time that would save her over and over again, day after day. What a wonderful invention the typewriter was.

Light flickered against the darkness outside the window. A low rumble sounded. She turned down the wick on the lamp, pushed back from the desk and walked to the window. It was storming in the distance. Probably at the other end of the lake. But it could be headed their way. There was a chill to the air.

She ran her fingers through her long, unrestrained hair to massage her scalp where the heavy roll of her hair was pinned every day, then brushed the silky, wavy mass off of her shoulders to hang down her back and crossed to her mother's bed.

The bouquet of straw flowers glowed rusty red and golden yellow in the dim light of the trimmed oil lamp on the night table. A frown drew her brows down. Why had Charles brought her mother flowers? What had he hoped to gain? She touched the papery petals of one of the red flowers, glanced at her closed writing case. Why hadn't he mentioned taking the fillers for use at the newspaper?

"I'm sorry I let Mr. Thornberg discover your secret, Clarice. It was careless of me."

She jerked, pressed her hand to her throat. "Gracious, Mama, you startled me. I thought you were asleep long ago."

"The thunder woke me." Her mother gave her a tired smile. "I sleep light. From all those years of taking care of babies, I expect."

"No doubt." She reached for the blanket folded at

the foot of the bed. "I just wanted to pull this up where you can reach it should the night turn cold."

"You're a good daughter, Clarice. I'm blessed to have you."

"It's the other way around, Mama. Sleep well." She bent down and kissed her mother's cheek, headed for her bed.

"Why don't you take this blanket, Clarice? I'm plenty warm under this quilt, and you have to sleep against those cold windows."

She shook her head, shrugged out of her dressing gown and slipped beneath the covers, shivering as the cold penetrated her nightgown. "I'll put my dressing gown back on if I get cold."

Light flickered through the darkened room. Thunder grumbled louder.

"Looks as if the storm is headed our way. I hope Mr. Thornberg's little brother isn't afraid of the thunder and lightning—a lot of little ones are."

Her mother's voice, soft, comforting as a warm, safe shelter, whispered through the darkness and wrapped itself around her.

"I know, Mama. I've been thinking about him." Tears stung her eyes. "He's not had anyone to love and comfort him when he's hurt or afraid…" Her throat tightened.

"He does now, Clarice. Mr. Thornberg is a caring man."

For the money. She held her tongue, stared into the darkness and tried not to think about Jonathan being afraid. Her mother's breathing came soft and even with sleep. The storm crept closer.

Rain splattered against the window, ran in rivulets down the small panes and dripped off the wood. Lightning flashed its watery gleam on the glass. Thunder cracked and rattled the panes.

She pushed herself to a sitting position and leaned back against the deep frame that housed the windows and the window seat. Cold penetrated the fabric of her cotton gown and chilled her shoulders where they pressed against the glass. She rubbed warmth into her arms and stared out into the darkness. Jonathan was a sound sleeper, but the thunder was getting louder. Would he sleep through the storm? Would he waken and be frightened? Would Charles hear him and comfort him?

She sighed, forced the questions from her mind. There was nothing she could do about it even if Jonathan were frightened.

Lightning streaked across the sky. Thunder crashed. *Don't let him wake and be frightened. Please don't let him be afraid.*

The words echoed back into her mind, empty, hollow…useless. She frowned, pulled the covers closer around her. It was almost as if the prayer— Thought. An aimless thought.

She stiffened, sucked in a breath as Scriptures learned in childhood flooded her mind… *Whatsoever ye shall ask the Father in my name… Ye ask, and receive not, because ye ask amiss… I am the way, the truth, and the life: no man cometh unto the Father, but by me.*

Tears stung her eyes. She shivered and wrapped her arms about herself, shamed by a sudden awareness of her petulant behavior in refusing to speak the Lord's name over the years. Had she really thought to punish Him by such childish action?

She closed her eyes and opened her heart, painfully aware of the emptiness that had been there for so long. "I've been so wrong. Please forgive me, Father God. Please forgive me, Lord Jesus. I will never deny You again."

The patter of the rain slowed, quieted. Peace settled over her, a contentment filling her heart. She breathed out a soft sigh, opened her eyes and watched the storm drift away into the distance.

Chapter Ten

"Me see horsey!" Jonathan bounced up and down on Charles's shoulders, his pudgy hands holding fistfuls of hair.

"Whoa! Easy on the hair, Skipper!" Charles laughed, took a firmer grip on Jonathan's chunky little legs and held them away from his healing blister. "We'll be aboard the *Jamestown* in a few minutes, and you can bounce all you want then."

He aimed a grin at Clarice. "Whose idea was this, anyway?"

Her gray eyes, shadowed by long lashes, sparkled with amusement. "Are you speaking of showing Jonathan the steamers? Or of carrying him on your shoulders?" Her lips curved. "Which—you may recall—I warned you might not be the best idea."

"He couldn't see anything in this crowd."

"Doggy! Me see doggy."

"Ow!" He stretched his neck, trying to ease Jonathan's pull on his hair.

"He can now." She grinned and looked up. "We're nearing the dock. I suggest you lift him down before he catches sight of the steamer and snatches you bald."

"I think you might be right. Down you come, Skipper…" He slid his hands up to Jonathan's waist, ducked, hoisted him over his head and settled him on his arm. He combed the fingers of his free hand through his hair to restore some semblance of neatness and looked down at her. "I can take that basket now. It must be getting heavy for you."

She shook her head and shifted the basket handles on her forearm. "I'm doing fine. And you have your hands full."

"I can handle this guy." He tugged the flat top of Jonathan's sailor hat straight and grinned. "You can't see everything at once, Skipper, no matter how much you twist and turn."

"Me see boat?"

"Yes. We're almost there. You'll see the boat we're going to ride on as soon as we turn this corner."

Jonathan stilled, looked up at him, his eyes wary. "Brover go on boat?"

He sucked in a breath, hugged Jonathan close and nodded reassurance. "I sure am, Skipper. And Clarice is coming on the boat, too." He glanced her way. She was smiling, but the same anger heating his blood flickered in the depths of her eyes. It was obvious she shared his fury at the way Jonathan had been treated. The worry he carried eased a little. Maybe everything would be all right.

"C'rice come?"

"I am." She reached out and straightened the wide collar with white trim that flowed over Jonathan's little shoulders and hung against his back. "We're going to have a picnic, remember?"

"Me have cookies!"

"That's right." Clarice laughed and patted the basket dangling from her arm. "I have them right here. And there—" she gestured toward the water as they turned the corner onto the less populated street leading to the dock "—is the boat."

Jonathan twisted around. "Boat!"

"It's a steamer, Skipper. See the smoke coming out of the tall stack?" He took a firmer grip on his brother, placed his free hand at the small of Clarice's back and guided her onto the long dock. Water lapped at the pilings.

"Tickets! Get your tickets for the *Jamestown* here."

He pulled the tickets he had bought yesterday afternoon from his pocket, showed them to the man in the booth and was waved forward.

"Water." Jonathan leaned sideways, pointed down at the lake water between the dock and the steamer.

"Lots of water. You sit still, Skipper." He kept a tight grip on Jonathan and again placed his hand at Clarice's back to help her, though she showed no hesitation at walking up the slightly sloping gangplank to the steamer deck.

"Good morning, Miss Gordon." The ticket taker doffed his hat. "You're off to Chautauqua to write another article, are you?"

"Good morning, Mr. Dewy."

She knew his name? Charles stared at the man concentrating his attention on Clarice. His back stiffened. The man's smile was too friendly for his liking. Didn't a captain have rules about maintaining correct decorum between the crew and the passengers? He cleared his throat and held out the boarding passes.

The man glanced at him.

"I have Miss Gordon's ticket. She's with me."

The man locked gazes with him, glanced back at Clarice.

She patted the basket. "No writing for me today. We're going on a picnic, aren't we, Jonathan?"

The ties on Jonathan's sailor hat bounced with his nod. "Me have cookies."

"Cookies, is it? Well, then…" The man took his offered tickets with a concession in the gesture. "Have a pleasant journey, sir."

He nodded, placed a proprietary hand at Clarice's back and urged her forward to the open staircase. She had been sitting on the upper deck the day he first saw her. "The upper deck has a better view." He held out his free hand. "Give me the basket."

She shook her head and gripped the banister. "You have Jonathan to carry."

"Clarice—" He shot out his hand, held her from climbing the stairs and leaned close to her ear. "You are the most obstinate, *independent* woman I have ever met. Please *allow* me to be a *gentleman* and help you." He took hold of the basket handles ground out quiet words. "I know you are a very capable young woman, and that you would likely make it safely to the top of the stairs. But you have long skirts you can trip on, and I am not willing to take that chance. Jonathan can hold on around my neck. Now give me the basket so we do not continue to hold up this line of people."

"Your blister—"

"Hang the blister! Give me the *basket*." He took a breath, reining in the explosion of frustrated male pride. "If I must make it an order as your employer, consider it so. But you will not carry that basket up those open stairs. Not while you are with me."

An odd expression he could not identify flashed in her eyes. She glanced at the people massing behind them, handed him the basket, lifted her hems and started up the stairs. He stared after her, let out a low growl, hoisted Jonathan into position on his arm and gripped the basket. "Put your arms around my neck and hold on tight, Skipper." He took hold of the railing with his free hand and followed her up the stairs, puzzling over her expression and whether he'd won or lost the basket battle. Either way, he'd likely made it highly improbable that she'd accept the position of Jonathan's guardian should anything happen to him. He should have held his temper.

"Do you wish to go forward or aft?"

Her voice pulled him from his sour musings. He looked at her in her dark blue dress with the little white dots on the bodice that put him in the mind of stars and wished, for a foolish instant, that things were different—that she truly were *with* him. "Forward. I want Jonathan to see what's ahead, not what's behind."

She nodded and reached for the basket. "I'll take

this. I'm in no danger of falling now." Her voice was soft, controlled, her expression an enigma he couldn't solve. Was she angry with him? No doubt. He deserved it.

He released his grip on the basket and moved forward to stand by the railing. The sun sparkled on the water. White clouds drifted in lazy splendor against the blue sky. There was no trace of last night's storm—unless it was in Clarice's gray eyes.

"Ocean." Jonathan pointed, looked up at him.

He shook his head, thought of what the little guy had seen on his way to him in America. Who had been taking care of him? "No. That's Chautauqua Lake."

"Chau'qua Lake."

"Close enough." He grinned, spread his legs for a more sure stance when the whistle blew. The engine throbbed through the deck beneath his feet. The steamer lurched. He glanced at Clarice standing beside him holding on to the railing, the picnic basket at her feet, and ached to put his arm around her, to share the moment with her. There was a hunger, an emptiness inside him he hadn't been aware of before Jonathan came into his life. Or had he?

An image of Clarice looking up at him when he had walked her home in the rainstorm slipped into his mind, and the truth hit him with the power of the steam engine's thrust. The hunger, the emptiness, had been there since that moment.

He stiffened, his thoughts churning like the foaming water sluicing off the paddle wheel. He held back a scowl, watched the *Jamestown* crawl away from the dock. What was he thinking? He was lonely, that was all. But he had family now. Jonathan was enough.

A whistle sounded in the distance. He looked down at his brother and smiled. "You hear that whistle, Skipper? That's another steamer telling us to get out of her way—that she's coming into the dock."

"Me see boat!" Jonathan twisted around and pointed out on the lake.

"That's it. That's the steamer." He looked out over the water, focused his attention on the other vessel.

Clarice turned to face them, smiled and straightened Jonathan's stocking. He glanced down, met her gaze, and the oneness, the sharing of the moment he'd craved, happened.

"I think he could wiggle right out of his clothes."

A proprietary tone, a touch of motherly pride, sounded in her soft words. She smiled and the warmth in her eyes, the gentleness in the curve of her lips sailed right by his common sense and lodged firmly in his heart.

Clarice crumbled the biscuit, tossed it out onto the strip of grassy shore and smiled as birds flew down from the surrounding trees to dine on the offered morsels.

"Me get bird."

Jonathan ran onto the grass dodging this way and that trying to catch hold of a bird. She laughed and returned to the blanket, glad that they'd traded the comfort of a table and benches for this secluded part of the shore. She glanced over at Charles to see if he was enjoying his brother's futile efforts. "The birds don't seem a bit intimidated by Jonathan's attempts at capture."

"Not in the least. How long do you suppose he can keep on running like that?"

His gaze fastened on her. She looked down and brushed her hands free of crumbs, quelled a sudden urge to check her hair and straighten her gown. "Probably until we board the *Jamestown* for our return trip. He never seems to run out of energy." She waved her hand toward the remnants of their picnic. "The chicken is gone. But there is another biscuit with sliced beef." His gaze didn't waver. She held still, refused to fidget, though she had the strongest urge to turn and run. The man made her *nervous*.

"I've had enough, thank you. Though I might find room for one of those ginger cookies Jonathan has been devouring." He took a cookie from the towel-covered plate.

She took a breath and sank to her knees on the blanket to clear away the picnic things.

"Umm, no wonder he keeps coming back for more. This is delicious." He glanced toward the shore and chuckled. "If you threw one of these cookies out there, those birds wouldn't stand a chance. They'd stay right there and eat and let themselves be captured by Jonathan's grasping little hands."

"I didn't know cookies could be used as bird lures." His chuckle made her stomach go all quivery. She pressed her hand against it and took a breath.

"It turned out to be a beautiful day. The weather couldn't be better for our outing." He grabbed another cookie then handed her the plate. "I was afraid when that rainstorm rolled in last night it might ruin our plans for today."

"I thought the same." She stacked the dirty plates, looked askance at the one holding the remaining biscuit with sliced beef.

"I'll get rid of that. I'm sure some beast will appreciate a good meal." Charles grabbed the biscuit and threw it into the woods.

She put the empty plate atop the others, folded a towel around the pile and placed it in the basket. "I wondered if Jonathan would be fearful of the storm— some children are."

"I know." He nodded, brushed cookie crumbs off of his shirt. "I remembered how some of the kids in boarding school would hide beneath their blankets and cry during rainstorms, so I went and sat in his room until the storm passed. He slept straight through it."

I remembered... She closed the top on the basket and secured the latch, told herself it was none of her business but couldn't resist asking. "You attended a boarding school?"

He glanced over at her, gave a curt nod. "From the time I was five years old. That's when my father died, and my mother decided she preferred a career over motherhood." He shoved to his feet and stood watching Jonathan, who had stopped chasing birds to examine a stone. "A stranger came and took me off to boarding school the day after we buried my father. I never saw my mother or my home again—though she kindly paid for my schooling." He shoved his hands in his pockets, shook his head. "Those first few years I would lie in bed at night and wonder where she was and what had happened to her—why she didn't come for me. At least Jonathan has been spared that."

There was such bitterness in his voice. She stared up at him remembering how lost and alone and fearful she had felt when her mother had sent her away to protect her from her father. But she had been old enough to understand. And she'd had her mother's love to sustain her. Charles had been *abandoned*. And he'd been only a little older than— She stiffened, glanced at Jonathan, then back at Charles. His words when he'd read the letter left with Jonathan slipped into her head. *So, Mother, you've done it again.*

He turned, his lips slanted in an acrid smile. "Sounds familiar, doesn't it?" The smile faded; his eyes darkened. "She thought she'd throw Jonathan into boarding school and be rid of him the same way she'd gotten rid of me. Not that I would expect anything different of her." The muscle along his jaw twitched. "What *galls* me is that she thinks *I* am like her. That *I*, too, would toss Jonathan into a school somewhere so he won't interfere with my life."

He shook his head, looked back toward the shore. "That will never happen. That little guy is my brother." He strode out onto the grass, squatted down in front of Jonathan, picked up something and held it between them on his upturned palm, poked at it with his finger. Jonathan laughed, stuck out his pudgy finger and poked whatever it was, too.

Her heart ached at the sight of them together. Both

of them—*discarded*. Charles's word. His voice, angry and fiercely protective, rang in her mind. *It's all right, Jonathan, everything is all right. You have a home now. No one will ever discard you again. I give you my word on it.* She caught her breath, stared at Charles. Perhaps the money *wasn't* the reason he was keeping Jonathan. Perhaps she had misjudged him.

She bent and picked up the blanket, gave it a sharp shake to rid it of dirt and grass.

The blast of a steamer whistle rent the air.

She glanced down the shore toward the dock. The *Jamestown* was slowing, preparing to dock. Their picnic was over. She glanced at Jonathan looking up at Charles and pointing toward the steamer, folded the blanket and packed it away.

"Ball…go in water." Jonathan yawned, leaned his head on Charles's shoulder and rubbed his eyes with a pudgy fist.

Clarice glanced back over her shoulder at the sun hanging between the shimmering reflection of its light on the water, the dark jagged line of treetops on the far shore and the red-streaked graying sky above. "It looks that way, doesn't it?"

She reached up and removed his sailor hat, which had gone askew, brushed a soft black curl off his forehead. "That 'ball' is the sun. He's been working hard all day keeping it bright and warm so you could play. Now it's time for little boys to rest."

He blew out a soft breath, nodded. "Me go bed."

"In a few minutes, Skipper. We're home."

Charles's footsteps mingled with the brush of her hems against the wood as they crossed the porch. The door latch clicked. She stepped into the entrance hall, warm with the light from the oil lamp that Charles always kept burning, looked at the stairs, the hall that led to the kitchen. *Home.* It was starting to feel like it. She had best guard her heart. She was becoming too… comfortable with…everything.

She held her glance from Charles, set the picnic basket down and led the way up the stairs to put Jonathan to bed.

Chapter Eleven

Clarice pulled the pan from the rinse water, placed it on the wood drainboard, threw a towel over the washed dishes and took off the apron. Now to begin work on the new pile of CLSC letters Charles had brought for her when he'd come home for dinner.

She dipped a finger in Mrs. Hotchkiss's honey-and-almond cream, rubbed it into her hands and hurried to the stairs. The ticking of the sitting room clock urged her forward. Jonathan should sleep for— She stopped, turned at the sound of the front door opening. "Charles! Did you forget something?"

He stepped to the bottom of the stairs, looked up at her. "No. I came back to talk to you, Clarice. Come into the sitting room, please."

She took in his sober expression, gripped the banister and descended the stairs. Had she done something to displease him at dinner? "Is something wrong?"

"I'm hoping not." He gestured toward the sitting room. What did *that* mean? She moved forward, the hem of her long skirt whispering an accompaniment to her racing thoughts—there was nothing this morning. She sifted memories of yesterday's picnic, came up with nothing but the incident on the stairs. Surely that wouldn't explain his terse words and tense expression. She stopped by one of the wingback chairs in front of the fireplace where she could hear if Jonathan stirred.

"Please, have a seat." His lips curved in a polite smile. "This may take a little time."

Why draw things out? She squared her shoulders and lifted her chin. "Perhaps I can save you some time. Have I done something to displease you?"

"What? No. Quite the opposite. I apologize if I gave you that impression." He scrubbed a hand over the back of his neck. "You have been wonderful with Jonathan."

Her work! She stiffened. "If it's my work for the *Assembly Herald*, I assure you I will be finished—"

"I'm not concerned with your work, Clarice. It's something I have done."

"You?" His pronouncement knocked her thinking askew. "But what does what you—?"

"It concerns you."

"Me?" She stared, snapped her mouth closed. "How does—?"

"I think this will go faster if you simply let me explain."

Warmth climbed into her cheeks. "Yes, of course. Forgive me for interrupting."

"You've every right. Please feel free to do so if, at any point, I do not make myself clear." He took a deep breath, exhaled. "To begin, let me apologize for my delay in speaking with you about this matter. I meant to tell you the other day, but my intent was lost in Jonathan's fear of being moved to a different place."

She stared at him, intrigued by his discomfort. She'd never seen Charles Thornberg look anything but self-confident—except with Jonathan, and even that was waning. She glanced at the charming dimple at the side of Charles's mouth. Jonathan had one also. It deepened when he smiled. And she was quite certain Charles's dark hair would curl like Jonathan's if it weren't cut so short. It was quite wavy. And it did curl a bit when he got frustrated and ran his fingers through it…

"And then again, yesterday, I— But I digress."

His gaze locked on hers, and the heat in her cheeks returned. He'd caught her staring. Did he realize she'd been admiring his good looks? Only in comparison to Jonathan, of course. He looked away, cleared his throat. She touched her hair, wiped her palms down the sides of her skirt.

"Do you remember what I told you yesterday about my childhood? Of how, when my father died, my mother sent me off to boarding school, and I never saw her or my home again?"

"Yes." She remembered perfectly. The melancholy look on his face had almost broken her heart. Her throat tightened with the memory.

"Perhaps you surmised, but it's important for you to know that I have no other family."

Her attention sharpened. What did his family, or the lack thereof, have to do with her?

"My life was spent in boarding schools. It's a…

lonely existence. And when I read in my mother's letter of her intent to do the same thing to Jonathan—" anger swept like a cloud across his face, darkened his eyes "—I promised Jonathan that would not happen to him. That I would take care of him, that he would not ever be *discarded* like an unwanted possession."

She blinked, rubbed at a sudden fullness in her chest. "I remember."

The muscle along his jaw twitched. "And do you remember the bank draft my mother enclosed to pay for Jonathan's life in boarding school?"

She gazed at him and nodded, a wariness worming its way through the tightness in her chest.

He pulled in a breath, exhaled. "The day I graduated, I was called to the headmaster's office and given an envelope my mother had sent along with me when I arrived at the boarding school. It contained information about a trust fund my father had left for me that I was to receive on my graduation." His face and voice softened. "It was as if my father had reached out after all those years since his death and touched me."

He looked down, cleared his throat and rolled his shoulders, then fastened his gaze on hers again. "If anything happens to me, I want that for Jonathan. I want him to know that I cared about him, and that I kept my word to take care of him. So I turned that bank draft into a trust fund for him to receive on the day he graduates from school."

Her heart jolted at the unselfishness behind his act. Her father would never—

"Now, here's the part where you come in."

She'd forgotten about that. She looked at his wry smile, the hint of guilt in his eyes and squared her shoulders. What could it be?

"Jonathan's just a little guy. And it dawned on me, when I was in the bank setting up the trust fund, that an accident could take my life the same as happened to my father when I was five years old."

Her heart gave another jolt at that thought.

"Anyway, the how isn't important. It's the fact that I could die at any time that matters." His eyes darkened. He lifted his hand and combed his fingers through his hair. "The point is—I need to know that if something happens to me, Jonathan will be taken care of."

He came and stood in front of her, fastened his gaze on hers. "Another thing I inherited from my father was his business skills. I found that out when I took that small trust he left me and invested it. I did very well on those investments, and since I was making my living as a roving reporter, I invested my earnings, as well. And then—" He gave a little shrug. "Suffice to say, I am a wealthy man. And I expect to be wealthier yet when I turn the *Jamestown* into a prosperous daily newspaper."

There was an energy, a *vitality* coming from him that made her tremble. She tried to step back, to put some space between them, but the chair was behind her. She took a breath, made herself stand still and not flinch away from the power of his gaze, grabbed for the safety of words. "What has any of that to do with me?"

He studied her for a moment, a *long* moment, then turned away.

She sagged with relief, mustered her scattered thoughts.

"On Robert Tyner's advice, I created a second trust containing any and all monies, savings and assets in my possession on my death. That trust will be available immediately for Jonathan's care."

"How good of you."

He turned back. "There was one small problem—"

The look in his eyes took her breath. *Concentrate!* "A problem?"

"Yes. I needed to name an administrator. Someone I trust to do what is right for Jonathan."

She stared into his eyes, raised her hand to the base of her throat and pressed against her suddenly racing pulse. *It couldn't be...*

"I named you."

Her knees gave way. She plopped into the chair, shaking her head.

"Before you refuse, let me tell you that the bank president and my lawyer would maintain control over my investments and those sorts of things. But as the administrator of the trust, you would have the say over the running of this house—which I hope you would choose to move into, and your mother, as well—and the monies that would be placed at your disposal every month to see to Jonathan's needs…and yours. Plus, you would receive a monthly wage commensurate with your duties."

"I—I don't know what to say…"

"I hope you will say yes, Clarice."

"But I know nothing about handling large sums of money or running a grand house like this one."

"You can always ask Robert Tyner for advice about the money, as long as you realize *you* have the final say as to its disbursement. I trust you to know what is best for Jonathan. And I'm certain your mother would be helpful in guiding you in overseeing the house. You would have a housekeeper and a maid to do the work, of course."

He turned away, shoved his hands in his pockets. "I realize I would be asking you to give up the full pursuit of your career as a journalist, but I would be willing to stipulate that you could continue to write articles for publication from home, as long as Jonathan's care came first."

Did he think that was why she was hesitating? That she was like his mother, who put her career ahead of her own children? She rose, stared around the lovely, well-furnished room and shook her head. "What you are proposing is too much for me." She lifted her hand, smoothed back her hair. "I'm not qualified—"

"The only qualification I require is that you care about Jonathan." He turned back, locked his gaze on hers. "Do you?"

She lifted her chin. "Of course I do! But—"

"And do you care what would happen to him if I were no longer alive to take care of him?"

"Stop saying that!"

Something flickered deep in his eyes. That *energy* radiated off him again. Her breath caught and she turned away, put her arms about herself to stop the trembling spreading through her. She had to get away from him so she could *think*. "All right, you may leave my name in place as the administrator of the trust. You need a name, and I have no reason to worry that I will ever have to take on the task. You are a young, healthy man."

"Thank you, Clarice."

She nodded, started for the doorway into the entrance hall. "If you will excuse me—"

"Actually, I have two papers for you to sign."

She looked at him.

He pulled two folded papers from his pocket. "One is for the bank and one is for my lawyer."

What was she getting herself into? "Very well. I'll sign them—for Jonathan's sake."

"There is pen and ink here in the secretary." He crossed to the bookshelf desk, pulled down the slanted front to form the writing surface, took the pen and ink out of their cubbyhole and smoothed out the papers.

She let out a sigh, walked over and sat on the chair he held for her, willed her hand to stop shaking.

"There's no reason to be nervous—truly."

I wouldn't be if you would move away. She signed the first paper then signed the second while he blotted the first dry.

"There." She rose and started for the doorway again.

"Clarice, there is one other thing I wanted to ask you…"

No. She couldn't take any more. All she wanted was to escape his presence and—

"How long has your mother been bedridden?"

"My *mother*?" She turned and looked at him. "Why do you ask?"

"I thought perhaps it hasn't been very long." He tucked the folded papers into his pocket and closed the desk. "When I went to see her the other day, I noticed that her hands are still calloused."

Tears sprang to her eyes. "I don't know if they will ever soften. I cream them every morning and night. But Mother did almost all of the work on the farm by herself since she sent me away nine years ago and her hands have suffered for it." *Along with the rest of her body.*

"Then your father is dead. I thought as much."

Anger stopped the tears, stiffened her spine. "My *father* is in perfect health. He works in the oil fields, as do my three brothers. But he refuses to give up the farm, so my mother and I, when I was home, were made to tend the crops and the animals, along with doing the housework and everything else. If the work was not done to his satisfaction, a hard, quick slap let you know." Bitterness soured her voice. "My mother was carrying a basketful of their heavy work clothes she'd just washed and scrubbed to hang out on the line to dry when she became crippled."

"What happened?"

"I don't know." She took a breath to calm her anger. "All I know is that when Miss Hartmore—she's the teacher that rescued me from Father's cruelty—went to read my latest letter to my mother, she found her on the ground beside the laundry basket unable to rise. I guess her body just gave out. With the help of another neighbor, she took my mother to her house to care for her." The anger surged. She lifted her chin and clenched her hands. "When Miss Hartmore went to the farm that night and told my father what had happened, he declared he had no use for a *cripple* and no time or money to care for one. He told her to keep Mother at her house."

Charles sucked in air so sharply she heard it hiss through his teeth. *"Unconscionable!"*

"Yes."

Two of his long strides brought him to stand in front of her. "How did your mother come to live with you?"

She took another breath but couldn't stop the shaking. "Miss Hartmore wrote me of what had happened, and I went and, with Miss Hartmore's help, brought Mother here to live with me." Tears welled. He reached for her. She glanced down, and he dropped his hands. The tears pushed upward, overflowed. For the first time in her life, she wanted a man to hold her. She wanted *him* to hold her. His arms looked so strong, his shoulder so comforting. She blinked, wiped away the tears and straightened her shoulders.

"We took pillows so Mother could lie down on the train, but moving her caused her great pain. I thought she was going to faint when we carried her up the stairs to my room. But, as you've seen, she's much better now. The pain in her back has subsided."

He flexed his fingers, nodded. "And what does the doctor say? Would it harm her to move her? Does he hold hope that she may yet recover?"

Guilt rose. She stared at him. *How simple life was for the wealthy.* "I'm saving money to pay for a doctor. I hope to be able to get one for her soon. Now, if you'll excuse me, I have work to do to earn that money." She whirled and started for the doorway.

"Wait!" He caught her arm, turned her around, then quickly let go of her. "I wasn't merely being curious, Clarice. I had a purpose for asking those questions."

She stared at her arm, warm and tingling where he had touched her. Where was the anger that should have gushed when he grabbed her arm? What was happening to her? She lifted her gaze to meet his. "And that is?"

"I want to send Dr. Reese to see your mother. He has a reputation for restoring strength, and even mobility, to the infirm."

"I'm aware of Dr. Reese, but I haven't yet saved enough money to pay his—"

"I will pay the doctor."

Her back stiffened. "No. I do not accept charity, Mr. Thornberg. I refuse to be indebted to you or any other *man*." She swallowed back the tears that again threatened and lifted her chin. "However, I cannot refuse your offer when the doctor may help my mother walk again. Therefore, I will accept your kindness with the understanding that I will repay you."

"The name is Charles." His gaze captured hers, held it prisoner. "And I'm not offering you charity, Clarice. Nor would you accrue any debt. I'm simply trying to discharge *my* debt to your mother."

"Your debt to Mother?" She couldn't keep the skepticism from her voice.

His eyes narrowed. "Yes. I need the fillers she wrote for the newspaper, but she refuses payment. So, as I don't accept charity, either, I thought I would use the money I would have paid her to pay for the doctor. However, if that is not acceptable, I will have to think of something else." He shrugged and moved beyond her into the entrance hall.

She spun about. Her skirt billowed out around her; the hems whispered across the rug. "Charles…"

He paused in the open front door, glanced over his shoulder.

"I accept your offer on Mother's behalf." Her voice broke. She swallowed hard, lifted her hand to press against the pressure in her chest. "Thank you."

He nodded, yanked his gaze from hers and stepped outside.

The clock in the sitting room gonged.

She stared at the closed door and took a deep breath to calm her racing pulse. In the course of a half hour, Charles Thornberg had changed her life.

Chapter Twelve

"Does your head pain you, Clarice?"

"A little, Mama. It does every night." She closed her eyes and ran her fingers through her hair, massaging her scalp, winced when she touched a tender spot.

"It's likely because you wear your hair pulled so tight. Why don't you wear it a bit looser as long as you're not going to the newspaper to work? I'm sure Jonathan wouldn't mind." Her mother smiled and held out her hand. "Come sit on the edge of the bed and let me brush your hair for you."

She handed her mother the brush and sat, rubbing at her temples while the brush stroked through her long hair. "I did something today I'm not sure was wise, Mama."

"I find that hard to believe, Clarice. You're a very sensible girl."

"Usually, I am. But things have gotten all mixed up since I've been caring for Jonathan."

"Mixed up in what way?"

"I let my heart get involved in my decisions." She reached back, halted the brush and turned her head. "Mama, I signed a legal paper today naming me the administrator of a trust account Mr. Thornberg has set up for Jonathan."

"Administrator of a trust account? What's that mean?"

"It means if something happens to Mr. Thornberg, *I* will be in charge of Jonathan and that grand house and all of Mr. Thornberg's money! To be used for Jonathan's benefit, of course. But still…"

"Gracious me…"

"Exactly."

"Well…" Her mother motioned her to turn around with the brush then drew it through her hair again. "How did all this come about?"

"I'm not sure, Mama. I said no. I told him I wasn't qualified to do all of that. But then he said all he cared about was that I cared for Jonathan. And he asked me if I did. And, of course, I had to say yes. And then he *looked* at me—" she tipped her head down and buried her face in her hands "—and I got all confused, and— He makes me *nervous.*"

She sighed, lowered her hands into her lap and sighed again. "So I told him yes. He needed to name an administrator to make the trust valid. And I will probably never have to do it, anyway. He's a young, healthy man. But he kept saying he needed to know Jonathan would be taken care of if he died. And—"

She grabbed the brush from her mother's hand and jumped to her feet. "And I kept thinking about what you used to tell me…that the Bible says 'be it unto thee according to your words' or something like that, and I just wanted him to stop talking about his dying!"

She stormed over to the dressing table, tossed down the brush, gathered her hair into a mass at the nape of her neck and tied it with a ribbon. "Anyway, that's why I did it. I agreed because I love Jonathan. He's quite stolen my heart. And if anything…untoward did happen, I want Jonathan to be all right."

She whirled and faced her mother. "Do you understand?"

Her mother nodded and smiled. "I believe I do."

"Good." She sank onto the dressing table bench. "Did I do the right thing, Mama?"

"I believe you did, Clarice."

"Good. Thank you. That makes me feel better." She rose, rubbed her scalp at the hairline and walked back to her mother's bed. "Time for your back rub."

"Not tonight, Clarice. You need to go to bed with a cold cloth on your head to get rid of that headache."

She looked down at her mother's work-worn hand resting on hers and smiled. "Not yet, Mama. I have more news to share with you. Important news." She pulled the pillows out of her way and handed them to her mother.

"What is it?"

She smiled and began kneading the tight muscles beside her mother's spine. "Remember the other day when Mr. Thornberg discovered you were making fillers for his newspaper and offered to pay you for them, and you refused?"

"Yes, of course. What about it?"

"He told me today that he needs the fillers, but he doesn't accept charity, and he won't use them unless he pays for them."

"That's nonsense!" Her mother dropped her head forward as she started massaging her shoulders. "I told him I was only helping you. That the fillers were included in your wage."

"But they're not, Mama." She moved back down her mother's spine, noting with satisfaction that it was not quite as protuberant as it had been when she came. Her mother had put on a little much-needed weight. She'd been so frail…

"Well, that doesn't matter. He didn't ask me to write the fillers, and it's not right that he should pay for them. But he will pay for the next batch…we agreed." She craned her head around and smiled. "I can't believe I'm earning money just writing down the stuff I know about cleaning a house and putting up food."

"That's valuable information to a young housewife just starting to keep house."

"I suppose. But you haven't told me what your important news is."

"Well…" She grabbed a pillow and put it behind her mother's back. "Mr. Thornberg has been pondering the problem of using the fillers without paying for them." She shoved the second pillow in place. "And he's come up with a solution."

"Thank you, dear." Her mother leaned back, looked up at her. "What sort of solution?"

"He's paying a doctor to come and see you."

"A *doctor*." Hope filled her mother's eyes, but she

shook her head. "You tell him no, Clarice. Doctors are costly. That's too much—"

"It's already been done, Mama. I agreed on your behalf. You earned that money and you should get the benefit of it. Dr. Reese will be here in the morning."

"But, Clarice—"

"It's done, Mama. Now, you get a good night's sleep so you will be well rested when Dr. Reese comes." She smiled and turned down the wick on the oil lamp, stepped to the dressing table and poured cold water on the cloth in the washbowl.

"Clarice…"

"Yes, Mama?" She took the wet cloth to the window seat in the turret.

"Mr. Thornberg thinks very highly of you."

She froze, thought of the way Charles had looked at her that afternoon, then shook her head at her foolishness and kept on walking. "Mr. Thornberg knows I take good care of his little brother, Mama. That's what he likes. He doesn't care for me personally." A rush of hurt accompanied that thought, catching her off guard.

She lifted the blanket on her window-seat bed and slipped beneath it, made herself as comfortable as possible and placed the cold cloth on her forehead. "He has a low opinion of career women. And I can't blame him after what I've learned of his mother." *That's when my father died, and my mother decided she preferred a career over motherhood.* "She's a terribly selfish, *heartless* woman who puts her own desires and goals above her children."

She rubbed at her temples and wished she felt well

enough to work on her article for the *Assembly Herald*. It would get her mind off Charles and the way she had felt this afternoon—still felt, if she were honest about it. "What he doesn't understand is that it isn't the same for me as it is for his mother. It isn't the same at all. His mother is wealthy, with a husband who takes care of her. I'm poor, with a father who cares nothing for you and me and would take every penny I earn, given the chance."

She forced back tears. She'd learned long ago that there was no profit in self-pity. It only made one feel worse. "Mr. Thornberg is a wealthy man. He doesn't understand that sometimes life just doesn't give you a choice."

Which would she choose if she had a choice? She wasn't certain now. Charles treated her with respect and—and what? Her breath snagged at the memory of the look that came into his eyes when he gazed at her. And his touch. So different from anything she had ever known. What would it be like if he—

"Perhaps not, Clarice. But God does."

Her mother's words were soft, quiet and hopeful. She sighed and closed her eyes. It was a pleasant thought to sleep on. And perhaps it would keep away other impossible dreams.

It was no use. Sleep was impossible. Charles threw off the covers, shrugged into his dressing gown and stepped out onto the balcony. The moon was a silver sliver in the night sky. Warm air caressed the skin on his face, throat and hands. The quietness settled around him like a caress, and a hunger rose to share such moments with a wife. No, not just any wife. Clarice.

He let out a low growl, stepped forward to the railing and stared up at the stars strewn across the heavens. It had finally happened. He was right the other day—he was falling in love. With a *career* woman. How could he have let that happen? He barked out a laugh, shoved his fingers through his hair. How could it *not* happen? She was intelligent, beautiful, warm… And when she looked at Jonathan…

That had been his undoing. He had been able to hold his feelings at bay until he saw the way she was with Jonathan.

No. There was no use in trying to fool himself. That was not all it was. It was her eyes. If he hadn't looked into her eyes, hadn't let himself sink into the beauty in their depths, he wouldn't have known. But yesterday on the steamer and during their picnic, he'd caught a glimpse of something in her eyes that had awakened a longing in him. And then this afternoon in the sitting room when she had looked at him, he'd seen it again, stronger, purer. And when she had *blushed*— He blew out a breath, shoved his hands in the pockets of his dressing gown. It had taken all of his self-control to not take her in his arms and try and waken what he saw in her eyes. But it was a contradiction of everything else about her. Her coolness. Her independence…

If the work was not done to his satisfaction, a hard, quick slap let you know… She's the teacher that res-

cued me from Father's cruelty... She found her on the ground beside the laundry basket unable to rise... He declared he had no use for a cripple *and no time or money to care for one...*

What kind of a man treated his wife and child like that? He leaned down and gripped the railing, wished it were the neck of the man who had put the fear in Clarice's eyes and the wall around her heart. It was no wonder she was an independent career woman. She had to earn a living for herself and her mother. With a father like that, why would she ever trust a man to take care of her?

The wren. He flinched at the memory. He could understand her plain appearance and her cool, standoffish way now. She didn't want to attract a man's attention. She had certainly quelled his with a cool look. It was clear Clarice didn't want a man in her life. Including him. She had chosen her path. Or perhaps it had been chosen for her by the cruelty of her father. But either way, there was no place in her life for him.

He straightened, shoved his hands back in his pockets and stared out at a future void of love. There no place in his life for her. He wanted no part of a career woman, whether by choice or by circumstance. He'd had enough of that with his mother. And he had Jonathan to think about.

Odd how certain he was that Clarice would take good care of Jonathan if anything happened to him. But he had no doubt about that…none at all.

If only.

* * *

"Does the forward movement cause you pain, Mrs. Gordon?"

"No, none at all, Dr. Reese."

"Very good. Miss Gordon, if you would assist me, please?"

"Of course, Doctor." Clarice left Jonathan sitting on the window seat watching the people passing by on the street below and hurried to her mother's bed, her heart pounding.

"I am going to lift your mother and turn her so that she may sit on the edge of the bed. I will need you to pull the blankets out of the way and place the pillows behind her so that she cannot topple backward when she is seated."

She nodded, her throat too constricted to speak.

"And you, Mrs. Gordon. Do you understand what I am going to do?"

"Yes."

"And are you afraid?'

"No. It will feel good to move out of this position— even if it is by your strength."

"Good, because I think your daughter is fearful enough for both of you."

The doctor smiled, reached out and patted her hand. "There is nothing to be afraid of, Miss Gordon. I will not hurt your mother. I give you my word. Now, are you ready?"

"Yes." It was a little shaky, but at least she managed to speak.

"Very well." The doctor leaned forward, slipped

one arm behind her mother's back and one arm beneath her legs. "Put your left arm around my neck, Mrs. Gordon. Good. Now, do not attempt to help me lift or move you. I do not want you to twist or turn at all. Ready? Here we go."

The doctor lifted her mother as if she were a feather. She swallowed back her fear and yanked the covers out of his way, grabbed hold of a pillow.

"There." The doctor straightened, held her mother by the upper arms. "Are you in any pain or discomfort of any kind?"

She swallowed hard at the kindness in his voice, shoved the pillow behind her mother, grabbed the second and put it in place.

"No. There is a tingling in my limbs but it's not painful." Her mother smiled, blinked back tears. "It's good to feel my feet again."

"Indeed." The doctor nodded. "Miss Gordon, I am going to perform a few range-of-motion exercises. Please stand behind your mother and brace her by the shoulders should she start to topple." His gaze shifted and his expression softened. "Mrs. Gordon, I want you to tell me immediately if you feel any pain or discomfort."

She took her place, stared at her mother's narrow shoulders. Her stomach churned. *Please, Lord Jesus, don't let him hurt her. Let her be all right.*

"Me see doggy!" Jonathan turned from the window and grinned at her.

She took a breath, focused on his adorable face. "What color is the doggy?"

He turned back, pressed his nose against the window. "Him gots spots."

"Did any of that hurt at all?"

She jerked her gaze back to her mother, held her breath.

"No. But the prickly tingling feeling is stronger."

"That's a good sign. All right, I'm going to lift you back into bed now. And we'll do it the same as before, only in reverse. Ready? Here we go."

She propped the pillows against the headboard, let out her breath as the doctor rested her mother against them, pulled the blankets up and waited.

"I have good news for you, Mrs. Gordon." The doctor smiled and picked up his leather bag. "It is my belief that your inability to walk was caused by an injury to your back when you lifted that heavy basket of wet laundry. That injury has healed itself. The tingling in your legs and feet tells me there is nothing wrong with them. A few daily exercises will help them regain their strength and you will soon be walking again."

"Thank You, Lord Jesus, thank You."

Her mother's soft words brought thanksgiving flowing into her heart. She grabbed hold of the bedpost, blinked the tears back. *Thank You, Lord.*

"I will come tomorrow at this same time, and we will begin the exercise program. Until then, please do not try to get out of bed or sit on the edge as I had you do. That will all come very quickly, but only with my supervision at first."

"I'll do as you say, Dr. Reese. Thank you for coming."

He put on his hat, looked over at her and smiled.

"Thank you for your assistance, Miss Gordon. I'll see myself out."

She lasted until he reached the door. "Oh, Mama…" She fell into her mother's open arms sobbing out her fear, her relief and joy. Something pulled on her skirt. She lifted her head and looked down at Jonathan tugging at her dress, his little mouth quivering.

"You hurted?"

"No, my sweetie." She leaned down and scooped Jonathan into her arms. "I'm very happy." He hugged her tight, twisted around and pointed at her mother.

"Mama hurted?"

"I was, but I'm getting better." Her mother laughed and held out her arms. "A hug would make me much better."

Jonathan looked back at her, wiggled to be free. "Me hug Mama."

She lowered him to her mother's waiting arms, looked away from the sheen of tears in her blue eyes, laughed and wiped the tears from her own cheeks. "There's a lot of crying going on for such a happy occasion."

Jonathan straightened, peered into her mother's face, his little brow knit in concern. "Mama better?"

Her mother nodded and smiled. "Much better, thank you. And my name is Gramma to you. I'm Clarice's mama."

He thought that over for a moment. "You Gamma?"

Her mother gave an emphatic nod. "I'm Gramma."

Jonathan grinned, scooted closer, settled himself in

the curve of her mother's arm, looked up at her and patted her mother's shoulder. "Me *Gamma*. You Mama."

He didn't mean it the way it sounded, of course, but for a minute her heart wished it were so. And then she heard her mother's whisper. It was too faint for her to hear clearly, but it sounded like "'And a little child shall lead them.'"

Chapter Thirteen

"Have a good nap, Skipper. I'll see you when I come home tonight." Charles kissed Jonathan's cheek and straightened.

"Me go for walk?"

"I can't promise, Skipper. But if I get home in time, we will."

Clarice's chest tightened. She pulled the covers up over Jonathan and promised herself she would not do this again. Charles was comfortable enough now to put Jonathan down for his nap by himself. And these moments were too…heart touching. "Happy dreams, Jonathan. I'll be here when you waken." She kissed his soft, warm cheek, touched his silky curls then turned and walked from the room. Charles fell into step beside her.

She pressed her hand to her chest to calm her skipping pulse. The sound of his footsteps, the sense of strength emanating from him made her chest tighter. He paused, waited for her to precede him through the doorway into the hall. She'd grown used to his good manners—the small courtesies he performed for her, like pouring her coffee. Tears stung her eyes. She blinked and hurried down the stairs. He trotted by her, positioned himself in her way at the bottom.

"Are you all right, Clarice?"

The kindness, the concern in his voice made everything worse. Why did she want to cry every time he was nice to her? She nodded, swallowed back the tears. "Yes. It's only… I've had a happy but difficult morning." She gave a little laugh. "Which I suppose makes no sense at all." She managed a breath and a smile. "I've been waiting for an uninterrupted time to thank you again for sending Dr. Reese to see my mother."

"It went well?"

The tears gushed. She couldn't stop them, couldn't even speak. She looked into his eyes, gulped and nodded.

"Ah, Clarice…"

His arms slid around her, pulled her close against him. His cheek pressed against her hair. His heart beat beneath her ear. The gentleness in his strong arms offered a safety she'd never known. Her tears fell faster. His arms tightened. His hand lifted, brushed over her hair, and she had the sudden wild wish that she had heeded her mother's suggestion and softened her hair style, let its wavy fullness free. It sobered her. She fought the tears back, struggled to get her trembling under control and pushed lightly against his hard chest. His arms relaxed their hold.

She stepped back, swiped at her cheeks with her hands. "I'm sorry. Please forgive me. I don't know wh-why

I—" She stopped, stared at the linen handkerchief he held out to her and gulped back another rush of tears.

"You've been carrying a heavy burden." He took one of her hands in his, placed the handkerchief on her palm and curled her fingers over it, let go. She wished he'd kept holding her hand...kept holding her.

Her chest filled. "But it's o-over now." She dabbed at her eyes and cheeks, chided herself for her behavior. It helped. "Dr. Reese s-said—" She squared her shoulders and tried again. "Dr. Reese said Mama would soon be w-walking again."

"That's wonderful news, Clarice. I'm glad for you both."

The sincerity in his voice threatened to undo what little composure she had regained. She focused on the details. "He said that to start, she will need to do exercises every day to strengthen her legs. I'll help her with those, of course. And then—"

"How are you going to help your mother with her exercises if you are here, caring for Jonathan?"

She lifted her head and stared at him. She had learned that Charles did not ask idle questions. "I haven't had time to plan..." She pursed her lips, tugged at the damp handkerchief wadded in her hand. "It's only a few more days. I believe the easiest solution would be if I take Jonathan with me to the boardinghouse—with your permission, of course."

He shook his head. "That would put you at the mercy of the weather." He gazed at her, and the memory of that stormy morning he'd walked her home flashed into her mind. That had been the first time she felt...*drawn* to him. "Also, it would take additional time away from your work for the *Assembly Herald*."

She couldn't deny that what he said was true. Her heart sank. "I cannot do anything about the weather. But you needn't be concerned about my work. I will make up the time at night."

His brows lowered. Clearly, he did not like her answer. She ignored her disappointment, her yearning to be back in his arms, and braced herself to do battle. Her mother's welfare came first.

"Is your mother able to be moved?"

"With care, yes. But—"

"Then it seems the best solution would be for me to hire a carriage and bring your mother here with me each day when I come home for dinner. You can prepare the bed for her in the bedroom where you are working. That way, when you are through with her exercises, you can work while she rests and Jonathan naps. I will take her home after supper. From what I have learned of your mother, she will appreciate being outside for a short time each day. Do you agree?"

Once again he had rendered her speechless. She nodded.

"Good."

The sitting room clock gonged.

He frowned and headed for the front door. "I may be late tonight. We have to get out tomorrow's issue. Don't wait supper." He grabbed his hat, stepped outside and glanced back. "I will check with Dr. Reese to be certain moving your mother is possible. Good afternoon, Clarice."

"Good afternoon."

The door closed. His footsteps faded away across the porch. She sank onto a step, leaned her elbows on her knees and stared at his handkerchief in her hand.

Clarice brushed her still-damp hair to the crown of her head, loosened her grip until it puffed in loose waves around her face and neck, twisted the long strands into a loose, soft coil and held it in place while she studied her image in the mirror. She looked… softer, prettier. She turned her head and slanted a side-wise look into the mirror.

"I like it."

Warmth flooded her cheeks. She glanced at her mother's reflection in the mirror. "I remembered what you said about a looser hair style easing my headaches, and I thought I would experiment." She opened her hand and let her hair fall free. "I thought you were asleep, Mama."

"I'm too excited to sleep." Her mother smiled and glanced toward the windows in the turret. "I can't wait until I go for my carriage ride tomorrow."

"It's only a little more than three blocks, Mama."

"I don't care. It's outside in the fresh air, with trees and fall flowers." She gave her a cheeky grin. "And the return trip will make it seven blocks. It was so kind of Mr. Thornberg to offer to have me at his home. I'm so glad Dr. Reese agreed. He's a very nice man."

"He can come to Mr. Thornberg's house and show us the exercises you're to do as easy as to come here tomorrow, Mama. It works out better for everyone.

Charles's plans always seem to work out better for everyone."

Her mother's brows rose, and her lips curved into a small smile. "I agree."

Did her mother suspect the emotions troubling her since Charles had held her in his arms? Warmth crawled into her cheeks. "What dress are you going to wear? Not that you have much choice. Father only allowed you two. As he allowed me." Anger shook her voice.

Her mother gave a soft sigh. "I managed, Clarice."

"Well, when I'm a journalist on a daily newspaper, you won't have to *manage* anymore. I'll buy you lots of pretty dresses, Mama. And fancy hats to wear with them." She rose from the dressing-table bench and stepped to the wardrobe, braced herself for the screech and opened the doors.

"I thought the blue cotton—"

"All right. I'll brush it to make it— What is this?" She pulled out the bodice of her brown dress, fingered the new cream-colored ruffle that edged the high collar and the three tabs that fell from its base, eyed the new bone buttons that marched from beneath the tabs to the waist. Her throat tightened. Everything lately seemed to make her want to cry, either from anger or from a full heart or both. "Mama, I gave you that money in case you had a need and I wasn't here to go to the store for you."

"Well, I *needed* something besides writing fillers to do. I enjoy sewing, so I asked Mrs. Duncan to buy me a few notions at the store and I took the liberty of adding a touch of decoration to your dress." Her mother sighed, stretched out her hand and lifted her sewing box off the nightstand. "I know you don't want to look pretty, Clarice. That you want men to take you as a serious career woman instead of wanting to court you—but that dress was so drab and bare it was just plain ugly. And there's so little I can do for you now…" Her mother heaved another sigh. "Give me the bodice. I can take the edging off. And I saved the old brown buttons. They're here in my sewing box."

She looked from her mother to the bodice, touched the new buttons. It *was* pretty. She turned to the mirror and held the bodice up to her, studied her reflection. "Never mind, Mama. I think I like it this way." *Would Charles? Not that it mattered.*

"Truly?"

She gave another glance in the mirror and nodded. "Truly."

"Then I can leave the brown-eyed Susans on your hat?"

"Mama!" She whirled about, looked from her mother's guilty expression to her flower-bedecked hat in her hands and burst into laughter. "Leave the flowers, Mama—they look lovely. I shall wear the hat proudly."

She hung her bodice back in the wardrobe and glanced at the desk in the turret area. "I'm going to work on my article for the *Assembly Herald* for a while before I turn in. I'll keep the lamp turned low."

"Clarice, before you begin your work… You received a letter today."

"A letter?" She halted, stepped to the bed and reached

for the envelope her mother held out to her. It was Miss Hartmore's writing. "Why didn't you tell me earlier, Mama?" She broke the seal and unfolded the letter. Another folded piece of paper fell to the floor. She stooped to retrieve it.

"You were late coming home. You'd had a long day and you had another headache. I decided to keep it until morning, when you would feel better. But if you're going to work—"

She sucked in air, clenched her hands. The papers crunched, rattled with her shaking.

"What is it?" Her mother's voice sharpened. "Clarice, tell me what's wrong!"

"You're a divorced woman, Mama." The words hissed through her teeth, choked with bitterness. "Miss Hartmore has sent us a copy of a decree of divorce granted to Father on the grounds that you are an 'unfit wife' unable to carry out your 'wifely duties.' After he crippled you!" She handed her the paper she had dropped, fisted her hands to stop their trembling. "You've been *discarded*, Mama."

Blessed.

The word slipped into her mind, turned her thinking about. If her mother had not been crippled, she would not be free. A bittersweet smile touched her lips. "Or blessed." She stared down at the paper in her mother's hands, her heart swelling with gratitude. "Only think, Mama—you will soon be walking again. And you are now free to do whatever you wish. Father cannot hurt you. He can never treat you as his personal servant again."

* * *

Clarice bent over the paper on the desk, penning a vivid description of Chautauqua lecturer Miss Louise Moore and her subject of woman's suffrage. She paused only to check her notes for accuracy. There was little doubt that Charles would be displeased with her championing the cause for equality for women in the workplace and voting booth, but Charles did not have the right of selection of material for the articles printed in the *Assembly Herald*.

She blinked her dry, burning eyes, rubbed her throbbing temples and the tired muscles at the back of her neck then picked up her pen again. The nib scratched across the paper, the sound loud in the silence. Every word was a repudiation of the superiority of men her father stood for.

Her head drooped. She snapped erect, frowned at the streak of ink left by the pen in her slipping hand, glanced at her mother asleep in her bed and forced herself to concentrate, to write on. She had to finish this article and the answers to the CLSC letters by her submission date, and time was running out.

A frown pulled her brows down, increased the pain pounding at her temples. She had allowed herself to become distracted by Charles's pleas for help with Jonathan, but no more. She could not afford to go on steamer rides and picnics. She had her career to consider. And her heart. She would never put herself under some man's grinding thumb only to be cast aside like a worn-out shoe!

Her head drooped again. She jerked awake, scowled

at the new ink smear and pushed back from the desk. She walked the length of the room and back, swinging her arms and stepping on tiptoe to force herself to concentrate on her balance, then paced the room again. She would finish this tonight. And tomorrow she would tell Charles that in order to do her work for the newspaper *and* care for Jonathan and her mother, she would need the use of a typewriter at home. A typewriter would help her finish her work on time.

She rubbed her temples and sank back down onto the chair. She would *not* be some man's personal servant. She was a journalist. How could she have thought, for even a second, that she might be wrong about Charles? Everything he had done for her had benefited him, as well.

She shoved the memory of those moments in his arms today from her thoughts and picked up her pen. It had been a moment of weakness she would not repeat. She knew what men were really like. It would take more than good manners and a few acts of kindness meant to get her to agree to his plans for Jonathan to fool her! And should she ever weaken again, she had only to look at that paper tucked in her mother's sewing case to set her straight.

Jonathan left the toy horse he was playing with, came and tugged at her skirt. "Brover get Gamma? Me see Gamma?"

Clarice smiled and nodded. He had asked her the same question at least four times in the past ten minutes. "Yes. They will be here soon." She set a plate, flatware and a napkin on the tray waiting on the work table, glanced over at the table set for three. How long would it be before her mother would be able to sit at the table with them? Or would Mrs. Hotchkiss have returned by then to be—

The front door opened, closed.

"They're here, Jonathan."

She leaned down, scooped him into her arms and rushed into the entrance hall, halted at the sight of Charles holding her mother, both of them smiling. Her mother's cheeks were pink, her blue eyes shining.

"Me see Brover! Me see Gamma!" Jonathan leaned forward, his little arms outstretched.

"Hold on, Skipper." Charles's deep voice settled the boy in her arms. "Let Clarice and me get this lady settled before you start visiting with her." His gaze shifted to her, his lips slanted in a smile that set her stomach aquiver.

She tightened her grip on Jonathan. "The bed is ready."

Charles nodded and started for the stairs. "Here we go, Mrs. Gordon. You tell me if I do anything that hurts you."

Clarice gripped the banister with her free hand and followed, his shoulders so broad she couldn't see her mother, only her arm around his neck and her black shoes peeking out from under the hem of her long blue skirt. Her mother was wearing shoes!

She hurried by them in the hallway and rushed to the bed. "You stay here beside me while I help brother settle Gramma, and then I will lift you up to visit with her." She gave Jonathan a hug, set him on the floor and held the propped pillows in place then searched her mother's face for any sign of pain as Charles lowered her to the bed.

"There you are, Mrs. Gordon. Are you comfortable?"

Her mother nodded and smiled. "Very much so. Thank you, Mr. Thornberg, for all you have done for me. I so enjoyed the carriage ride." Her eyes twinkled up at him. "And you make a very acceptable pack mule."

He chuckled, gave a rueful shake of his head. "I have come down in the world. Jonathan thinks I make a great horse." He sobered, looked across the bed at her. "If you've no further need for me, I have to be going. But I'd like a word with you, please." He shifted his gaze back to her mother. "Best wishes for your exercises, Mrs. Gordon."

"Brover give me horsey ride."

She stepped back as Charles came around the bed. He scooped Jonathan up and tossed him into the air, laughed at his squeal and caught him on the way down. "I have to go back to work right now, Skipper, but if I get home before dark tonight, I'll give you two horsey rides around the backyard. How's that?"

Jonathan's black curls bounced with his nod. "Me see Gamma now?"

Charles glanced at her mother. "Mrs. Gordon?"

"I should love to visit with Jonathan."

"All right, Skipper. But you must sit still and not climb around on Mrs. Gordon or try to get off the bed."

The curls bobbed again.

Charles set Jonathan on the bed, lifted his gaze to her.

She nodded, glanced toward the bed. "I'll be right back, Mama."

"There's no hurry, Clarice. It's been too long since I've known the joy of being with a little one. And we have to get acquainted. Don't we, Jonathan?"

She pulled her gaze from the sight of her mother and Jonathan smiling at one another and led the way to the hall. She turned too quickly and her shoulder brushed against Charles. Her heart lurched, quickened at thoughts of yesterday. She set her mind against them. "I thought I'd close the door. If Jonathan does climb off the bed, I don't want him to come out here and fall down the stairs."

"I'll get it." He turned and pulled the door closed.

She edged closer to the wall to put space between them.

"I'm sorry I have to leave you, Clarice." His gaze sought hers, held it. And in spite of her best effort to keep calm, her pulse skipped out an accelerated beat. "That wasn't my intent when I suggested bringing your mother here. But there is a big political meeting this afternoon that I need to cover, I have no editorial written, and I'm far behind in the composing of the pages for tomorrow's printing." He frowned, combed his fingers through his hair. "I may not be home for supper, either, but I give you my word, I will come home long enough to take your mother home. I just wanted you to know so you wouldn't be concerned about her."

"Thank you for telling me." She started to smooth back her hair, remembered it was arranged in the looser style she'd experimented with last night and lowered her hand. "There are ham sandwiches prepared for dinner. I can wrap some up for you to take along." She pushed away from the wall and started for the stairs.

He shook his head. "You stay with your mother and Jonathan. I'll get one of the sandwiches." He started down the stairs, stopped and looked over his shoulder. "And, Clarice…"

"Yes?"

"I like your hair that way."

The look in his eyes stole her breath.

Chapter Fourteen

The shaking woke him. *No.* He couldn't have a bout of malaria now. He hadn't finished the page layouts for tonight's printing. Charles gritted his teeth against the pain he knew would streak through his muscles and rolled onto his side. Hopefully, the medicine would hold off the worst of the attack so he could get to the *Journal* building and finish the composing.

He shoved his arm out from under the blanket and reached for the knob on the drawer in the stand by his bed. A shudder shook him. He yanked the drawer opened, grabbed the bottle of tonic and pulled it to him. His fingers were shaking so hard he couldn't make them obey. He fumbled with the cork, finally got it out, sucked in a breath and held it to steady his hand. The bottle shook. He lifted it to his mouth, tilted it up. A small bit of liquid trickled onto his tongue.

Empty.

"No!" He tried again, scowled. He'd been so taken up with Jonathan he'd forgotten he needed to get another bottle. Another shudder took him. The bottle fell from his hand, hit the floor with a thunk. The bell on the mantel clock chimed out the hour.

Six o'clock. He bit back a moan, curled into a ball and tugged the blankets close around him, shivering and shaking. *Let it be a short, mild attack, Lord. I have to get out the paper. Jonathan! Clarice. Clarice would take care of Jonathan.* He closed his eyes, set his jaw to stop his teeth from chattering and waited for sleep to take him.

Clarice settled her hat forward of her new swept-up coiffure, pinned it in place and turned from the mirror. She didn't want to confront the accusation in her eyes concerning the real reason she'd let her mother leave the trim on her dress and the flowers on her hat. She was having a hard enough time with her jumbled emotions. "I'm ready to leave, Mama."

Her mother stared up at her, smiled. "You look beautiful, Clarice."

"Thank you, Mama. But I think your opinion may be just a tiny bit influenced by the fact that I'm your daughter." She swept her gaze over the table beside the bed. "Do you need anything before I go?"

"Not a thing. I'm all dressed and ready for breakfast." Her mother patted the writing box on her lap. "I'm going to work on fillers until it's time for my carriage ride."

"What?" She gave her a teasing grin and pulled on her gloves. "No more clandestine sewing?"

"Not unless you hand me that green wool dress

you'll be wearing when the weather cools. A touch of ivory ruching at the neck and cuffs would be just the thing to brighten it up a bit."

She laughed and shook her head. "You're incorrigible, Mama."

"Whatever that means."

"It means I love you." She opened the door, wiggled her fingers in farewell and closed it behind her.

The stairwell was dimly lit by the trimmed oil lamp on the wall shelf. She cast a sidewise glance at it, her fingers itching to turn up the wick. She would— the day she moved out. Whenever that might be. She crossed the entrance hall, the light of its oil lamp already snuffed at the first hint of dawn, and stepped out onto the porch. A shiver chased down her spine at the touch of the chilly predawn air. She might be needing that green wool dress soon.

She hurried down the porch steps and out to the gate, quickened her steps as she started up the sidewalk. A brisk walk would warm her.

Fingers of gold probed through slits in the gray sky, feathered out into beams of morning light. Birds twittered their wake-up songs. In the shadowy light ahead the lamplighter snuffed the flame of a street lamp, shouldered his tool and strode on to the next.

She crossed the intersection, glanced at the dark facade of the *Journal* building as she walked by. It would be busy there today. Charles hadn't finished composing the pages for today's issue before he came home last night. She would enjoy doing that job. But even though Charles approved of the work she'd done in her accidental foray into composing, with his attitude toward career women, that would never happen.

She paused at the next intersection, waited for a wagon to pass, then hurried across the street. But one thing was certain. When Mrs. Hotchkiss returned— Her heart squeezed at the thought. She ignored the pain. She had to be prepared for the day when Mrs. Hotchkiss took over Jonathan's care, and she returned to the full pursuit of her career. The day was fast approaching. Too fast. It was only two days from now. She jerked her thoughts away from leaving Jonathan. When she went back to work at the *Journal* building, she was going to visit Clicker's "domain" and have him show her how to run the printing machine. She'd coax if she had to. Those clicking sounds were intriguing.

The sun's rays had widened. They gleamed on the windows of Charles's home. It was a beautiful house. She glanced up at the balcony that formed the roof of the porch. How lovely it would be to stand there in the moonlight with Charles when Jonathan was sleeping and— *Stop it!*

She hurried up the steps and into the entrance hall. No dimmed lamps here—the oil lamp poured out warm, welcoming light. She paused by the stairs to listen for voices, though it was still early for Jonathan to be awake. All was silent.

Time to fix breakfast. She moved on to the kitchen, removed her hat, laid it on the step-back cupboard and slipped on the apron.

He should be up and stirring by now. She must have been making too much noise to hear him. Clarice slid the griddle of sausage and potatoes to the back of the stove to keep warm, moved the coffee to sit beside it and stirred the oats.

The clock in the sitting room gonged. Uneasiness gripped her. She added a pat of butter to the oats, slid them to the back of the stove and adjusted the dampers for a slow burn. She glanced at the table set for three, looked up at the ceiling and strained to hear any sound from above.

A faint sort of sliding sound followed by a soft thump caught her attention. But it wasn't coming from above. She frowned, tiptoed toward the doorway to the entrance hall, paused as the odd sound grew louder. What—

She hurried toward the front door. *Slip—thump.*

She halted, turned toward the stairs. *"Jonathan!"* She stared at the toddler, sliding down the stairs on his rump, his nightshirt wrinkled up around his waist and his bare chunky legs stretching down for the tread below him. Her heart froze. "Stop! Don't move, Jonathan!"

She lifted her hems and ran up the stairs, pulled the toddler into her arms and held him tight against her pounding heart. "Jonathan, you must never do that again! You could fall and hurt yourself! Do you *understand* me?" She loosened her grip, looked down at him then pulled him tight into her arms again. "What were you doing? Why—"

"Me get you." His words were muffled by the apron bib over her bodice.

She relaxed her grip, struggled to get beyond her fright to common sense. "You were coming to get me?"

His black curls bobbed agreement. "Brover no get up. Me do—" He grabbed a fistful of the apron bib and tugged.

"You tried to wake brother, but he won't get up?"

He nodded. His blue eyes studied her. "You get brover."

"Oh. No, I can't—" She clamped her lips shut on the foolish words. Jonathan would not understand propriety. She glanced up the stairs. Why wasn't Charles awake? What if he was ill? She'd never known him to imbibe. Her stomach clenched.

She settled Jonathan on her hip, gripped the banister and climbed the stairs, turning to the left at the top. There were two bedroom doors ahead, one closed and one open. Perhaps he was awake now. She stopped outside the open door, rapped her knuckles against the frame. "Charles…"

No answer.

She rapped again. "Charles…"

There was a low moan.

He *was* ill. Her heart leaped into her throat. She stepped into the dark bedroom, spotted a bed against the far wall. Her eyes adjusted to the darkness, and she saw the covers twisted, hanging over the side of the bed, one arm dangling. "Charles…"

"Brover get up?"

"Not now, Jonathan." She carried him to a wing-back chair in front of a fireplace and lowered him to the seat, struggling to stay calm, to fight back a rising fear. *Why would Charles not answer her?* "I need to help brother. You sit here and wait for me."

Sunlight peeked in through the slats of a shuttered window beside the bed. She undid the latch and folded the shutters back, turned to the bed. Fear crawled up her spine. Charles stared up at the ceiling, his eyes glassy, his face flushed. His damp hair was plastered to his head and beads of sweat clung to his forehead. His body, twisted in the covers, shook so hard his teeth clattered.

She laid her hand on his damp forehead, drew it back. He was burning up! She leaned over where he could see her. "Charles, it's Clarice. Tell me what's wrong. How can I help you?"

He turned his head toward her, shuddered. "M-ma-lar-ia. No m-medi-cine." His eyes closed, opened again, focused on her. "T-take c-care of Jona-th-than."

"It's you who needs care." She looked around then ran and peeked in a door on the other side of the room. Jonathan's dressing room! She filled a washbowl, tossed in some washcloths, grabbed a towel and carried them all back to the table under the window.

"Me go potty?"

She glanced at Jonathan and nodded. "Yes, you may go potty—" she squeezed out a washcloth "—but come right back here to me." She shook out the towel and tossed it over her shoulder. "Can you get down out of the chair?"

"Me do it." He flopped onto his belly and wiggled backward, his chunky legs stretched down, his little feet groping for the floor. He touched wood with his toes, pushed away from the chair and padded off to the dressing room.

"Charles…"

His eyes were closed. She leaned over the bed and touched his cheek. "Charles, do you hear me?"

His eyes opened, searched for her. "I'm going to wash your face with a cool cloth." She wiped his forehead and temples, his cheeks and mouth and chin, drew the cloth down his neck to the hollow at its base. His pulse throbbed. She could see the skin rising and falling. *Too fast.* She dabbed his face dry with the towel, squeezed out another washcloth, folded it and placed it on his forehead then tucked the ends against his temples.

"Th-thank—"

"Hush." She touched her fingertip against his lips, quickly lifted it away. "You need to save your strength. I'm going to straighten the covers now. I'll be as quick about it as I can. I don't want to chill you more."

She freed the sheet and blankets that were twisted around him, pulled them straight and tucked them in close. "Now I'm going to go and wash and dress Jonathan and give him his breakfast. Try to sleep. I'll be back as soon as possible."

"Dr. Reese. Come in!" Clarice stepped back, pulled the door wide. The tightness in her chest released. "I'm so glad to see you!"

"Is there something wrong?" The doctor stepped into the entrance hall, glanced toward the stairs. "Have the exercises harmed your mother, Miss Gordon?"

"Mother isn't here, Doctor. It's Cha—Mr. Thornberg." She closed the door, fought to keep the quaver from her voice. "He's very sick, and I don't know what to do for him."

"His malaria acting up again, is it?"

"Yes, that's what he said."

"Well, I'll go up and take a look at him." He headed for the stairs, glanced back and motioned her forward. "Come along. If you're going to be nursing him through a bad spell, you might as well learn how to do it right. Did he take his medicine?"

She lifted her hems and climbed, grateful that she had closed Jonathan's bedroom door. Hopefully, he would nap through the doctor's visit. He'd been very upset about Charles being sick. "He told me he had no medicine."

"Let it run out, did he?" The doctor shook his head and motioned her through the bedroom doorway ahead of him. "I warned him about that." He stepped to the bed, looked down at Charles shivering and shaking, laid the back of his hand against his cheek.

She took up a position on the opposite side of the bed. The toe of her shoe hit something, sent it skidding over the floor. She went to retrieve it, read the legend imprinted in the glass. *Grove's Tasteless Chill Tonic.*

"He ran out of medicine, all right. That's the bottle."

She set it on the stand by the bed, closed the partially open drawer and watched the doctor uncover Charles's arm and wrap his fingers around his wrist. The clock on the mantel ticked away the seconds, the sound ominous in the silence. The doctor frowned, covered Charles's arm again. "Looks like this is going to be a bad one."

The words sent alarm skittering through her. She stared down at Charles's flushed face, lifted the cloth on his forehead and turned it over to the cool side. *Heal Charles, Lord. Please heal Charles.* "What can I do to help him?"

"There's not much you can do but try and keep him comfortable."

Her stomach churned. *Lord, there has to be something that will help him. Please help him.*

The doctor reached for his bag, looked her way. "See that he rests. And keep up the cold cloths—they help fight the fever and any headache and keep him from being so restless. And get as much water in him as you can. That's important. I don't want him losing body fluids and getting dehydrated. And give him two tablespoons of this three times a day." He pulled a bottle of Grove's Tasteless Chill Tonic from his bag and handed it to her. "It has to be shaken well before you pour out the dose then taken quickly so the medicine doesn't settle. It's bitter stuff. If you'll get a spoon, we'll start that immediately." He gave her a smile and closed his bag.

"Of course, Doctor." She turned for the door.

"It looks as if you are in for a sleepless night."

She froze, struck immobile by his words. She'd been so busy and so frightened she hadn't considered anything beyond the moment. She turned back and lowered her gaze to Charles. He was so strong, so competent. And now he was so *sick*. Tears stung her eyes.

"I'm sorry, Miss Gordon, I forgot you're a young, single woman with a reputation to maintain. You can't stay here alone with Charles, even if he *is* ill. I'll have to find someone to nurse him." The doctor's brow furrowed. "You'll have to stay with him meantime. It may take me a while—"

Her chest tightened at the thought of a stranger tending to Charles's needs. He should have someone who— who *cared* about him. The thought took her breath. She shook her head. "I will take care of him."

The doctor peered across the bed at her. "Are you certain?"

Was she? She thought about Charles taking off his suit coat and wrapping it around her during the rainstorm…taking the basket from her on the stairs… pouring her coffee…holding her in his arms to comfort her… Yes. She was certain. But she couldn't tell the doctor why. The perfect answer slipped into her head. She met the doctor's gaze and nodded. "I would have to stay anyway to care for Jonathan."

"Ah. I had forgotten about the boy. Of course, you must stay and care for him. The matter is settled. Do you wish me to convey the message to your mother? I shall go to conduct her exercises—"

"Mama…" It was a choked whisper of guilt. How could she have forgotten her *mother*?

"Or…perhaps not."

She looked at him, her head spinning, her heart aching. Charles and Jonathan and her mother… How could she choose?

Charles moaned and curled into a ball. Shivers shook his body.

She stared down at his flushed face, the perspiration on his forehead even with the cool cloth. He was in agony. His distress tore at her heart. She ached to comfort him, to ease his pain. "The matter is settled, Doctor. I'm staying." She blinked her eyes, turned from his steady gaze. "Now... I'm going to get that spoon for Charles's medicine. And water for him to drink."

"And I, Miss Gordon, am going to give this matter some additional thought."

She glanced back at him. He smiled, waved her on her way, then clasped his hands behind his back and began to pace the room, staring down at the floor.

Clarice ran down the stairs and into the kitchen, tears flowing down her cheeks. She wiped them away, grabbed a glass and set it on a tray on the work table, snatched a tablespoon from a drawer and stuck it in the glass. How was she to manage care for her mother? Mrs. Duncan would help, but where was she to find the money to pay her? And how would that help her mother's loneliness, stuck alone in that room all night? Oh, what was she to *do*?

Lord Jesus, I need an answer. Please give me an answer.

She lifted down a pitcher from the shelf over the refrigerator, froze. The *refrigerator*! She pumped water into the pitcher, set it on the tray, then ran to the pantry, grabbed a large deep bowl and set it on the floor in front of the refrigerator. A few quick moves had the front board off and the drip tray half-full of melted ice water in her hands. She poured the ice melt into the bowl, replaced the drip tray and board, added the bowl to the tray and hurried for the stairs.

She would find a way to earn the money to pay Mrs. Duncan to care for her mother. But there was nothing she could do about leaving her mother alone. Still, the doctor would explain, and her mother would understand that she couldn't leave Jonathan and Charles.

She caught her breath and carried the tray into Charles's bedroom, set it on the table under the window and tossed a washcloth into the cold ice-melt water. There had to be a way to keep her mother from being lonely. Charles… Jonathan…her mother… How could she possibly help them all? *Lord, please show me the way—*

"I have the answer to your dilemma, Miss Gordon."

She snatched the spoon out of the glass, turned and looked at the doctor.

"Charles was to go and bring your mother here today. Correct?"

"Yes. But—"

His raised hand stopped her. "So I will go in his stead." He smiled and nodded, picked up his bag. "It is the perfect solution. I will bring your mother to stay here and that will solve the problem. She is the perfect chaperone. You will be able to stay here and care for Charles and Jonathan without risk to your reputation, and I will come to check on Charles and help your mother with her exercises."

"But…"

"Yes?"

She stared at him while his perfect solution crumbled into ashes at her feet. "I have no money to pay you."

"And I have not mentioned a fee. Now, get that medicine into Charles while I go and bring your mother here."

Chapter Fifteen

"Papa…" Charles bolted upright, yanked his hand from beneath the covers and clenched it into a fist. "Papa…cuff…links…" He flopped back onto his pillow, shivering from the chills that chased up and down his spine, spread painful prickles over his skin.

"I don't understand, Charles. Do you want your father's cuff links? Tell me where to find them and I'll bring them to you. Charles? Do you hear me, Charles?"

The voice lured him from the darkness. He opened his eyes, stared at Clarice's face floating above him, struggled against the pull of oblivion. "Jonathan…"

"He's down for his nap. You were talking about your father's cuff links. Do you want them?"

He shook his head, winced. "Dreaming…"

"You need to drink some water, Charles. Dr. Reese says it's important."

Her face disappeared. He ignored his disappointment and took inventory. Heat radiated off his body—so a high fever. Chills…bad ones. Muscle pain. Headache. The attack was a severe one.

"Charles…"

He opened his eyes, forced them to focus. She was there again, hovering above him.

"If I help you, can you lift your head and drink some water?"

"Y-yes."

Her arm slipped behind his shoulders. Chills exploded up his neck, down his back and into his arms at the contact. He mustered his strength, drew his elbows back to lean on them and lifted his head. She touched the glass to his dry lips. He drank the water, shivered as it slid down his throat.

"Do you want more?"

"L-later."

"All right." She withdrew her arm, set the glass back on the table under the window. "Is there anything I can do to make you more comfortable?"

He shoved himself back higher on the pillows, used the pain that streaked through his muscles to hold off the darkness that beckoned. "I n-need you to get out the p-paper."

"What?" Shock spread across her face, widened her eyes.

"Listen…I haven't st-strength to argue or re-repeat." He made his gaze meet hers, held it there. "Tomorrow's issue gets p-printed tonight. Editorial on d-desk. P-pages aren't r-ready. You are o-only o-one who can d-do them."

Her eyes clouded. She shook her head. "No, Charles. You're too sick. I can't leave you here alone."

"I've g-gone through this b-before." He poured all the persuasion he had into his voice. "I'll be all r-right. I need you t-to do this. I'll p-pay—"

She jerked back, caught her breath.

"Wh-what—"

"Nothing. I'll do as you ask. I'll have to take Jonathan with me, so I will leave as soon as he wakes from his nap." She turned away.

"W-wait." He reached for her hand, but she stepped back, and he hadn't the strength to raise himself higher.

"Don't waste your strength talking, Charles. Dr. Reese says you need your rest."

The hurt in her voice was disguised by her cool tone, but he knew her now. He tried to think of what he had done to cause her hurt, but his mind wouldn't work. Darkness slid over his thoughts, carried them away. He fought to grasp them, fought to hold on to consciousness…lost his grip and slipped into obscurity.

"Me no go! Me no go!"

Jonathan tugged his hand out of hers and ran, his chunky little legs pumping.

"Jonathan, wh— Wait! Come back!" Clarice dropped the bag she carried and ran, caught the fleeing toddler up in her arms.

"No! Me no go!" He twisted and turned, kicked his feet and pummeled her with his little fists. Ragged sobs shook him. "Me want brover! Me no go!"

"Jonathan, stop! Listen to me!" She tugged his small

writhing body close against her, held him tight so he
could not move. "I am *not* taking you away from brother."
Her eyes teared at his fear. What had happened that he no
longer trusted her? *Lord, help me understand. Give me
the words to reassure him.* "Brother is sick. He can't do
his work and I need to do it for him. See that big building...?" She turned so he could see without her releas-
ing her confining grip.

He shoved his face against her shoulder, trembled
and sobbed. "Me n-no go..."

She stared at the *Journal* building and understanding burst upon her, made her heart ache for the child in
her arms. "Jonathan, that big building is where brother
works. You know how he leaves every day to go to
work? This is where he comes." She took a breath,
made her voice soft and calm the way she did when
she was teaching him his colors or numbers. "Brother
is sick, and so he asked me to come here to this building and do his work. When I am finished, I promise
I will take you back to *your* house...back to brother,
just like I did the last time."

She blinked the tears from her eyes, kissed his
cheek. "You don't have to be afraid anymore, Jonathan.
Remember what brother promised you? He promised
you he would take care of you always. That he would
never let anyone take you away from him. Not ever.
And he never will. Brother loves you. You don't have
to be afraid anymore."

She'd run out of words. She held him and hoped he
would feel her love for him.

"What love?"

What I feel for you. Her throat constricted. How did you explain love to a toddler? "Love is when you want to be with somebody forever and ever." He stirred, lifted his head and looked at her.

"Me love brover."

She smiled and nodded. He understood.

"Me love you."

Her heart swelled. It took a minute to find her voice. "And I love you." She kissed the tip of his nose, hugged him tight, then stood him on the sidewalk, picked up her bag and held out her hand. "Let's go do brother's work so we can go back home."

Clarice read the report Boyd Willard had left on Charles's desk, frowned and picked up a pen. Did the man not know how to use a dictionary? She struck a line through several of the words, made the spelling and misuse corrections and glanced at Jonathan on his stomach on the floor drawing wiggles and squiggles on a piece of paper. A smile curved her lips. "Jonathan, I'm going in the other room to finish brother's work. Do you want to bring your pencil and paper and come with me?"

He nodded, scrambled to his feet, followed her into the composing room and flopped back down on the floor.

She scanned the tables. The pages on the far tables were finished—except for the editorial page. There was a blank area on the white paper. She carried his editorial to the last table, placed it in the blank spot, scanned the pages to make sure she wasn't missing anything then walked back to the front tables. Most of the second page was also finished. There was one blank area blocked out for a picture. The white paper on the first table was blank, except for a wide piece of dark paper across the top that represented the *Journal*'s masthead. And a second strip of paper that bore the legend Lead Story. There was a stack of papers on the table.

Her stomach flopped. It looked like too many articles to fit on the available space. Was she supposed to pick and choose? Had Charles already decided which he wanted to use? How could she know? She stared at the pile, everything in her rebelling. How long would it take to do the work? She didn't want to be here. She wanted to be caring for Charles. Was he all right? *Lord Jesus, please watch over Charles. Please keep him safe. And please help me to do this job quickly and well so that I can go home and take care of him.*

The prayer rose straight from her heart. And brought her face-to-face with the truth she'd been trying not to see. In spite of all her protestations and proclamations, she was falling in love with Charles Thornberg. She glanced at the windows in the editorial room, remembered the rain splatting against them and their walk home beneath his umbrella. It had started that day. She knew that now. She'd never known a man to be caring and protective until then. And now— Now she must face the fact that he was only being kind, that it was his nature and meant nothing special to him. He had little regard for a career woman.

Oh, how that thought hurt. She pushed beyond her personal feelings and set her thoughts on the job she had to do. At least she could earn his respect. She set Boyd Willard's article aside and thumbed through the pile. Two of them had "LS?" scrawled on the top right corner. She scanned the stories, one a national political piece about the ongoing dispute between President Rutherford B. Hayes and the Congress over the Bland-Allison Act, the other a local piece about proposed improvements to the docking area on Chautauqua Lake. She nibbled at the corner of her lip, wondered which of the two Charles would choose. There were both advantages and disadvantages to using either piece. In the end, she decided the national piece had more relevance since it was about the American monetary system, which touched every citizen, not just the few who owned the property along the waterfront. She set it in place as the lead story. The waterfront piece held the second most important place. She chose the articles, lined them up on the white paper, tucked in fillers—smiling with pride when she found her mother's offerings among them in the baskets—and wondered what came next.

"Come along, Jonathan." She lifted him into her arms, took one last look at the composed pages and headed for the stairs. She needed some advice.

"Me go see brover?"

"In a little while. First I must talk to a man called Clicker."

The house was silent.

"Me hungry. Me want biscuit."

"I know, Jonathan. I'm sorry—it's far past supper

time." She set her bag on the floor and settled him on her hip. "Let's go see brother, and then I will fix you some biscuits and jam. Would you like that?"

"An' milk?"

"And milk." She forced a smile, stepped into the hallway and looked at the open bedroom doors, torn between whom to check on first, her mother or Charles. Of course, her mother would know her choice—and then she would guess. She made her feet turn right. "I have a surprise. Gramma is here."

"Gamma!"

"Well, it's about time you came home, young man. I've been waiting for you." Her mother smiled and held out her arms.

"Remember to be careful of Gramma, Jonathan." She lowered him to the bed, watched him snuggle up close to her mother.

"Me see Clicker. Him gots dirty hands."

"He *does*?"

"An' him gots a big 'chine!" Jonathan spread his arms as wide as they could reach.

"My, my…" Her mother glanced up, made a small nudging motion with her chin toward the door and turned her attention back to the toddler in her arms. "And what does this machine do?"

She mouthed, "Thank you," and hurried back into the hall, her heart pounding. *Please let him be all right. Please, Lord, let Charles be all right.*

He was on his side, shivering and muttering. She rushed to his bed, snatched the blankets up off the floor and spread them over him then tucked them close to his back and shoved them under the mattress at the foot of the bed so he could not pull them off. "I told you I should have stayed here with you. Only look at the mess you've made of things."

"…mother…gone…" He flopped onto his back, yanked an arm free of the covers and waved it in the air. "…never come…never…"

She poured water into the glass, dodged beneath his flailing arm and held it to his lips. "Drink this, Char— Oh!" His wildly waving hand smacked against her shoulder, knocked her backward and sent the glass flying from her hand. Her heel caught in the hem of her skirt and she sat down hard on the floor, her heart pounding. Bile surged into her throat. *It was an accident. Only an accident.*

"Clarice…"

"I'm fine, Mama! I dropped the glass and it smashed on the hearth." She struggled to her feet, hurried to the dressing room and grabbed the glass off the washstand then walked back to his bedside and poured more water.

Charles lay still, muttering about a horse.

She pulled the covers back up over his arm, sat on the edge of the bed to hold them down with her weight and slipped her free arm behind his shoulder. "Charles, please drink this water." She dribbled a little on his lips and he swallowed. She tipped the glass and he drank it all, quieted. Perhaps he would sleep peacefully now. She squeezed out a washcloth and put it on his forehead. A quick sweep with the hearth broom and use of the ash shovel got rid of the broken glass.

There's was nothing more she could do. She hurried toward the other end of the hall, her hems whispering against the rug.

"And what does a cow say?"

A smile curved her lips at her mother's question. She quickened her steps, waited by the door.

"Cow say moo."

"That's right! Now, can you answer this? Bossy-cow, bossy-cow, where do you lie?"

"In the green meadow, under the sky." She chanted the answer, stepped into the room and made a small curtsy.

Her mother laughed. Jonathan wiggled toward the edge of the bed and held up his arms.

"Me want biscuit."

"And you shall have one." She lifted him off the bed. "Thank you for entertaining Jonathan, Mama. I shall reward you with a lovely supper, as soon as I feed this hungry little bear."

"Me not a bear. Me Jonathan!"

"Why, so you are. I guess I'll just have to give Mr. Bear's biscuit to you."

"Don't fuss, Clarice. You have your hands full."

Yes, I do. If only it could stay this way.

"God bless brover an' make him all better."

"Amen." Clarice's heart swelled at Jonathan's prayer. His little heart was so ready to give and accept love now. He was a different little boy since Charles had "inherited" him. What a blessing that was for them both. And for her, though for her it would soon be over.

She mustn't let herself forget that. She leaned down and kissed Jonathan's soft, warm cheek. "Happy drea—"

"An' C'rice." He blinked his eyes and yawned.

"Thank you." Her heart filled. So did her eyes. She blinked them clear.

"An' Gamma."

"Yes, and Gramma." Oh, dear. She drew in a breath, blinked again.

"Her in bed."

"Yes. She's going to sleep here in *your* house tonight. You will see her in the morning. Perhaps if you ask her nicely, she will tell you a story about the birds and who gave them their songs."

"Birdies…go bed…nest…" His eyes closed, his lashes lying against his rosy cheeks. He gave a soft sigh, rolled onto his side and fisted his hand beneath his chin.

"Sleep well, Jonathan. May the Lord whisper happy dreams in your ears tonight." She tucked the covers close around him, touched his silky curls then rose and walked through the connecting dressing room into Charles's bedroom.

"…lead…" He frowned, rolled his head against the pillow. "…set bold…"

The clock on the mantel chimed, the notes soft against the hush of the room.

Time for his medicine. She shook the bottle, filled the tablespoon and dumped it into the small glass she'd brought up for the purpose, repeated it a second time and swirled it around. *It's bitter stuff.* She poured water into the larger glass, set it on the table within easy reach and perched on the edge of the bed.

"… Clarice…typewriter…"

He was thinking of *her*? Her breath caught. She lowered the glass of medicine to her lap, waited.

"…help…" He rolled his head, scowled. "…stubborn…obstinate…"

Well, really. "Charles…Charles, wake up. It's time for your medicine." She leaned forward and gently shook his shoulder. "Charles…"

He opened his eyes, looked straight at her. "Clarice?" He blinked, looked at her again. "What—" Awareness flashed into his eyes. He swept a glance around the room, tried to sit up, bit off a moan and sank back down against his pillow. "How—" He cleared his throat, turned his head toward the table. "I'd like that water, please."

She rose from the bed, held out the glass in her hand. "Medicine first."

He curled his lip.

"I know—bitter stuff. Nonetheless…"

He tried to lift his head, winced and raised his hand to cover his eyes.

"Have you a headache?"

"A symphony of drums—none of them in rhythm."

"Don't try to lift yourself. Let me help you." She slipped her free hand under his shoulders. Heat poured though his nightshirt, scorched her arm. He might be conscious, but he was not well. "Drink this." She swirled the medicine in the glass and held it to his opened lips, poured it in his mouth. "Now the water."

She switched glasses, held the water to his mouth until it was gone, then withdrew her arm and let him sink back into his pillow. His face was taut, his eyes shut tight. The covers over his chest rose and fell with his quick, shallow breaths.

"I'm going to put a wet cloth on your head to help with the pain." She squeezed out a washcloth, folded it and placed it on his forehead. "This won't help much. The water is tepid from sitting out all day. I'll go get some cold water and—"

"No." He opened his eyes. "It's late. You need to go. Close Jonathan's bedroom door, leave the doors to the dressing room open then—" he drew a shallow breath "—close my door when you leave. That way he can't get out of our bedrooms, and I will hear him if he needs me."

"I'll do no such thing! You're in no condition—" She stopped, stared down at his long fingers wrapped around her wrist and marveled that she felt no fear.

"I'm in no shape to argue the point, Clarice." He dragged in a breath, closed his eyes. His hand dropped to the bed. "Please do as I ask. I'll not have your reputation compromised because of me."

He was still thinking of her, protecting her, even in his illness. She cleared the lump from her throat, forced out words. "There is no danger of that. Mama is here."

He opened his eyes and fastened a disbelieving gaze on her. "How—"

"Dr. Reese brought her. It was his idea. Now stop talking and sleep. I'm going to get that cold water."

She blinked away tears, picked up the deep bowl and hurried into the dressing room before she lost control in front of him.

Chapter Sixteen

It didn't mean anything. It wasn't *personal*. It was just Charles being Charles. He was thoughtful of everyone.

Clarice lifted the cold cloth from her tired, burning eyes, slipped it back in the cold water and returned to curl up in the wingback chair in front of the stone fireplace. Telling herself the truth wasn't helping. Nothing helped. No matter. It would soon be over. Mrs. Hotchkiss was supposed to return from her visit with her daughter today.

The thought drove her to her feet. It was time she stopped dreaming over things that would never be and turned her attention to the things that were. She didn't even know how she'd come to feel like this. Or what it was she was "dreaming" for. It was only a nebulous *something*. A yearning that Charles had awakened in her when he had taken off his suit coat and wrapped it around her.

Oh, she wished it had never rained that day! Or that she had walked home by herself in the storm. The misery of being soaked by a cold rain would have been over as soon as she went in the house and changed out of her wet clothes. *This* ache went on and on, grew deeper and deeper. Well, it was going to stop!

She strode out of Charles's bedroom, down the hallway and into the bedroom where her mother was sleeping. A quick twist raised the wick and spread the circle of lamplight over the table covered with her stacks of CLSC letters. She had promised herself she would never marry—would never subject herself to some man's "rule" over her. She had planned to be a career woman, to make her own way in the world—to earn a living and provide for herself and her mother. She was doing that. True, it was a miserly living right now. But no man could take it away from her simply because she was a woman! And it would get better. She would be a journalist!

She plunked down on the chair, grabbed the top letter off the pile in front of her and prepared to go to work. It was a sure way to keep her mind focused on the things that mattered. If she held a steady pace, she could have these letters finished by morning. She wasn't sleeping, anyway.

Dear Chautauqua Literary and Scientific Circle teacher:
I am having difficulty understanding the principle behind—

Charles's clock.
She listened to the faint chiming hovering on the

silence. Would it wake him? Was he all right? The question hovered in her mind, refused to be dislodged. She laid the letter on the table, dimmed the lamp and headed for his bedroom, chiding herself for her weakness.

The light filtering in from the hallway and from the dressing room was enough to enable her to see the pain on his face. His eyes were closed tight, his face taut and flushed, his lips pressed into a thin line. She shouldn't have left him. She spoke softly to let him know she was there. "Charles, I'm going to change the cloth on your head. And I'm going to put a cold cloth on the back of your neck to try and bring down the fever."

He drew breath, opened his mouth to speak.

She touched his shoulder. "Don't try to talk unless you need something."

The washcloths were in the bowl. She squeezed out one, folded it and replaced the warm, drying one on his forehead. His skin was hot and dry against her hands.

And get as much water in him as you can. That's important. I don't want him losing body fluids and getting dehydrated.

Fear clutched at her heart. Was he becoming dehydrated? Was that dangerous? She folded the towel and placed it on the bed, poured a glass of water to have ready, then twisted the excess water from another washcloth and folded it in half. "Charles, I'm ready to put the cold cloth behind your neck. But first, when I raise your head, I want you to drink some water."

She slipped her arm beneath his shoulders, alarmed by the heat pouring from his body. "I'm going to lift your head off the pillow now." His jaw tensed. "Here's the water." She held the glass to his lips until it was empty then dropped it on the bed, pulled the folded towel over his pillow, placed the cold cloth on top of it and lowered him down onto it. A shiver ran through him. Air hissed through his teeth.

Her stomach knotted. "I'm sorry—is that too much? Do you want me to remove it?"

"No. Better…"

"All right, then… Try to sleep. I'm going to stay here and keep changing these cloths. I'll try not to disturb you."

"You…soothing…"

She touched the cloth on his forehead—it was already warm. He was so hot even the ice melt from the refrigerator warmed after a few minutes. The refrigerator! She touched his shoulder, leaned over him. "Charles, I have an idea that may help your fever. I'll be back in a few minutes."

She lifted her hems and ran on tiptoe into the hallway and down the stairs, snatched the oil lamp from the entrance hall and carried it to the work table in the kitchen. She pulled open drawer after drawer in the cupboards, searched through them and finally found the ice pick she wanted.

Please let this work, Lord. She pulled a big bowl off a shelf in the pantry, carried it to the refrigerator and opened the door to the ice compartment. The block of ice delivered that morning still had a rough edge on the bottom side. She slid it forward until it hung over the bowl and hacked at it with the ice pick. *Please, Lord.*

Please! A small piece of ice hit the bowl with a clink. Another…another…

She chopped at the ice until her fingers refused to grip the pick any longer then shoved the ice block back into place and closed and latched the door. *Please let it work… Please let it work…*

The prayer accompanied the tap of her shoes on the stairs, the whisper of her hems on the rugs. Was he sleeping?

"…discarded…gone…"

His muttering twisted the knots in her stomach tighter. Her chest constricted.

"I'm back, Charles." She set the bowl down, removed the cloth from his head and dipped it in the cold water. "Remember I told you I had an idea I hoped would help your fever? Well, it's ice. I've got ice—" Her voice broke. She blinked tears from her eyes, squeezed out the cloth, scooped small bits of ice onto it, folded it in half and placed it on his pillow beside his neck.

"…got…favorite ones… Skipper…"

"I'm going to lift you now." He was deadweight. She climbed onto the bed, braced herself with her knees and pulled him toward her, held him with one hand, slipped the washcloth holding the ice into place and lowered him onto it. A shiver shook him. She squeezed out another cloth, added ice, folded it and placed it on his forehead. The last cloth she filled with ice and put on his chest.

The blankets were a tangled mess. She straightened one over him and tossed the others off the end of his bed. It was all she could think of to do. She grabbed the bowl and ran to get more ice.

She was beginning to hate the steady ticktock of the clock. At least Charles had stopped mumbling and fallen asleep. The medicine had taken down his fever at last. Either the medicine or those three bowls of ice. How frantic she must have looked down on her hands and knees in front of the refrigerator hacking away at that ice block, and then running through the house like a demented person.

What if he had died? Was this why he had asked her to take care of Jonathan if something happened to him? *Was* he better? Or would the malaria return again? A trembling took her. She pushed to her feet and went to his bed, placed her hand against his cheek and listened to his even breathing. He was much cooler.

She sighed, returned to the wingback chair, curled up in the corner and closed her eyes.

Charles!

Clarice jerked upright and rushed to his bed, shook her head and blinked to clear her vision. It was empty. Her heart jolted. Fear exploded. She threw herself across the bed to look on the floor on the opposite side, dreading what she might find. Nothing. Her stomach rolled. Where—

A chuckle…faint, weak.

Her pulse stuttered, raced. *He was out of his head with fever again.* She shoved off the bed and whipped around toward the partially open dressing room door, thrust conventional niceties aside and shoved it open.

"Him gots dirty hands."

Jonathan.

"That's from the ink he uses to print the newspaper."

Charles.

She burst through the door to Jonathan's bedroom, stared. He was sitting in the chair in his dressing gown with Jonathan on his lap. "You're *sick*! What do you think you're doing?" Her voice trembled almost as much as her body. She marched toward them on shaky legs. "You need to be resting in bed not—" she stared at the small buckled shoes in his hand "—dressing Jonathan…"

"He's hungry and I didn't want him to wake you, so—"

"So you decided to *scare* me half to death instead! Do you *know what I*—" Tears gushed. She choked, spun toward the hallway door. "Fine. *Carry on!*"

"Clarice, wait…"

"I have to take care of my mother!" She slammed the door, ran across the hall into the bedroom, slammed that door and leaned back against it, fighting for control.

"What was that uproar about?"

She shot a glance toward her mother. "He—" Her control fell apart. "Oh, Mama, he *frightened* me!" She rushed to the bed and threw herself into the safe haven of her mother's arms.

"So you yelled at him." Her mother drew her close,

rubbed her back. "You've always gotten angry ~~when~~ you're frightened, Clarice…"

"I thought—" She choked on the words. Shuddered.

"I know… I know…" Her mother crooned the words, stroked her hair. "You've grown to care a great deal for Mr. Thornberg, haven't you, Clarice?"

"I—I suppose." She straightened, wiped the tears from her cheeks and made an effort at obfuscation. "He's been kind to you, and—" She stopped, squared her shoulders. *She* didn't even believe what she was saying—and judging from the look on her face, neither did her mother. She took a breath, tucked back a strand of hair that had come loose and lifted her chin. "And none of it matters, because Mr. Thornberg has little regard for a career woman."

"You're wrong, Clarice."

"No, Mother, I'm not." *I need you to do this. I'll pay…* "He—he thinks I'm greedy and selfish like his mother." She swallowed the hurt and headed for the dressing room connected to the bedroom. "Now, let's get you prepared for the day, and then I'll—"

"Go apologize for shouting at him?"

"No. I'll go and fix breakfast." *For one last time.* "Jonathan is hungry."

The knock shot through her like a bolt of lightning. She whirled, stared at the door.

"Talk to him, Clarice."

She stiffened her spine and moved to stand facing the closed door. "Yes? What is it?"

"I need to talk to you, Clarice…"

How many times had those words led her to do what

she knew would end in pain for her? "I'm busy." She held her breath, hoped.

"My strength is going. I can't take care of Jonathan."

So it wasn't about... She released the breath, blinked the tears from her eyes. "Take him to your room. I'll come for him as soon as I get my mother settled."

She smelled the coffee and bacon as soon as she opened the door. Her chest tightened; her stomach sank. *It was over.* She stepped to Charles's closed bedroom door, rapped lightly and entered. He was in bed with Jonathan beside him. She steeled her emotions, avoided looking directly at Charles. This was going to be hard enough.

"Good morning, Jonathan. Are you ready to have your breakfast?"

He scrambled to his feet, held up his arms. "Me hungry. Me want biscuit!"

She scooped him up, her heart breaking at the feel of him in her arms.

"Clarice—"

"Mrs. Hotchkiss has returned." She glanced down, met Charles's gaze and jerked hers away then burst into speech so he wouldn't have time to talk. "She will be startled to see Jonathan and me, I'm sure. I'll tend to him downstairs and send her up with your breakfast so you can explain everything to her." She turned away, unable to face him any longer without breaking down. "I'll bring Jonathan up so you can explain to him as soon as she returns to the kitchen."

She took a breath, glanced back over her shoulder. "Please tell him that I can no longer come to care for him, because I have to take care of my mother. I don't want him to think I have *discarded* him." She couldn't hide the bitterness of the words.

"Clarice, wait!"

Not this time. She closed the door, stiffened her spine and carried Jonathan downstairs.

"Dr. Reese is with Charles, Mama. He will be in to do your exercises and bring you home when he finishes examining him."

"Jonathan—" Clarice smiled down at the toddler in her arms "—you are going to stay here with…with Gramma until the doctor is through with brother. I have to pack up my work and take it home." Her chest and throat tightened, shut off her air. She forced her lungs to work, forced out the words she needed to say. "Do you remember how I told you brother and I work in the big building?"

"An' Clicker."

She managed a smile. "Yes, and Clicker, too. Well, I have to go back to work now that Mrs. Hotchkiss is going to take care of you."

"Me go too."

Jonathan's lower lip turned down, quivered. Her heart splintered into a thousand aching pieces. "But there's no toys to play with in the big building. And there's no backyard where you can run around and chase birdies. And brother will be here. He needs you to be with him. Remember, you're *family*. He belongs to you, and you belong to him. He wants to take care of you." She was going to break down! She cast a pleading look at her mother.

"Jonathan, come sit with me while I tell you a story." Her mother smiled and held out her arms.

She kissed Jonathan's cheeks and lowered him to the bed, hurried to the table and began shoving the CLSC letters into the bag, heedless of the piles they were in.

"Who taught the birds their pretty songs…whose notes so sweetly vary?"

Tears flowed; sobs pushed up her throat. She shoved the letters into the bag faster.

"The skylark, robin, nightingale…the goldfinch and canary."

She lifted the bag into her arms, oblivious to its weight, and walked to the door.

"All through the pleasant summer days…we hear their voices ringing…"

Goodbye, Jonathan.

"And know when wintry days appear…that somewhere they are singing."

She closed the door and stumbled for the stairs, blinded by her tears.

Chapter Seventeen

Clarice walked through the entrance hall, trudged up the stairs and headed for her room, thoroughly disgusted with herself. For the past two days she had stepped into Charles's shoes and taken over the running of the paper, as the note he had sent requested. She should be elated. Instead, she was heartsick, wondering if his recovery was going well and if Jonathan was happy.

She refused to listen to the reports on his recovery her mother elicited from Dr. Reese during his daily visit.

...stubborn...obstinate...

Her heart lurched at Charles's indictment. Well, maybe she was. But so was he, clinging to his wrongheaded opinions about all career women being as selfish and uncaring and greedy as his mother.

How could he think that of *her* after— No! No remembering. She had to protect her heart. She lifted her hands and removed her hat, once again devoid of decoration. She'd removed the flowers the day she'd come home from Charles's house. And then she had gone to work on the CLSC letters. The work had helped her to get through the day. They were all answered now. All she had left to do was type the answers into a column for the *Assembly Herald*. She should have time to do that tomorrow—barring any unforeseen emergency reporting needs.

When would he be back? How would she endure the pain of seeing him again when he did return? She sighed and rubbed at the pain in her temples. The headaches had returned along with the skimmed-back coiffure she'd resumed for her work at the *Journal*. Boyd Willard would flirt with anything wearing a dress and she refused to encourage his obnoxious behavior. Or the attentions of any other man. There was only one man she wanted to find her attractive.

Tears filmed her eyes. She blinked them away, squared her shoulders and opened the door. "I'm home, Mama. I'm sorry I'm so late but I had to finish composing the pages for tomorrow's printing. I don't want to be caught—" She stared, blinked, stared again. "Mama... Oh, Mama, you're *standing*!"

"That's not all, Clarice. Watch..."

Her heart leaped into her throat and lodged there as her mother walked slowly to the turret area, turned and walked back to her bed, her face a picture of joy.

She rushed over and gave her mother a fierce hug. Tears poured down her cheeks. "When did this happen, Mama? Why didn't you tell me?"

"You've been very busy, Clarice, and I wanted to be

sure it would last. That I would truly walk again. And I know now that I will." Her mother smiled and blinked tears from her eyes. "I'm getting stronger every day, Clarice. And Arthur—Dr. Reese—says I will soon be normal. Though he has ordered me not to lift anything."

Her mind raced, struggled to assimilate all that she was hearing and seeing—especially the blush on her mother's cheeks. "*Arthur*, Mama?"

Her mother's chin lifted. "Dr. Reese is a widower, Clarice."

"Mama!" She sank onto the edge of the bed and stared at a woman she had never before seen. How had she not noticed the happy sparkle in her mother's blue eyes or the soft curve to her lips? She looked younger… prettier. "You…you *care* for Dr. Reese, Mama?"

"I do. And he cares for me, Clarice. We're going to be married." The blush rose into her mother's cheeks again. "At our age, it's foolish to wait when you know you've found something lovely and lasting." Her mother's smile settled in her heart, dissolved the anger that had resided there for so long. "And Arthur wants you to come and live with us." Her mother placed her hand on hers. "He greatly admires the way you cared for Mr. Thornberg, Clarice."

The name stabbed deep into her heart. She rose and stepped to the dressing table, tossed her hat on it and began pulling the pins from her hair. "I—I don't know what to say, Mama. I—" she gave a little laugh, shook her hair free "—I think I'm too astounded to think straight."

"Well, I have given you a bit of a surprise."

"*A* surprise?" She laughed and pulled open the wardrobe to get her nightclothes. "You have given me a plethora of surprises, Mama. But— Oh, Mama, are you certain?" Tears clogged her throat. "I couldn't bear for you to be hurt again."

"Dr. Reese helps people, Clarice. He doesn't hurt them." Her mother took three careful steps, reached out and took hold of her hands. "And Mr. Thornberg is the same sort of fine gentleman. He doesn't hurt people, either."

"I don't want to talk about Mr. Thornberg, Mama." She turned and picked up her soap and towel and started for the door. "My head hurts. I'm going to the dressing room to wash this ink off my fingers and then I'm going to bed."

Him gots dirty hands.

The sound of Jonathan's voice filled her memory. How would she ever get the toddler out of her heart?

Clarice hurried across the intersection and continued on toward the *Journal* building, her umbrella clutched tight in her hand. It wasn't raining, but the massing of gray clouds and the cold mist that hung in the air did not bode well for a warm autumn day. She had come prepared for a storm.

She rejected the memory that rode the coattail of the thought and quickened her pace. The chill in the air penetrated the fabric of her midnight-blue cotton, but she was loath to begin wearing her green wool dress too soon. Her wardrobe was so scant she had to stretch the seasons to make it do. And it would be warm enough inside.

She turned onto the *Journal*'s sidewalk, lifted her gaze to read the legend on the building and jerked to a halt. Light streamed out of the second-floor windows of the editorial and composing rooms into the gray morning light. Someone had lit the chandeliers.

He was back.

Her heart reeled. She wanted to turn and walk away, but that wasn't possible. She had to be available to answer any questions he might have as to what she had done in his absence. And she had a living to make and a career to build. Unfortunately, Charles Thornberg held the keys to those things. That he also held the key to her heart was something she would simply have to overcome.

She stiffened her back and entered the building, walked through the entrance and climbed the stairs determined to hide her feelings behind a thoroughly professional persona. He thought she was a coldhearted career woman who did things only for monetary gain— so be it!

The editorial room was empty. She took a breath and hurried to her desk, leaned her umbrella in the corner, removed her hat and tossed it in the bottom drawer. A quick flip of the latch opened the box that protected the typewriter. She pulled the sliding shelf forward and locked it in place, inserted a piece of paper, pulled her handwritten notes on her Chautauqua Experience article and began to type, the rapid click of the keys striking the paper on the roller filling the silence.

She felt him coming before she heard his footsteps. She lost her place on her notes and her rhythm on the keys. She picked up the pile of papers, tapped them against the desk as if to even them in order to cover her faltering and began typing again. His shadow fell across her desk. Pain stabbed deep in her heart. She schooled her features into a pleasant politeness and looked up. "Good morning, Mr. Thornberg. I see you have fully recovered."

"Yes. Thanks to your care."

She lowered her hands out of sight on her lap and clenched them, forced a cool, detached tone into her voice. "I only did what Dr. Reese instructed."

He narrowed his gaze on her. "That's not true, Clarice. Dr. Reese told me it was the ice that brought the fever down and—"

"Well, ice is cold." *If he offered to pay her, she'd...* She pulled in a breath, placed her fingers back on the typewriter keys and looked up. "Was there something you wanted?"

"Good morning, chief."

She sagged with relief when Boyd Willard entered the room. The reporter tossed his hat on his desk and strode down the length of the room, a smile on his face.

"It's good to see you back, boss." He dropped his gaze to rest on her. "Not that this little lady hasn't done a good job running things in your absence. But there are other things women are better suited—"

"If you want to keep your job, I'd swallow the rest of that sentence, Willard."

Charles sounded ominous. She looked up. The muscle along his jaw was twitching.

"Ah, I didn't mean anything by that, chief. I was just—"

"I know what you were 'just,' Willard. And I wouldn't make the mistake of bringing that subject up again. I do not consider a woman's reputation a joking matter."

"Yes, sir." Willard shot her a look then turned his attention back to Charles. "I've heard rumors of a couple of the waterfront property owners giving bribes to some of the town officials so they would swing their votes their way at the next council meeting. It's only a rumor, but I thought I might look into it—see if there's any truth to it."

Charles nodded, clapped his hand on Boyd's shoulder and walked him toward the stairs. "A good idea. But I don't want you to bring back word-of-mouth suppositions. If I'm going to print a piece on graft among the town officials, I want proof."

She breathed a sigh of relief that Charles had shifted his attention from her, lifted the carriage frame on the typewriter and peered at the words she had typed. The last lines, the ones she had typed after his appearance, were full of mistakes.

"If there is any, I'll find it. I'll start searching as soon as I get my piece on the new Presbyterian church written." Boyd sat down at his desk and dragged a tablet and a pencil toward him.

"That piece can wait, Willard. Get started on the graft investigation."

They would be alone. She grabbed the end of the paper, rolled the cylinder toward her to remove it, then slipped in a new piece of paper, adjusted it, lowered the carriage into place and began typing again. If she was busy, perhaps—

"Miss Gordon…"

It had been too much to hope for. She took a firm grip on her emotions and looked up. "Yes, Mr. Thornberg?"

"I have a notice I wish you to write and have ready for tonight's edition. I will give you the gist of it and let you put it into printable copy."

He was all business. She had nothing to worry about. He was not going to pursue the conversation about her caring for him when he was ill. She released a sigh of relief and reached for her pad and pencil. "I'm ready."

"The notice is to state that I have a position open for a nanny to a two-year-old toddler."

Jonathan. She gasped, looked up at him. "But Mrs. Hotchkiss…"

"Mrs. Hotchkiss does not watch children. In truth, she doesn't particularly like them." He gestured toward her pad.

She looked down, poised her pencil to write. *Who was watching Jonathan today? Was he unhappy or—*

"The applicant must be experienced in caring for small children, and they must be available to begin work immediately. The wage will be generous. The hours of employment will be from eight in the morning until five at night six days a week. However, they must be able to stay beyond that time if I am delayed at my work. They may apply for the position here at the *Journal* building. Have you got all of that?"

How could he be so businesslike when this concerned Jonathan? She caught her breath, looked up at him. "The facts, yes. But—"

"Good. Then I shall expect you to have the copy for that notice ready by the time we go to print." His gaze held hers. Her pulse skipped, raced. Perhaps— "I want to thank you for getting the paper out on time when I was ill. I commend you on your work on the layout. You did an excellent job." She looked down, fought for composure. What did that matter if he— If Jonathan—

"And you've done an excellent job with the layout for tonight's printing, but I'd like to speak with you about the second page, please. We will have to do some rearranging to fit the notice on the page. If you would come into the composing room..." He turned and walked away.

She stared after him—her vision blurred and her chest constricted. How could he be so matter-of-fact about a nanny for Jonathan?

He paused, glanced over his shoulder. "Miss Gordon..."

She blinked her eyes and rose to her feet, her hands clenched and her stomach knotted. "Yes, Mr. Thornberg, I'm coming."

The day was endless. She couldn't concentrate. He kept asking her questions about something that had happened at the paper during his absence the past few days, and all she wanted was to go to his home and take Jonathan into her arms. How could he expect her to think about the *newspaper* when he treated her like any other employee, and Jonathan was being watched by a woman who didn't like children.

She stared at her notepad, poised her fingers on the typewriter keys, but the words wouldn't come. How could he let some *stranger* take care of Jonathan? How could *she*?

The idea burst upon her. She pushed back from the typewriter and walked to his desk. "May I speak with you, Mr. Thornberg?"

He shook his head, struck a line through a sentence on the paper on his desk. "I haven't time now, Miss Gordon. We'll talk later."

Dismissed. As if the time they had spent together had never happened. As if he'd never held her in his arms. She took a deep breath and dug her fingernails into her palms to quell the sobs clawing at her throat. "Very well." She spun away.

"Have you finished that notice, Miss Gordon?"

So polite and correct. How she longed to hear him call her Clarice. But that was over. She squared her shoulders and turned back. "Not yet—that's what I wanted to talk with you about."

He kept reading, waved a hand through the air. "Just follow my instructions. I'm sure you'll do an excellent job. But you'll have to hurry. I'll need it shortly. When I've edited this piece, I'll be ready to finish composing the pages." He glanced up. "I do appreciate your staying to help me. It's already past the supper hour and Mrs. Hotchkiss is— Well, she doesn't like having to stay late." He returned to his work.

She gritted her teeth and walked back to her desk. A few strokes of her pen scratched out the notes she'd written. She shoved her pen and pad in the drawer, fed a clean piece of paper into the typewriter and began typing. When she finished, she set the paper aside and pulled the article forward that she'd been working on when he interrupted her that morning.

The click of her typing filled the room. Charles stole a glance at Clarice sitting prim and proper at her desk with her fingers flying over the typewriter keys, and his stomach knotted. Had he misjudged her? Was she actually typing out the notice?

He took a breath, ran his fingers through his hair and shoved away from his desk. The click of her typing followed him into the composing room. He affixed the article he had edited to the second page, glanced toward the clock then thumbed through the fillers in the basket. The one Clarice's mother had written about cleaning mica was the right size. He stuck it in place, rolled the paper, snapped a rubber band around both ends to secure it and wedged it under his arm.

It was only a moment's work to snuff the chandeliers. He grabbed the other pages he'd rolled earlier and walked back into the editorial room. She was still typing as if the work was all that mattered to her. A heaviness settled over him. He'd thought that having to write that notice would awaken a desire in her for them all to become a family. How could he have been so wrong?

"It's time to take these pages to Clicker, Miss Gordon. Bring the notice you've written and come with me."

"Very well."

He watched her snatch a paper off her desk, then reach up and snuff her chandelier. He snuffed the others. Darkness crept in. How would he explain Clarice's abandonment to Jonathan? He kept asking for her.

Her skirt hems whispered an accompaniment to his footsteps as they walked down the stairs. He shoved open the door to the printing room, stepped back to let her precede him. "Here are the pages, Clicker."

"'Bout time." The printer took the pages in his ink-stained hands, carried them to a long table and began to unroll them.

"Give him the notice, Miss Gordon."

She nodded, stepped forward.

"On second thought, I'll give it to him." He held out his hand.

She looked down at it, lifted her chin and placed the paper in her hand on his upraised palm.

He glanced down. *Who taught the birds their pretty songs...whose notes so sweetly vary?*

He looked up, met her defiant gaze.

"Well, are you gonna give me that notice or not?"

He shook his head and stuck the paper in his pocket. "I believe I'll keep this for another time, Clicker. Print page two as is."

Her eyes glistened with tears. He took hold of her arm and ushered her out of the building, paused beneath a street lamp and stepped back from her, held himself from taking her in his arms. He had to be sure. "Would you like to tell me why you typed that poem?"

She tilted her head up and met his gaze full on. His heart jolted at her beauty. His pulse thudded. "Because you wouldn't listen to me." She drew a breath, rushed into speech. "I have a proposition for you."

His gaze captured hers. "Which is?"

"I will take the position as Jonathan's nanny."

It wasn't good enough...not by half. Not now. He looked off into the distance, shook his head. "I'm not sure that's the best idea."

"I believe it is." She shivered, rubbed her arms.

"You're cold." He took off his suit jacket, wrapped it around her and held it close beneath her chin. She looked down, drew a shaky breath. His pulse quickened at her tremble.

"Jonathan already knows and trusts me, and I love him." Her voice was a soft whisper. She looked up. The lamplight glowed on her beautiful face, gleamed on the tears in her eyes. "The only thing I ask is that you continue to let me answer the CLSC letters at home. And, of course, I will be available should you ever need my help at the newspaper."

He cleared his throat. "You would make yourself available to help me?"

"Of course. I lo—" She clamped her lips together. Pink bloomed across her cheekbones. She looked down, gripped the edges of his coat. "Of course I would."

His heart lurched. He was sure now. How could he ever have doubted her? "Your offer is a very tempting one. There's only one problem." He stepped closer.

"Wh-what?"

"The position is no longer open." He cleared the gruffness from his voice, tugged on the jacket lapels and pulled her close. "I think Jonathan needs something more permanent than a nanny." He released the lapels, slipped his hands up and cupped her face.

"Y-you do?" The words were barely a whisper.

He nodded, tipped her face up and bent his head. His lips hovered over hers, touched their warm softness. "I think the only solution is for you to marry me." He brushed his lips over hers again, tasted of their sweetness, the saltiness of her tears. His heart pounded. "I love you, Clarice."

She drew a ragged breath, looked into his eyes. "I love you, Charles."

Time stopped. He slid his arms inside his coat and wrapped them around her, drew her against him. "Will you be my wife?"

She placed her hand over his thudding heart and gave him a smile that sent joy exploding through him. "Yes. With all of my heart." Her arms slipped up around his neck and the coat fell unheeded into a pile at their feet as he claimed her lips in a kiss that promised forever.

Epilogue

Clarice brushed her hair up to the top of her head, gathered it into her hand, then loosened it until it fell in a pouf of soft waves against her temples and forehead. The length of hair still in her hand she twisted into a soft pile at her crown and pinned it in place.

"Here's the ribbon."

"Thank you, Mama." She took the length of wide ivory silk into her hands and wound it around the base of the puffed black mass of hair at her crown, tied it into a bow and let the ends fall down the back of her head. They just touched the top of her gown's high collar.

"And one more thing…" Her mother opened the drawer of the dressing table, pulled out a cluster of white silk flowers and tucked the stems beneath the ribbon at the front of her twisted puff of hair. "There. They look beautiful and the ribbon will hold them in place."

Clarice sat back and gazed at herself in the mirror, marveling at how different she looked. She hardly recognized herself since Charles had declared his love for her. The happiness inside glowed in her gray eyes, making them look wider and brighter, and turned the corners of her mouth up into the hint of a smile. All the shadows of bitterness and fear caused by the cruelty of her father were gone.

She took a breath, rose, spread out the ivory gown's short train and smoothed her hands down the front of the long ruffled skirt. "I guess I'm ready." She gave her mother a shaky smile. "Thank you for making my gown, Mama. It's lovely."

"*You're* lovely, Clarice. Charles will not be able to take his eyes off you during the ceremony. Or after."

Heat climbed into her cheeks.

Her mother cupped her face in her hands and gave her a loving smile. "Especially if you blush like that."

"Mama!" The heat in her cheeks increased. She raised her hands to cover her mother's, admiring their softness, thinking of how dry and calloused they had been for as long as she could remember. Tears stung her eyes. "I'm so happy for you, Mama. And so *thankful* that you can walk beside me."

Her mother sighed and nodded. "The Lord has richly blessed us, Clarice. He has taken all of our hurt and fear away and replaced it with the amazing love of two wonderful men—and one adorable little boy."

"I know, Mama. It's wondrous how the Lord took something as selfish and heartless as Mrs. Thornberg's—or whatever her name is now—*discarding* of her sons and turned it around for their good. Whoever would have thought God would use her cruelty to bring Jonathan and Charles together. To give them both the family they otherwise would never have known. He turned her selfishness around for their good."

"And for ours."

"Oh, yes, most definitely for ours." She looked at her mother and laughed. "I guess there are times when being poor and having to make a living for yourself is a good thing."

"And when being crippled and unable to walk is a blessing."

She nodded, sobered by the memory. "I was so *angry* with God because all of the hard work Father demanded of you crippled you. But that is what set you free from a life of drudgery and pain, Mama." She passed the button hook to her mother and smiled. "And it brought you the man you are about to marry."

"Indeed it did." Her mother buttoned her shoes, rose and donned the jacket that went over the blue gown she had made for her wedding day. "A widowed doctor..." She pinned her small flower-trimmed hat in place, her blue eyes sparkling with happiness. "God truly does work in mysterious ways."

"He truly does." She drew a breath, smoothed the front of her gown one more time. "Are you ready, Mama?"

"Never more so, Clarice. Are you?"

"I truly am, Mama. I can't wait to be Charles's bride—" the joy in her heart broke out in a huge smile "—*and* Jonathan's sis'er."

They walked downstairs, the hems of their gowns

whispering softly against the polished oak treads then crossed the entrance hall. Side by side they stepped through the door into the sitting room. Mrs. Duncan was there wearing a happy smile. And Jonathan, wide-eyed and adorable beside her. But it was the men standing by the fireplace waiting for them who captured and held their gazes.

They walked forward, each drawn by the love of the man waiting for her. Charles, breathtakingly handsome in his new dark suit, stepped forward and held out his hand. She looked into his eyes, warm with love, and placed her hand in his safe, loving grasp.

"Me too!"

The whisper brought a shared smile—the oneness that would be theirs from this moment on. Charles looked down at Jonathan, and that slow lopsided smile that made her stomach quiver tilted his mouth. "Not this time, Skipper. This time, she's all mine." He met her gaze, placed his mouth by her ear and whispered, "And forever more." The words settled in her heart, a promise of the love and happiness to come, as they stepped forward to stand beside her mother and Dr. Reese in front of the minister waiting to perform the double ceremony.

* * * * *

Dear Reader,

Clarice Gordon made her appearance in *An Unlikely Love*, my first book with a Chautauqua Lake setting. She was such an intriguing character in that book that I knew I had to write her story. I also knew, because of her nature, she had to have a self-confident, strong yet gentle hero to win her heart. Charles Thornberg was the perfect man for her. I enjoyed writing their story and, once again, giving two wounded people a happy-ever-after ending by God gently leading them into the knowledge of His love.

I'm going to miss the steamer rides on beautiful Chautauqua Lake. But I *think* the mode of transportation in my next book will be a train. At least until my heroine reaches her destination. I'm looking forward to that. I've always wished I could ride one of the old trains and experience the sway of the car, the clickety-clack of the wheels against the track and the faint smell of smoke as the steam engine chugged its way west. How about you, dear reader? Would you like to come along?

Thank you, dear reader, for choosing to read *His Precious Inheritance*. I hope you enjoyed Clarice and Charles's story. I truly appreciate hearing from my readers. If you care to share your thoughts about this story, I may be reached at dorothyjclark@hotmail.com or www.dorothyjclark.com.

Until the "All aboard" call sounds,

Dorothy Clark

COMING NEXT MONTH FROM
Love Inspired® Historical

Available October 6, 2015

A DADDY FOR CHRISTMAS
Christmas in Eden Valley
by Linda Ford

Chivalry demands cowboy Blue Lyons help any woman in need, so he offers widow Clara Weston—and her daughters—shelter and food when they have nowhere to go. And whether he wants it or not, Clara and her daughters are soon chipping away at his guarded heart.

A WESTERN CHRISTMAS
by Renee Ryan & Louise M. Gouge

In two brand-new novellas, Christmas comes to the West and brings with it the chance for love, both old and new.

HER COWBOY DEPUTY
Wyoming Legacy
by Lacy Williams

Injured and far from home, sheriff's deputy Matt White finds love in the most unexpected of places with a former childhood friend.

FAMILY IN THE MAKING
Matchmaking Babies
by Jo Ann Brown

Arthur, Lord Trelawney, needs lessons in caring for children, so he decides to practice with the rescued orphans sheltering at his family estate. A practical idea...until he meets their lovely nurse, Maris Oliver.

LIHCNM0915

REQUEST YOUR FREE BOOKS!

2 FREE INSPIRATIONAL NOVELS
PLUS 2 *FREE* MYSTERY GIFTS

Love Inspired® H I S T O R I C A L

LIH15

Will a young Amish widow's life change when her brother-in-law arrives unexpectedly at her farm?

Read on for a sneak preview of
THE AMISH MOTHER
The second book in the brand-new trilogy
LANCASTER COURTSHIPS

"You're living here with the children," Zack said. *"Alone?"*

"This is our home." Lizzie faced him, a petite woman whose auburn hair suddenly appeared as if streaked with various shades of reds under the autumn sun. Her vivid green eyes and young, innocent face made her seem vulnerable, but she must be a strong woman if she could manage all seven of his nieces and nephews—and stand defiantly before him as she was now without backing down. He felt a glimmer of admiration for her.

"Koom. We're about to have our midday meal. Join us. You must have come a long way." She bit her lip as she briefly met his gaze.

Zack still couldn't believe that Abraham was dead. His older brother had been only thirty-five years old. "What happened to my *brooder*?"

Lizzie went pale. "He fell," she said in a choked voice, "from the barn loft." He saw her hands clutch at the hem of her apron. "He broke his neck and died instantly."

Zack felt shaken by the mental image. "I'm sorry. I know it's hard." He, too, felt the loss. It hurt to realize that he'd never see Abraham again.

"He was a *goot* man." She didn't look at him when she bent to pick up her basket, then straightened. "Are you coming in?" she asked as she finally met his gaze.

He nodded and then followed her as she started toward the house. He was surprised to see her uneven gait as she walked ahead of him, as if she'd injured her leg and limped because of the pain. "Lizzie, are *ya* hurt?" he asked compassionately.

She halted, then faced him with her chin tilted high, her eyes less than warm. "I'm not hurt," she said crisply. "I'm a cripple." And with that, she turned away and continued toward the house, leaving him to follow her.

Zack studied her back with mixed feelings. Concern. Worry. Uneasiness. He frowned as he watched her struggle to open the door. He stopped himself from helping, sensing that she wouldn't be pleased. Could a crippled, young nineteen-year-old woman raise a passel of *kinner* alone?

Don't miss
THE AMISH MOTHER by Rebecca Kertz,
available October 2015 wherever
Love Inspired® books and ebooks are sold.

JUST CAN'T GET ENOUGH OF INSPIRATIONAL ROMANCE?

Join our social communities
and talk to us online!
You will have access to the latest
news on upcoming titles and special
promotions, but most important,
you can talk to other fans about your
favorite Love Inspired® reads.

 www.Facebook.com/LoveInspiredBooks

 www.Twitter.com/LoveInspiredBks

Harlequin.com/Community

LISOCIAL